TO SLEEP, PERCHANCE TO DREAM . . . OR KILL

Antony said, "You're telling me your brother was sleep-walking that night? That the police think—?"

Timmy shook his head. "The police just say he shot Uncle William, thinking it was Grandfather. Grandfather says Paul was mad. Paul says he was asleep." His look was defiant. "I know it doesn't *sound* true."

"Never mind how it sounds. Exactly what happened?"

"As Grandfather and I went outside, I heard my cousin Brent call out, 'Drop it, you fool, drop it!' Paul was standing with the rifle in his hand. We all looked past him through the study window; Uncle William was there, and he'd fallen across the desk and you couldn't mistake what had happened. Then Grandfather turned on Paul and screamed at him, 'You damned, murdering young swine! So you wanted to kill me!'

"And Paul turned and looked straight at him as though he was dreaming; and he said very slowly, 'I don't understand. I thought it was you!' "

Other Avon Books by
Sara Woods

BLOODY INSTRUCTIONS

Coming Soon

THE THIRD ENCOUNTER
LET'S CHOOSE EXECUTORS

MALICE DOMESTIC

Sara Woods

AVON
PUBLISHERS OF BARD, CAMELOT, DISCUS AND FLARE BOOKS

AVON BOOKS
A division of
The Hearst Corporation
1790 Broadway
New York, New York 10019

First Avon Printing, February 1986

AVON TRADEMARK REG. U. S. PAT. OFF. AND IN OTHER
COUNTRIES, MARCA REGISTRADA, HECHO EN U. S. A.

Printed in the U. S. A.

WFH 10 9 8 7 6 5 4 3 2 1

". . . Duncan is in his grave;
After life's fitful fever he sleeps well;
Treason has done his worst; nor steel, nor poison,
Malice domestic, foreign levy, nothing
Can touch him further."

MACBETH, ACT III, SC. II.

List of Characters

AMBROSE CASSELL, Managing Director of the firm of Cassell & Company, Vintners
MARIAN CASSELL, his unmarried daughter
RUTH HERRON (dec'd), his married daughter
MATTHEW HERRON (dec'd), her husband
PAUL HERRON } their sons
TIMMY HERRON
MARK HERRON (dec'd), Matthew's twin brother

GREGORY CASSELL, Ambrose's son; junior partner of The Firm
AGNES CASSELL, his wife
BRENT CASSELL, their son

WILLIAM CASSELL (dec'd), Ambrose's brother; Manager of the Lisbon Office, and Chief Buyer

ROBERT WAYNE, cousin to Matthew and Mark Herron

JOHN BARCLAY, artist. An old friend of the Cassell family
ANN BARCLAY, his daughter; engaged to Paul Herron
AUDREY BARTON, his niece; engaged to Brent Cassell

MANUEL DA COSTA CALLEYA, of the Lisbon Office

ROSE, parlourmaid at The Laurels

DOCTOR HEARN, doctor to the Cassell family
ROBERT BELLERBY, their solicitor
GEOFFREY HORTON, solicitor; representing Paul Herron

SIR NICHOLAS HARDING, Q.C.
ANTONY MAITLAND, his nephew; barrister-at-law
JENNY MAITLAND, Antony's wife

MALLORY, Sir Nicholas's clerk
GIBBS, Sir Nicholas's butler

SUPERINTENDENT FORRESTER }
INSPECTOR CONWAY   }   of Scotland Yard

MALICE DOMESTIC

CHAPTER 1

"It sounds an interesting case, sir," said Antony Maitland, hopefully.

Sir Nicholas Harding regarded him in a considering way, and then remarked, "No doubt," in no very encouraging tone. After a moment he added, rather more emphatically, "I will not take a case involving an insanity plea. As you very well know." And with these words he transferred his gaze from his nephew to his clerk, Mallory, who in turn looked at Antony, silently reproachful. Antony fidgeted, and said:

"Yes, well, I know it was my responsibility . . ."

"The matter should not have been referred to you," interrupted his uncle, coldly. "Mallory could have refused the brief out-of-hand."

Old Mr. Mallory coughed, and eyed his employer with a look at once mulish and distressed. "Well, Sir Nicholas—" he began, but was interrupted without ceremony.

"You can't blame Mallory, sir. He knows your fads well enough by now, but I don't expect he could bring himself to pass up a chance of soaking Bellerby's client for some perfectly outrageous fee."

This remark was not well received by either of his hearers. Sir Nicholas contented himself with a sharp glance at his nephew, but the clerk, to whom the subject of fees was sacred, remarked severely, "I did not feel that you would wish me to disoblige Mr. Bellerby in this matter." But spoiled the effect a moment later by adding, "He intimated that money would not be a consideration to his client."

Sir Nicholas disposed of the solicitor, and his client, in one brief, all-embracing phrase. Antony murmured, "Bellerby—Mallory's translation,'' at which the old man showed some signs of being affronted; but before he could reply Sir Nicholas looked up and said with a calm that was natural in him only when he was becoming angry:

''All this is beside the point. I do not want the brief.''

Mr. Mallory threw a despairing glance at Antony, who fixed his eyes on a point above his uncle's head and remarked ingenuously, ''Bellerby said it would be tricky; he wanted you because nobody else would be able to get away with it.'' He paused invitingly, but Sir Nicholas was not to be drawn by so obvious an attempt at aggravation. ''At least, it can't do any harm to see what it's about.''

''You have told me the plea is one of insanity.'' The older man returned to his grievance. ''I won't have it! Anyway, why should I? As I understand it, there's a brief for you, whoever leads the defence.''

''Well, yes, sir.''

''But nobody else would be likely to tolerate your meddling, if you feel so inclined—is that it?''

''Something like that,'' agreed his nephew, cheerfully. ''I only said you'd see Bellerby. I didn't commit you to anything.''

''I should think not, indeed.''

Mr. Mallory, who had maintained his air of studied dignity during this exchange, moved towards the door. ''I fancy I hear Mr. Bellerby now, Sir Nicholas. Would you wish to see him immediately?''

''Very well.'' He cast an infuriated look at his nephew, on whom it had no apparent effect. ''I suppose there's no help for it.''

''I only said you'd see him,'' Antony reiterated, unmoved. His uncle gave an exasperated sigh, and leaned back in his chair.

As the clerk made his stately way out of the room Antony retreated a little, to his favourite position by the window. At the end of the long vacation, and a few days before the commencement of the Michaelmas term, Sir Nicholas's chambers presented an unwontedly orderly appearance; particularly as the owner (in his person the most tidy of men) had returned from Switzerland so recently as to have yet had no time to disorganise the careful arrangement of documents on his desk. That, no doubt, would be remedied before long. As for the coming interview, he hadn't given up hope yet; Uncle Nick was ruffled, that—after all—had been unavoidable, but perhaps his interest might yet be caught. If not . . . a brief was a brief, whoever was leading.

Mr. Bellerby came in just then: a stout and cheerful man, though rather more affable in his manner than either uncle or nephew relished. Sir Nicholas conducted the preliminaries politely enough, but showed a certain aloofness when the visitor settled himself to discuss the business in hand. Antony directed at him a look more exasperated than respectful, and turned back to address the solicitor.

"You understand that my uncle is disinclined to take the case?"

"Quite, quite." Bellerby looked from one to other of them with no diminution of joviality. "You made the matter perfectly clear to me. However, there are circumstances which make this case a very difficult one." He turned to address Sir Nicholas directly. "I feel—and I have advised my client accordingly—that you could present the matter more convincingly than anyone else; and that—er—Maitland's special talents would be well employed in the matter."

Sir Nicholas looked at his nephew with every appearance of loathing. "I've nothing against his accepting the brief, though I don't quite see—"

"There are reasons, very good reasons. As I shall explain." The solicitor paused a moment, but as his evasion was not called to question continued with more assurance, "I had better give you the facts."

"By all means," said Sir Nicholas courteously. "But bearing in mind, if you please, that I have given no encouragement for you to waste your time."

"Very well." The solicitor nodded his concurrence. "You'll have heard something, I dare say, from Maitland of this unfortunate affair."

"No," said Sir Nicholas, unhelpfully.

Even Mr. Bellerby appeared a little daunted. He looked across at Antony, who grimaced at him over his uncle's head, and remarked, "if you imagine the words 'Without Prejudice' writ large in front of everything that is said, we shall get on wonderfully well."

"My client," said the solicitor, speaking now with some determination, "is Mr. Ambrose Cassell, who is senior partner of Cassell and Company—a firm of the highest reputation, of whom you may have heard."

Sir Nicholas looked momentarily less austere. "They are importers of wine?" he inquired. "But it is not Mr. Cassell, I believe, who requires my services?"

"He has consulted me on behalf of his grandson, Paul Herron."

"I see."

"First, I must tell you something of the family background." He wriggled a little, seeking more comfort than his chair was willing to afford him. "The founder of the firm had two sons: my client, Ambrose Cassell, and his brother, William, who lived abroad and was unmarried."

"Was?" queried Sir Nicholas. Antony turned from the window and remarked casually:

"X marks the spot."

"Precisely." Mr. Bellerby beamed at him. "Ambrose is a widower. He has two children living: Gregory, who is a member of the firm, and Marian, who keeps house for her father. Another son was killed in the war, and his youngest daughter, Ruth, was the mother of the twins—Paul and Timothy Herron. Ambrose lives at Wimbledon, and these two have been with him since they were six years old. Gregory, his wife and son, make their home in the country." He paused, as though for comment. Antony glanced at his uncle, but finding him apparently oblivious remarked encouragingly:

"What about the grandsons—there are three, I think? Are they all devoted to the wine trade?"

"So far as Brent goes, that is a very apt phrase. Brent is Gregory's son, and he appears to find a business career congenial. About the twins—that's another story, from what I gather. Timmy has published a novel, and is quite open about his intention to quit the firm when he can afford to do so. Paul dislikes town life in general, and the wine trade in particular. I'm not sure what he would like to substitute, but I know he has disagreed most bitterly with his grandfather on this subject."

Sir Nicholas roused himself sufficiently to say acidly to

his nephew, "If your curiosity is sufficiently assuaged, perhaps you will permit Bellerby to proceed to the facts he promised us."

Antony grinned. "Intelligent interest," he corrected gently. "However—"

"On Tuesday last the whole family was gathered at the Wimbledon house to welcome William Cassell, who was coming 'home' for the first time for many years."

"Coming for good?"

"I believe not. He arrived about tea-time. Everything went normally, quite as could have been expected, until after dinner. At about ten-thirty William went to his brother's study to write letters. The family dispersed, but within a few minutes there was the sound of a shot. They found him dead."

"And the weapon?"

"A .22 rifle."

"I see. And for this murder his great-nephew, Paul Herron, has been arrested. Is there a financial motive?"

"No. The police believe that his intention was to kill Ambrose—there was a strong family likeness between the brothers."

"Hm. And the evidence?"

"Paul was found with the gun near the place from which the shot must have been fired. As near 'red-handed' as makes no matter. His fingerprints were on the stock, with others too smudged to identify."

"And he wishes to plead insanity. What grounds are there for such a plea?"

"I am following my client's instructions. I understand that Paul is obstinately opposed to such a course."

It was at this point that Sir Nicholas picked up a pencil and began to scribble obscurely on the blotting-pad. "But Mr. Cassell—I presume he has his reasons for saying his grandson is mad?"

"He tells me Paul has been odd from being a youngster: nervous, given to sleep-walking. Quite different from his brother, who is of an equable disposition, from what I am told."

"Is the brother relevant?"

"Not particularly. Except, of course, as I said before, that they are twins."

Sir Nicholas gave him a suspicious look, but refrained from comment. "I take it that is not the whole of the case you are proposing I should take to court?"

"There is, besides, the—er—the family history." Mr. Bellerby produced the phrase with an air that was faintly apologetic.

"Well?" said Sir Nicholas. His tone was sharp.

"Eighteen years ago Paul Herron's father shot and killed his wife, his twin brother, and then himself." The solicitor's tone was matter-of-fact. Antony murmured, "Women and children first," and his uncle exploded into violent speech.

"So this is your interesting case!" He turned an accusing glare on his nephew. "A case not only involving an insanity plea, but also two sets of twins (identical twins, in the best story-book tradition, I make no doubt!). And beyond all this—I am to involve myself in the investigation of a shooting eighteen years old!"

Antony looked apologetically at Mr. Bellerby. "Are they identical?" he inquired.

"What the hell does that matter?" said his uncle, unreasonably. "A jury won't believe young Herron is crazy just because I tell them so. I won't do it, I tell you."

"Nobody's asking you to, sir. Not the preliminaries."

"I see." Sir Nicholas swung round again to his visitor. "In any event, is Paul Herron insane?"

"My client is quite emphatic—"

"Damn your client! You've seen the boy, I suppose? What's your opinion?"

"He seemed distraught—I admit, in the circumstances, that wasn't perhaps surprising. Previously, I had never observed anything out of the way in his manner." The solicitor was picking his words carefully.

"And yet you see nothing unreasonable in this contention?"

"In view of what has happened, I feel it is a reasonable assumption for the family to make. As for the legal position, that," said Mr. Bellerby with an air of triumph, "is a matter for counsel's opinion, not mine."

"True enough." Sir Nicholas sat back, and thought for a moment. "Well, as there seems to be some doubt in the matter, it might be advisable to see this young man."

Mr. Bellerby, to Antony's relief, had the wisdom to leave well alone. He mopped his brow, and got up, puffing gently; though whether this was due to the heat of the day, or to the stress of the interview, it was impossible to decide. "When will it be convenient for you to see my client?"

"I see no need for that at this stage. It is the grandson, after all, with whom we are concerned."

The solicitor, urged gently towards the door, spoke over his shoulder: "Mr. Cassell is a difficult man!"

"That," said Sir Nicholas, with a bland lack of sympathy, "is not, I am glad to say, my affair."

Antony came back a few moments later, and looked with admiration at the tangle his uncle had already contrived among his papers. "I'll see Herron to-morrow morning, sir. Meanwhile, I told Bellerby I'd like to see the brother—Timothy his name is. He may be able to make things a bit clearer."

"Who am I," said his uncle, sourly, "to deny you your pleasure, however unnatural?"

"A brief is a brief, after all. Stop looking like a thundercloud, Uncle Nick, and think of the sunshine you'll be bringing into Mallory's life. Besides—"

"I know, you're interested! May heaven give me patience," said the older man, dispassionately.

Antony grinned. Sir Nicholas picked up a bulky, redtaped bundle, adding in the tone of one who can endure no more, "Try and make some sense of these—Watterson wants an opinion—and let me have some peace."

His nephew caught the package, a little clumsily; meditated a reply and thought better of it; and departed, obediently, for his own room, and the unrewarding consideration of an obscure title.

CHAPTER 2

TIMOTHY HERRON received his visitor that evening in a small, untidy room, that was basically more bedroom than sitting-room, though it obviously did duty for both. There was one easy-chair, and he perched himself on the window-seat again as soon as Antony was seated, and bent upon his companion a glance that was at once speculative and wary. He wasn't too sure that old Bellerby's choice was to be relied on, but this chap didn't in any way measure up to his expectations. He was younger, for one thing, and altogether more human.

Antony, for his part, was prepared to feel his way with some caution. Nothing in the description he had been given had prepared him for the young man who now confronted him: a Byronic type, definitely; dark, and handsome as the devil. If he had a temperament to match his looks, the outlook was probably stormy; but Bellerby, after all, had pronounced him "equable." His first words were deliberately trite:

"I'm sorry to intrude on you at such a time, Mr. Herron."

The other gave a quick frown of irritation, and made a disclamatory gesture. "Bellerby told me . . . of course I wanted to see you. He told me your name, too, only I'm afraid it didn't register."

"Maitland."

"Good lord, then you're the one who cleared up that business last year, when the police were all set to hang Joe Dowling."

"I was . . . connected with the case." Antony spoke unwillingly, and was only a little comforted by the reflection

that whatever his companion had read in the papers was nowhere near the truth. Timothy Herron gave him a look of
bright interest, and laughed unexpectedly.

"Well, now!" he said. "This opens up a new train of
thought."

"I think, you know, that possibly you underrate Bellerby.
He's shrewd enough, and he knows his job." Antony's tone
was mild, and he was answering the thought rather than the
words, so that the other glanced at him sharply.

"I wouldn't be surprised if you're right. He certainly sold
you to my grandfather. Only trouble is, you know . . . Paul
isn't mad. Sane as I am: sane as you are, if you like it better
that way."

"I understand that Mr. Cassell—" Antony began, and
was interrupted without ceremony.

"My grandfather feels, if we've got a murderer in the
family it's a bit more respectable if he's mad. Besides, it
wouldn't reflect on the Cassell side. You see?"

"Not altogether. To take first things first, however: the
question is, have you a murderer in the family?"

"Oh, I should think so!" Timmy's tone was off-hand.
"But not Paul, you know; certainly not Paul."

"Then . . . you must forgive me if I seem curious, but it
would certainly be helpful to know—"

"Of course it would." He sounded impatient; not
unnaturally, as his visitor considered. "But if I knew, d'you
think I'd wait to be asked?"

"No," said Antony.

"I'm only going by circumstances, and what I know of
Paul."

"You'd better tell me."

Timmy got up; realised as he did so that his room did not
afford sufficient space for restless movement; sat down
again, and looked rather helplessly at his companion.

"I don't know what my grandfather believes," he said.
"He says Paul's mad, and that's the line his defence must
take. But if he didn't do it—"

Antony said quietly: "You think your brother is innocent?"

"Yes, I do." He sounded defiant. "I suppose you think
I'm prejudiced?"

"Well, you know, I don't see how you could help it."

"Then what's the use of talking . . . if you've made up your mind?"

"I didn't say that. Besides—forgive me—I don't think you're telling me the truth."

"Oh, well!" said Timmy. After a moment he added, "In books people are always sure. 'I know his mind as I know my own', they say. How can one ever be sure . . . of anything?"

There was an uneasy silence. After a moment Antony said, with apparent irrelevance, "You must realise, I had never heard of your family until two days ago. They are only names to me even now. And I know less than nothing about what happened the day your uncle died. If you can help me, I shall be grateful. You can't help me if you're afraid of the truth."

"I don't know the truth."

"What I'm trying to get across is this: your brother has been arrested, that means the police think (and doubtless with good reason) that he had a motive. In talking to me, you will be tempted to gloss over that fact, and that's just what you must not do. I want to know everything the police know . . . more than they do, if possible. Anything that could conceivably be adduced against your brother. Do you understand?"

"Yes, I suppose so. Yes, of course, that's reasonable. Only I don't know where to begin."

"With the relations between your brother and grandfather. That's as good a place as any."

Timothy grimaced. "That's to plunge into the thick of it. Still, if you want it that way—"

"I do. We will then proceed to a detailed consideration of what happened the day your great-uncle was murdered."

"Yes, well—" Timmy was hesitant.

"I was told," said Antony, with a measure of tartness in his tone, "that you are a writer. I'm asking for a piece of straightforward narrative. Or is that too difficult?"

His companion looked startled. "People tell me my stuff doesn't make sense. How did you know?"

"I didn't," said Antony, briefly. "I don't want to hurry you, but—"

"Hell!" said Timmy, unemotionally; he caught his companion's eye, and added in a hurry, "You said, start with how things were between my grandfather and Paul, so I take it you know the police theory; that he meant to kill—"

"In outline only. But we'll come to that in a moment."

"Well, there were rows, of course. But Paul's like that, you know, says more than he means."

"What did he say?"

"I tell you, it didn't mean anything."

"That isn't the point." Antony sounded weary. "The point is, what can be made of it in court?"

"That's rather different. He didn't make threats, if that's what you mean. Paul's mind doesn't work that way."

"That's one thing to be thankful for, at least."

"He might have told him to go to the devil," added Timmy, with the air of one making a handsome admission. "But it doesn't follow he'd have taken steps to see he got there."

"Well, at least, we've decided there were quarrels."

"There were."

"And on . . . Tuesday, wasn't it? The day Mr. William Cassell came home?"

"Came home and went home," said Timmy, apparently much cheered by this callous piece of childishness. Most illogically Antony, who was blessed (or cursed) with rather more imagination than was good for him, began at this point to feel definitely in sympathy with his companion. Timmy added after a moment, "Well, I gather Tuesday's was rather a super effort. Paul told me—" He paused, and then added sheepishly, "I say, you know . . . I don't like this at all."

"I don't suppose you do." Antony spoke with exaggerated indifference, and noted with interest that for the first time one of his shafts went home. Timmy flushed scarlet, but after a moment's further hesitation embarked on his story without further delay.

"The cause of the trouble was the same as it always was; Grandfather is all for our making a career in the family business, and Paul couldn't care less about the idea. Well, I'm not keen myself, but there doesn't seem anything to make a song about. I'll get out when I'm ready, and he knows it.

But Paul can't leave well alone, and he wants to get married
. . . that rather brought matters to a head.''

"Mr. Cassell objected?"

"He did. It wasn't Ann, you know, nobody could object
to Ann. Only it was a matter of principle, whatever Paul
does is wrong. You know how it is when people get like
that?"

"Unfortunately, yes."

"Well, Paul thought it wasn't reasonable for him to have
to wait another year. When we are twenty-five we get what
my father left. It isn't much, but enough for Paul's plan,
which is to set up farming in a small way. I can't say I see it
myself, because Ann . . . but that isn't my business, I suppose."

"Am I to understand that your grandfather was in a position
to decide whether Paul got his money or not?"

"That's right. I could have told him it was no use, but it
isn't much good telling people things they don't want to
hear. He just shrugged, and talked about it being 'only fair'.
As if,'' said Timmy, suddenly bitter, ''Grandfather was the
least concerned with fairness, so long as he got what he
wanted. But I'm off the track again . . .

"So there you have Paul, demanding his rights; and
Grandfather improving the shining hour with a few home
truths. The hell of a shindy. That was just after lunch, which
we'd all had here at home. And Uncle William was expected
about three o'clock."

"All?" said Antony.

"Well, Grandfather, of course. And Aunt Marian, she
lives here, anyway. And Paul and me. That's residents.
Then there were Uncle Greg and Aunt Agnes. And Brent.''

"Brent?"

"My cousin. Just a happy family party. It made it worse,
him being there; he's so much my grandfather's ideal. I am
not,'' explained Timmy carefully, ''fond of Brent.''

"You surprise me," said Antony; and grinned at him.

Timmy said defensively, "That isn't altogether irrelevant. Paul hadn't meant to say anything about Ann, not just
then; with everyone there it would have been a fatheaded
thing to do. Brent knew all about it, of course: Ann had told
Audrey, and Audrey told *him*. She's quite bright normally,

but she's engaged to Brent, and I suppose that makes a difference.''

"Before we go any further, you'd better explain Ann and Audrey.''

"But I told you! Oh, I see, you mean who *are* they? Well, they're cousins—of each other, I mean, not ours. Though the families have known each other for ever. Ann's father is a painter, an odd, extravagant, likeable chap; poor as a church mouse, of course. Audrey is an orphan, and has lived with them for the past four or five years: pretty well keeps the household together, if the truth were known, I think her father left her quite comfortable, as the saying is. So when Brent got himself engaged, Grandfather was quite happy about it. All most suitable! I'd have thought Audrey'd have had more sense, but you never can tell with girls, what they'll fall for. However—''

"You were implying, I think, that your cousin Brent informed Mr. Cassell of Paul's engagement.''

"Well, not just like that. We were going in to lunch when Paul arrived; that's one of the things that infuriates Grandfather, Paul *will* be late. So there's Brent, full of hearty good will, 'hear I must congratulate you, old boy . . . wish you all the best'.''

"A very proper sentiment.''

"There's a time for everything," said Timmy, "and a place for everything. And this was neither. Not with Paul standing there looking stuffed; and Aunt Marian (who's a dear, but not always tactful) asking questions as fast as she could lay tongue to them; and Grandfather lapping up every word, and looking grimmer and grimmer. Oh, lord!''

"I seem to be getting the impression that Mr. Cassell is a somewhat formidable old gentleman.''

"He's . . . . I don't know . . . you'll see for yourself, anyway." He thought for a moment. "I don't think 'formidable' is quite venomous enough, but I expect you'll think I'm laying it on a bit thick.''

"I'll reserve judgment.''

"You'll see," warned Timmy. "Anyway, just then he didn't say anything, but the atmosphere at lunch was somewhat strained, and they went into the study afterwards to have it out. Paul was a bit rattled by that time, you know, and I expect he said more than he ought. He told me very little about it, but Grandfather has been quite vocal on the subject.''

''I rather gather he won't be giving evidence for the defence.''

''Not he! He's made up his mind Paul meant to kill him, and he's scared stiff in consequence.'' Timmy's tone was not without its meed of satisfaction.

''Is it a reasonable contention: that a mistake of that nature could have been made?''

''Oh, yes, I think so. Uncle William looked very like Grandfather, and just sitting at the desk in the study, where anyone would expect Grandfather to be . . . you wouldn't notice the difference, I think, and they were both in dinner jackets. I don't mean I think Paul killed him, you know; but it does seem more likely that someone had it in for Grandfather, than that they wanted to murder Uncle William who has been away for eighteen years.''

''As long as that?''

''Yes. He hasn't been in England since the year . . . since my parents died. So if anyone wanted to kill him, you'd think it would be someone in Portugal, where he has been living. Not here.''

''No, I see. You haven't told me what your grandfather says about the interview.''

''Well, he forbade the banns, of course. Told Paul he was deceitful, and underhand, and—'' He stopped, and after a moment went on carefully, ''There are . . . things . . . that always come up when there's trouble. It isn't easy—''

''Skip it for now,'' said Antony.

''He said Paul couldn't have the money. He wrapped it up in a lot of talk about 'fulfilling a trust', which I don't suppose made it any easier to take. So Paul said, all right, they'd get married anyway, and both go on working for the year, and then do what they wanted. But Grandfather said if they did he'd throw them both out of work, and then what would they do? And there wasn't any answer to that, because Paul is about as much use in an office as Farmer Giles's prize bull; and though I expect Ann could get another job, things being what they are, she's such a little ninny it would be dreadful for her to have to try; and then she'd most likely do something silly and get thrown out. She works for the firm at present, she's one of the typists. And about as bad a typist," he added, consideringly, "as you'd meet in a day's march."

"All very pretty," said Antony (reflecting a trifle dismally on his uncle's probable comments on the interview as it would later have to be reported). "Yes, indeed!"

"I'm glad you think so."

"Well, we'll worry about that later. What were the rest of you doing, while this was going on?"

"We were in the drawing-room, being polite to each other . . . more or less. Aunt Marian got out her knitting, but even she had noticed the atmosphere, and rows always make her jittery. Aunt Agnes sat down by her, and started pouring out her latest grievance, I didn't listen particularly. She's one of those querulous women, and there's always something. Aunt Marian gave her half an ear. Uncle Greg withdrew himself behind *The Times,* and that left Brent and me to amuse each other. I told him straight what I thought of him, but it never does any good. And then Uncle William arrived."

He paused a moment, apparently surveying the scene he had been painting. "He was a nice old boy, with a kindly humorous look. Very like Grandfather, but very unlike, too, when you were talking to him. Just at first, of course, I kept in the background. It was all the older ones talking, because they knew him, you see. After a bit Grandfather called Brent over, and there was a lot about the firm, and how he was the third generation. Uncle William looked across at me, and said, 'You must be Timothy. I remember you well. Another representative of the third generation.' And I said . . . I don't know why, I could have kicked myself afterwards . . . I said, 'I'm not a Cassell, sir'."

The pause lengthened. Antony held his tongue, and after a while the younger man went on, "I expect I deserved what happened; he was only being kind, and I might as well have hit him in the face. Brent said something about my ambitions lying in another direction; he said it with a sneer, but I hardly had time to notice because then Grandfather said, quite quietly and deliberately, 'And Timmy's family, as he has reminded us, are noted in quite another connection than

that of trade.' It was pretty awful. Aunt Marian went quite
white, I thought she was going to faint; I know I felt sick;
and Uncle William (bless him) looked all round in a vague
sort of way, which I don't for a moment think was genuine,
and asked why he didn't see Paul.

"The answer to that, of course, was that Paul wasn't
there. He'd taken himself and his troubles on to the common, and he didn't come back until much later, when we
were at dinner. Brent and I went back to work, I don't know
what the others did, when I got home they'd gone up to
dress. It was supposed to be a festive occasion. I nearly
ducked out, only I didn't quite know where to go. Audrey
was coming to dinner, and I suppose Paul was with Ann.

"It wasn't so bad, in the event. Grandfather was sticky,
but the rest were more or less normal, and Audrey being
there even Brent was almost human. Round about ten
o'clock the party broke up. Uncle Greg and Aunt Agnes always go to bed early, and I expect Aunt Marian thought
Grandfather and Uncle William would like a session alone.
Brent went off to see Audrey home, and I was glad enough
to come up here."

He turned a little, to stare out the window. After a time
Antony prompted gently, "There must be more you can tell
me?"

"I was just wondering. This is the important bit, but most
of it is hearsay, I'm afraid." He looked apologetic, and
Antony realised, with surprise, that he was genuinely expecting a snub. He said quickly:

"Still, I should like to hear it. We'll worry about the evidential value later."

Timmy turned back to him. His smile was a little uncertain. He said, "They talked for about half an hour,
Grandfather and Uncle William. I should explain that it was
Grandfather's habit to go into the study, last thing at night,
and write up his diary. On Tuesday, though, Uncle William
said he had a letter he must write, so he took him in there
and made him free of the desk. He left him there, and about
five minutes later we heard the shot."

"Where were you then? And what have the rest of the
family to say about it?"

"I was in here, I told you. I looked into Paul's room when

I came up. He'd come in, and gone to bed, and was fast asleep. So I came in here. I hadn't got undressed, I thought perhaps I could work but I don't think I'd got three words written. Aunt Agnes was in bed and asleep, and never heard a thing. Uncle Greg was in the bath, and didn't appear until later. Aunt Marian had also retired, and only came down when she heard the commotion. Brent had got back from taking Audrey home; I heard his car as a matter of fact, about five or six minutes earlier.''

"And what had Mr. Cassell done, after leaving his brother in the study?"

"He says he came up to see if Paul had got home, and found his room untidy, and his bed rumpled but empty. So he went downstairs again, meaning to offer Uncle William a nightcap after he had dealt with his correspondence.''

"So you heard the shot. What then?"

"Well, it made me wonder. I mean, it isn't what you expect round here. Still, you don't expect murder, either, so I wasn't particularly excited. I went in to see if Paul had wakened up, and found his room empty, as Grandfather says. So I went downstairs to see if anyone knew what was going on. I went to the front door, but all seemed quiet outside, and as I came in again Grandfather came through from the back hall. He'd had the same idea, I think, but gone to the side door. He said very sharply, 'What is the matter? What has happened?' And before I could say anything we heard a shout from outside.''

He had been speaking quickly, but stopped now as though there was nothing more that could be said. He picked up a book from the window-seat beside him, regarded it blankly, and put it down again. He said, at last, ''The next bit isn't hearsay.''

Antony waited, and the silence grew. After a time he said, with a carefully casual air, ''This isn't the first time you've had a tragedy to face; but this time there may still be something to be saved from the wreckage. It's up to you.'' As he spoke, the words set up a connection in his mind, some train of thought that was gone before it could be formulated.

Timmy said, with suppressed violence, ''You'll think I'm a fool. But it was like . . . like a nightmare that came to life.

I could have understood if it had been me; I think if I went mad I could kill somebody—Brent, for instance. But Paul isn't like that.'' He looked at his companion helplessly. ''Nobody will believe me; they say he was moody, that no one knew what he was really like. And it's true enough he used to walk in his sleep. But can I tell you what I've thought? They say if you hypnotise somebody you can make them do anything, but not something that is quite against their nature. Don't you think it would be the same for some-one who was asleep?''

Antony said slowly, ''You're telling me your brother was sleep-walking that night? That the police think—?''

Timmy shook his head. ''The police just say he shot Un-cle William, thinking it was Grandfather. Grandfather says the same, but that he was mad. Paul says he was asleep.'' His look was defiant. ''I know it doesn't *sound* true.''

''Never mind how it sounds. Do you believe it?''

''I—''

''Do you believe it?'' His tone was insistent. Timmy said helplessly:

''I told you . . . how can I know?''

''At least, if he was sleep-walking it wasn't the first time?''

''No, but he hadn't . . . not for years. I think the row might have started him off again, though, because—'' He broke off.

Antony said merely, ''I see.'' Timmy showed no sign of wishing to take advantage of the pause which followed, so he added after a while, ''But you still haven't told me the bit that wasn't hearsay.''

''I'm sorry. I . . . I said we heard a shout, didn't I? I pushed past Grandfather, and went out by the side door, but he was just behind me, I heard his footsteps on the gravel. Brent called out again, I knew then it was his voice I'd heard before, he was saying, 'Drop it, you fool, drop it!' and then I came round the side of the house, and I could see them in the light from the study window.

''Brent was standing with his back to me, as though he'd come round the front of the house from the garage. And Paul was standing with his back to the shrubbery, as though he'd just taken a few steps out of it, and he had the rifle in his hand. And none of us said anything for a moment because we were looking in through the study window; Uncle William was there, and he'd fallen across the desk, but the light was bright and you couldn't mistake what had happened. And then Grandfather came up beside me, and he looked into the study too, and then he turned on Paul and screamed at him, 'You damned, murdering young swine,' . . . I remember particularly,'' Timmy explained carefully, ''because I thought at the time how unlikely it sounded. But that's what he said. 'You damned, murdering young swine . . . so you wanted to kill me.' And Paul turned very slowly and looked straight at him.'' Timmy paused, and gulped, and looked at his companion. But finding no encouragement to have done with his narration he added resolutely:

''He turned and looked at Grandfather, and he looked as though he was dreaming; and he said very slowly, 'I don't understand. I thought it was you!' ''

CHAPTER 3

ANTONY REFLECTED, with a certain wry, inward amusement, that he was getting no more than he had asked for: the case against his client, served up with all the trimmings.

Timmy was regarding him anxiously. He said after a moment, "That was it, really. Paul said he woke up on the lawn near the shrubbery; he thought it must have been the sound of the shot that roused him (this was some time later, of course, when we'd had time to think about things a bit); anyway, he knows he felt startled. And he went into the bushes . . . you know, that is reasonable," said Timmy, eagerly. "If he heard the shot, even while he was asleep, he would turn automatically towards the place it came from. Don't you think?" Antony gave a grunt that he hoped might sound both encouraging and non-committal. "Anyway, that's what he did. Only there was nothing to see, so he turned towards the house again, and when he came to the edge of the bushes there was the rifle lying on the ground. He could see it quite clearly in the light from the study window. So he picked it up." Timmy paused, and said aggressively, "It was quite a natural thing to do."

"Quite natural."

"And then he looked in at the study window, and saw Uncle William; only, of course, he thought it was Grandfather. And, you see, that was one of the first things they said: that Paul was the only one of us who hadn't seen Uncle William, and didn't know how alike the two of them were."

"Yes, of course." Obviously, the right solution, he reflected, and why seek further? Why, indeed? "Well, I don't think," he added, aloud, "there's much point in taking this any further to-night."

Timmy got up. It was a sudden, jerky movement, as though a spring had been released. He said—and the words, too, were jerky and gave no evidence of forethought, "Do you mean, you've made up your mind you can't help Paul?"

"I hope all the conclusions you leap to aren't based on such faulty premises," said Antony. He spoke sharply, to cover a sudden urge of sympathy. On an impulse he added, "I'll talk to my uncle. I think Bellerby's right, and he's the man you want."

"Then . . . the only thing is, will he want to say Paul's mad?"

"That isn't a question I can possibly answer at this stage. When the time comes you can rely on him to do what seems best for your brother." He added, in reply to Timmy's look of discontent, "I know that's not much consolation, but you must realise I can't advise you until I know all the facts."

"I've told you—"

"Yes, I know. But you can't build a case on one witness."

"No, I see. Stupid of me," said Timmy.

Antony got up. "Anyway, I've by no means finished with you, I'm afraid. But I'd like to get Tuesday night clear, from all angles, before I dig any further. I'll keep you posted . . . I promise you that."

"Thank you." Timmy sounded subdued, and led the way downstairs in silence. As they reached the front door he roused himself to ask, "Did you come by car, or do you want a taxi?"

"I'll get a bus at the corner. It takes me nearly home."

"Then I'll walk to the gate with you."

They went down the drive together in a silence that was uneasy with unspoken thoughts. It was nearly dark now, and the light near the front door was soon obscured by the trees that overhung the path. They were in sight of the gate when Antony heard the footsteps, which seemed to be approaching diffidently. Then the latch clicked, and a girl was coming towards them under the trees.

It was too dark to see her face, but he guessed that she was young from the slightness of her figure and the lightness of her step, even before he heard her voice. When she spoke there was no doubt about it; twenty at the most, Antony decided. She said, "Timmy?" doubtfully. And then, with more assurance, "I'm glad I met you."

Timmy Herron had halted. "Ann, you shouldn't—" He, too, sounded uncertain, and there was no mistaking the strain in his voice.

The girl said, quickly, "I didn't want to come to the house. Only, I had to know—" She was close to him now, and said again, "Oh, Timmy!" Timmy's arms went round her.

It was at this point that Antony, who had cleared his throat to make his adieux, decided to make himself scarce without ceremony. He glanced back as he shut the gate, but they did not seem to have moved, nor had there been any further words between them.

Jenny Maitland was at home; curled up on the sofa, and half asleep over a book. Antony stood in the doorway for a moment, watching her: her brown curls were ruffled, but touched with gold in the lamp-light; she looked relaxed and contented as a kitten before a fire. He was feeling tired, and discouraged (most illogically), and his shoulder was aching; but he was comforted, as always, merely by finding her there among all the familiar things in the big shabby room. She looked up and smiled at him; and her grey eyes were welcoming, though her voice sounded lazy.

"You've been ages, darling. I ought to have brought the car."

He bent to kiss her, looked at and through her for a moment and then remarked, "Hell and damnation!" in a vague and dispassionate tone. Jenny sat up.

"Is it the Cassell brief, Antony? I thought—"

He came round the end of the sofa, and stood on the hearth-rug, looking down at her in a troubled way. "I'm theorising ahead of my data, love; but somehow I don't think I like our client."

"Have you seen Mr. Cassell, then?"

"No, only the other grandson—Paul's twin. Name of Timothy. A nice lad, and standing up pretty well to a dose of trouble that would make Job think twice. I told you what happened to them, didn't I? I haven't had the story in detail yet, but the inference is that their father shot his wife and brother out of jealousy, which isn't a nice background. As far as I can make out the old man brought them up, and hasn't let them forget about it for a moment. May Beelzebub and all demons haunt him!''

''Well, you know—this Mr. Cassell may be everything that's horrid, and still be right about Paul being mad.''

''I know. I think most probably he is right. In which case I shall have the devil's own job with Uncle Nick.''

''He seems very determined not to take the brief.''

''As to that,'' said Antony, ''we shall see!''

''I don't understand. Do you think he didn't do it?''

Antony sat down. ''There's every reason to believe him guilty, and nothing at all to be said for the defence, so far as I can see. As to whether he really is mad . . . well, I may be wiser after I've seen him to-morrow. Probably he is, as he seems to have killed the wrong man. But he wouldn't need to be mad, I should think, to have wanted to kill his grandfather.''

''You sound very bitter,'' said Jenny quietly.

''Yes, I'm sorry. Get me a drink, Jenny—something stronger than milk, if you love me. We'll see what happens to-morrow. Who lives may learn.''

Antony didn't realise, until he saw Paul Herron next morning, how firmly he had expected to find in him the counterpart of his brother. Not that he had consciously formulated the thought, but it was not the less real for that; and he was glad to have the opportunity, while Bellerby was greeting his client, of studying the young man and rearranging his ideas.

Paul was a little shorter than his brother; squarer both of face and figure; with hair no nearer dark than ''mouse-coloured,'' blue eyes and a pugnacious set to his chin. He came forward slowly into the bare room where they were to interview him, and did not seem aware of the door that slammed behind him. Antony himself was frankly oppressed by his surroundings and even the solicitor inclined to a more sedate attitude than was his wont; but the prisoner, apart from what might or might not have been an unnatural quietness, gave no sign of being affected by his situation.

Antony, meditating what he had heard of Paul Herron's "oddness," grew more and more bewildered.

Mr. Bellerby had got them settled to his satisfaction, and beamed from one to other of his companions. "Now, Maitland, I think we can get down to business."

"Yes, indeed," said Antony. As he turned to the younger man his tone was bland and friendly. "Well, Mr. Herron, you must be heartily sick of questions by this time—"

"Yes," said Paul. He said it flatly, without apparent malice; but the effect was disconcerting in the extreme. After a moment he added, looking at the solicitor, and speaking with the first sign of animation he had so far displayed: "I told you I wouldn't see another doctor. I'm rather ill-placed here to refuse visitors, but at least I don't have to talk to them."

"But—" said Mr. Bellerby, and looked helplessly at his colleague. Antony took up the protest.

"But I'm not a doctor. Merely a member of the legal profession. Does that make any difference?"

"No," said Paul, without turning his head.

Antony decided that if he were to allow these tactics to daunt him, he might as well give up and go home. He said, firmly, "I'm from my uncle's chambers: Sir Nicholas Harding, you've probably heard of him."

"No," said Paul again.

"Your brother had."

"Timmy? Have you seen Timmy?" He still displayed no real interest, but his look was—perhaps?—a little less wary.

"I talked with him yesterday evening."

"Did he say?. . . well no, of course he wouldn't—" He broke off, looking confused; and Antony's thoughts turned briefly to the two young people he had left last night, under the trees. Paul added slowly, "I suppose it can't do any harm. But it won't do any good either, that I can see."

"My dear boy," the solicitor cut in quickly, "we're only here to help you!"

"I know," retorted Paul, "that's what they all said."

Antony leaned back in his chair, and said with an air of casualness that only just missed being over-elaborate, "All? How many doctors have they unleashed on you, for goodness' sake?"

"Well . . . only two, as a matter of fact. First it was the police, and then he sent one." He nodded towards the solicitor, but without taking his eyes off the other man's face. For the first time Antony seemed to have his attention. "And *he* said he'd like another opinion. That's why I thought it was you. And they asked questions all right, and then the same ones over again. Only they wouldn't tell me anything."

"What did you want them to tell you?"

"Oh, I don't know . . . whether they thought—"

Antony removed his gaze from the ceiling. His tone was still casual, but his look was sharp and direct. "Whether you are mad or not? Is that what you're trying to say?" He had deliberately turned the phrase, and was interested to note that Paul, in replying, reverted to the words he had originally used.

"Well, I had some interest in knowing what they thought."

"Only that?"

"What else, then?"

"You didn't wonder, yourself—"

Paul broke in angrily, "Look, I've had time to think about this. About trying to kill my grandfather. I didn't, you know."

Antony was silent now. He could hear Mr. Bellerby, beside him, shift uneasily in his chair. After a moment Paul went on:

"Well, I couldn't have done, and not known it. Even if I am mad. I mean, I'd have known there was a gap . . . something missing." He paused, and went on in a tone that was suddenly uncertain, "It was . . . just like the other times."

"But it's a long time—isn't it?—since you did any sleep-walking."

"You can take it from me, it's not a thing you forget. You go to sleep, and that ought to be that; and then you wake up somewhere else. You wouldn't forget what it felt like, not in a thousand years."

"And this time, you say, your experience was in no way different from previous occasions?"

"No, it wasn't." Paul sounded dogged now. "Only nobody seems to believe that. And if you're here because my grandfather sent you, I don't suppose you will, either.''

"It doesn't seem to follow," said Antony, and his tone was dry. He added, after a moment, "Your grandfather is not exactly fond of you, is he?''

Paul looked startled. He said slowly, "If you mean—''

"I mean," said Antony, "precisely what I say. We'll get on a lot quicker if you'll just take that for granted.''

"But that wasn't—''

"Damn it all! Can't you get it into your head that I am not a doctor? I've no interest at all in your health, and very little in your state of mind. Have you got that?''

Paul smiled at him, and looked for the first time young enough to be Timothy Herron's twin. His smile was apologetic, and when he spoke again he sounded unsure of himself. "I'm sorry. But it isn't easy to tell you, really. I mean, I've always known how I felt about him, but I don't think I've ever thought about it the other way round.''

"Well, think about it now.''

"I'm trying to. I think," said Paul slowly, "that if you asked Grandfather that question he would say he had done his duty. I don't think he dislikes us exactly, Timmy and me; but we make him think of things he'd rather forget, so he doesn't like us either. I'll tell you something, though: he honestly thinks I tried to kill him.''

"So I gather.''

"I expect it was a relief when they arrested me . . . in a way. Only he doesn't want a scandal, not again, so that's why he wants to prove I'm mad.''

"He might even believe that, too.''

"Oh, I shouldn't think so. After all, he knows me." (And that, thought Antony, is a dangerous line of argument, my friend.) "But he thinks it's slightly more respectable to be mad than just to be a murderer.''

"He might even be thinking of your safety.''

"Well—'' Paul sounded doubtful. "He couldn't really think—'' He stopped speaking, and eyed his companions consideringly. "You'd better understand this once and for all. I know I'm in a spot, and I've got to take my chance when the trial comes on. But I will not plead insanity.'' He caught Antony's eye, and added truculently, "Yes, I know

I'm scared stiff. But I'm not mad. And I didn't kill Uncle William.''

Antony let the silence lengthen, and when he did speak it was with decision. ''Right!'' he said briskly. ''Then let's get down to business.''

CHAPTER 4

SIR NICHOLAS took the news that he was committed to acceptance of the Herron brief with surprising calmness. It was conveyed to him by his nephew when he reached the Temple again after regaling Mr. Bellerby with a somewhat lengthy luncheon, and after one brief, unemotional outburst he pushed all his other papers ruthlessly on to the floor, sharpened three pencils, and provided himself with a fresh foolscap pad from the drawer of his desk. Antony, who knew that all these preparations would result in nothing more momentous than the drawing of a series of rather unlikely-looking ducks, in solemn procession across the pad, watched him with patient amusement. Having donned a pair of dark-rimmed spectacles, which he had taken to for the first time during the previous Hilary term, Counsel found his preparations complete, and looked expectantly at the younger man.

"You are, I take it, satisfied as to the sanity of our client? Is he guilty, or not?"

"He says not. I'm inclined to believe him."

"That's just as well. It might be difficult to show mitigating circumstances."

"There's something singularly cold-blooded about potting your grandfather through his study window," Antony agreed. "Especially when you only succeed in killing your great-uncle." Sir Nicholas, who affected an extreme aversion to slang, winced slightly, but made no comment. Encouraged by this forbearance his nephew continued, "I wouldn't take an oath he didn't do it without knowing; but I'd lay a pretty stiff bet on it."

"That means you're not sure." Sir Nicholas scowled at

his pencil. After a moment he looked up. "Well, fair enough, I don't see how you could be. What do the doctors say?"

"Doctor MacSomething—Bellerby's chap—wouldn't commit himself. Wanted another opinion, said there were suggestive symptoms. Good heavens, Uncle Nick, aren't there always symptoms?" His uncle nodded absently, and provided his leading duck with a pair of pince-nez. "The other one—I think from what Paul said of the trend of his questions that he came to the conclusion an insanity plea would not be valid."

"And your own opinion . . . yes, I see. What does Bellerby say?"

"Well, it took me some time to get him to give an opinion of his own. Very full of what his client said . . . he sounds pretty much of a menace, sir. He insisted that Paul had been much calmer to-day than when he saw him previously. I don't think that means much, as things are. I'll tell you something, Uncle Nick; if the time comes to break it to old Cassell that his grandson will be giving a straight 'not guilty' plea, it won't be his solicitor who does it."

"Hum," said Sir Nicholas. "I suppose you don't think the fact the Bellerby is supposed to instruct us counts for anything."

"Not much, frankly. Well, you know I told him he couldn't have you *and* an insanity plea, but I didn't stress that to-day, of course."

"Quite right. Now, to get down to it: what relevant facts have you to give me?"

Antony considered. "Well, first there's what the prosecution will say. Paul quarrelled with his grandfather, constantly, over a period of years; and with especial bitterness on the day of the crime. Paul was the only member of the household who hadn't met Uncle William, and so had no idea how strongly he resembled Ambrose Cassell. Paul, whether sleep-walking or not, was present at the scene of the crime, where he was found immediately after the shooting with the gun in his hands (there's no doubt about that, they cited it when he came up before the magistrates). About the only thing to be said by way of answer is that the murder was not necessarily committed by a member of the household, and even one of them could have been misled by the fact that Uncle William was sitting where his brother might have been expected to be at that time of day. We can't deny Paul's presence, or that he was holding the gun, or (unfortunately) the fact of the quarrel.''

''Ambrose Cassell being still alive to tell the tale. Will he testify?''

''I don't see how he can help himself; apparently he gave his opinion pretty freely to the police. Bellerby says, unwillingly; Paul and Timmy both say he's scared because he really thinks Paul tried to kill him. If that's correct, I'd say he would trot out everything he can think of.''

''I see. And even if the prosecution assume that we are pleading insanity, they'll still call him to prove motive. Did you say you liked this case, Antony?''

His nephew grinned. ''It has its points. However, I'll not deny it's tricky.''

''Tricky!'' Sir Nicholas added a barrister's wig to the largest duck, and sat back to regard his handiwork critically. ''Well, my boy, it looks as if you're going to be busy. I refuse to go to court without something to say.''

''Oh, I'll dig around. I'm afraid I'm going to be unpopular in the Cassell family by the time I've finished.''

''They'll just have to put up with it. I've got to have something to construct a case of, after all.''

''Yes, I see that. I wonder if they will.'' Antony got up and stretched. ''I've a feeling they'll think it a pretty poor reason for parading the family skeletons for my inspection.''

His uncle tilted back his chair. ''Before you go, you might restore some of those no-doubt fascinating bundles of documents which Mallory insists on keeping on my desk. I take it you're off to see Mr. Cassell?''

''I think so, don't you?''

''Well, I see no reason to go into any detail—'' Antony, who was grovelling on hands and knees at the far side of the desk, gave a censorious grunt; his uncle added, defensively, ''After all, I don't know yet what will be best to do.''

''And that,'' said Antony, scrambling to his feet, ''is only too sadly true.'' He dumped the deeds he was holding in front of Sir Nicholas, who prodded at them idly with his pencil.

"By the way," he remarked, as the younger man turned to go, "what was William Cassell doing in the study in the five minutes before he died?"

Antony looked over his shoulder, but did not retrace his steps. "He'd started a letter," he said. "A personal letter, in Portuguese; I gather he hadn't got much further than 'dear Manuel'. And he had drawn a life-like sketch of his brother on the blotting-pad. Apparently he had quite a gift that way."

Sir Nicholas looked complacently at his parade of ducks. "Poor Uncle William," he sighed.

The offices of Messrs. Cassell and Company were of the old-fashioned variety. Antony's first impression was of masses of heavy mahogany, all dustless, all polished until it shone; even the dark linoleum showed no signs of wear, despite what was probably some fifty years' service, and had undergone such ruthless treatment at the hands of some over-zealous person that it now presented all the more inconvenient aspects of a skating rink.

The girl who preceded him down the corridor had bright hair and a demure frock. She walked confidently enough, despite high heels. No doubt the office boy, if there was one, would regard this passage as being specially constructed for him to slide along; or perhaps not, for here was a door with the discreet superscription "Managing Director." The girl paused and knocked; smiled briefly and encouragingly over her shoulder as a voice bade them enter; opened the door, announced, "Mr. Maitland," and stood back to let him pass. Though her manner was as demure as her dress, Antony was conscious that she regarded him with an air of amused sympathy, but he had no time to wonder why this should be so. A moment later the door closed behind her, and he was left with the absurd feeling of having been abandoned by his only friend. Well, he had faced more formidable lions than Ambrose Cassell in his time.

And first, he found, he must rearrange all the ideas he had had about the old man's appearance. From Paul and Timmy's description he had somehow created for himself a very formidable image, beetle-browed, and of gigantic stature. What he now saw was a man of rather less than middle height, slightly built, and fastidiously neat. He had a good deal of grey hair, very straight and sleek; a steely eye behind old-fashioned gold-rimmed spectacles; and a mouth like a rat-trap. Antony decided after one look that the creature of his imagination had been, after all, the less dangerous. He produced his most amiable smile.

Ambrose Cassell, for his part, took one look at the younger man, and it was apparent that his worst fears had been realised. He saw a tall young man, with a thin, intelligent face; clad with conventional sobriety, and concealing pretty well under a carefully professional manner his own preference for the casual. Characteristically, old Mr. Cassell discounted the intelligence and observed only the youth (which affronted him), and the amused look in the grey eyes (which he chose to regard as personally directed). He said, "Hmph," and was silent a moment; after a while he added in an accusing tone, "I've been talking to Bellerby."

"Then I expect he told you—"

"He talked a lot of nonsense," said Ambrose Cassell. "Professional etiquette, indeed." From which oblique remark Antony gathered that the present inaccessibility of Sir Nicholas was regarded as a cause of grievance. He contemplated some soothing remarks, but thought on the whole there was more to be gained by silence on this point. The old man showed no disposition to let the silence lengthen.

"Questions, Bellerby said. Thought he'd have told you it all; thought it was obvious, myself."

"I'm afraid," said Antony firmly, "we haven't anything like a case to take to court."

"Why not? Boy's mad, isn't he? Well then!"

"There's the little matter of legal proof, sir."

"Macintyre will swear—"

"It's not quite as easy as that."

Mr. Cassell seated himself again at his desk, and waved irritably towards a chair, which Antony took. He added, "May I explain?"

"I'm waiting."

"Well, sir, Doctor Macintyre is inclined to agree with you as to your grandson's state of mind. He'll give his opin-

ion in court, he'll give his reasons, and very impressive
they'll sound. That's before the prosecution have their
say.''

''What has that to do with it. The facts—''

''Facts in a court of law are what you can make the jury
believe: no more, no less.''

''You appear to me to be a very cynical young man,'' said
Ambrose Cassell severely. Antony was a trifle taken aback.
''And what,'' the older man added, ''could the prosecution
find to say that would discredit Doctor Macintyre?''

''You mistake me, sir. They wouldn't try to discredit
him, only to make the jury doubt if his opinions were the
right ones.''

''How could they do that?''

''One question would do it. 'When you saw Paul Herron,
Doctor, it was with full knowledge of his family background, and of the crime of which he is accused. I put it to
you, now, these things may well have influenced you.' By
the time that theme had been elaborated—''

''You are telling me, then, that it is a waste of time to call
expert evidence on this point?''

''Far from it. I'm only saying we can't rely on it exclusively. The police have had their doctor to see your grandson, too. It's our business to shake the jury's faith in what he
says. With luck, the two of them will cancel out with a slight
bias in our favour; but we've got to have more.''

''What are your questions, then?''

''I shall also want to talk to the other members of your
family,'' Antony warned him, feeling he had better get this
clear at the outset. ''But I felt I should see you first.''

''Very proper. That didn't stop you talking to young
Timmy last evening, though. What did he have to say for
himself?''

''He gave me a very helpful account of what happened at
your home last Tuesday.''

The old man looked at him suspiciously, but for once
made no direct comment. ''What's that to the point?''

''It seems to have a certain relevance, sir,'' said Antony,
at his most innocent.

''No good disputing facts. William's dead, that's a fact.
Paul shot him, meant to kill me. Father mad as a hatter,

must have been, stands to reason. Not good for a child, all that. Not to mention heredity.''

''Bellerby mentioned Paul's oddness as a boy. Can you tell me about that, sir?''

''He was a quiet, moody child. It is difficult to define such things; there was a quality of strangeness, of the unexpected.''

''Perhaps you can give me some particular instance?''

''I'm afraid not.'' He sounded impatient. ''There was the sleep-walking, of course.''

''But something he *did*, sir. Surely—''

''I think you must take my word, Mr. Maitland, that he was different from other boys.''

''It isn't my beliefs we're concerned with,'' said Antony, bluntly. ''It's what the jury will think that matters in the end.''

The old man's lips were a thin line. He was breathing rather quickly. ''Timmy was quite different,'' he insisted.

''That's hardly helpful, sir. A moment ago you were speaking of heredity.'' He caught his companion's eye, and added in a hurry, ''About Paul's father—''

''Handsome young devil. Good family. Not good enough for Ruth, of course.''

''And his brother—''

''Not a word of truth in what they said.'' He was on surer ground now, and gave his opinion firmly. ''Must have been mad to think it—Matthew, I mean. Let alone to do what he did.''

''You must remember, sir, this is all new ground to me. Matthew was your son-in-law, I take it.''

''That's right, Ruth's husband. Had a twin brother, Mark (like as two peas, they were). No saying anything to the girl, always thought the world of him, and went on that way, too, whatever nonsense he got into his head.''

''Then there had been trouble between them?''

''Nothing of the sort. Who told you that? Pack of lies.''

''I understood you to say, sir—''

''I'm telling you what we thought afterwards. There had to be some reason, even for a madman, to do that.''

''I'm sorry to harp on a painful subject, Mr. Cassell, but as you yourself pointed out, what happened to Paul's parents is of the utmost importance to the present issue. If you could give me a connected narrative—''

The old man glared. ''I've told you, haven't I? Twin brothers Matthew and Mark, inseparable. Matthew married my girl, Ruth. Still inseparable, the three of them. No sign of anything wrong, though Wayne said afterwards—''

''Wayne, sir?''

''Cousin of Matthew's. Only a lad then, but a sensible sort of fellow. Come to think of it, he'd be able to tell you more than anybody—if you must go into all this.''

''Thank you, I'll see him. But you were telling me—''

''Well, Wayne said Matt had been odd in his manner. Said he'd noticed it for some time, thought he was 'run down' or some such nonsense.''

''Did Matthew leave any statement?''

''Nothing like that. Didn't need to. Facts were obvious enough.''

''The facts, sir?''

''Neighbour woke early one morning. They lived in one of those blocks of flats, Plantagenet Mansions, over the other side of the common. Uncivilised sort of way to live. Neighbour heard one of the twins crying, thought it sounded queer, not natural. Went and banged on the door. After a bit Timmy opened it, he was the one that was doing the crying. Fellow went in, found the three of them in the living-room. Gun in Matt's hand.''

''The children were there?''

''Of course they were. Their home, wasn't it?''

''And there had been nothing to lead you to expect trouble?''

''I told you, nothing. Only what Wayne said.''

''Then may we turn to more recent events, sir? Had Mr. William Cassell's visit been long planned?''

''Three or four months, maybe longer.''

''Was he returning to England permanently?''

''He intended to stay about six weeks with us.''

''Was he married?''

''No.''

''Have you been in touch with his household, or his associates in Portugal, Mr. Cassell?''

''I have done all that was proper, I believe.''

"I was considering, sir, the question of motive."

"That need not concern us. The motive is here, in England; and it was a motive for my death, not his."

"Would it not be better to examine all possibilities?"

"Mr. Maitland!" His tone had a sharp edge to it. "The one thing we know beyond doubt is that Paul has committed murder. He was six years old when his uncle left England after his last visit. It is a little far-fetched—"

"The possibility I had in mind, sir, does not seem to have occurred to you. You did not see Paul fire the shot."

"I saw him a moment after, with the gun in his hand. Yes, and he turned and said to my face he thought he had killed me. That's all the proof I need, young man."

"That is your story as it stands in the police records? As you will tell it in court?"

"It is the truth."

Something in that calm persistence got under Antony's guard. He said, "Then you are not interested in the possibility that your grandson is innocent?" For the first time his voice had lost its level note, and held a certain tartness.

"It is not a possibility. He hated me. He tried to kill me."

"And you would rather see him proved mad, than Not Guilty?"

There was a silence. Antony realised for the first time that Timmy Herron's use of the word "venomous" had been all too apt. After a while the old man spoke, and his tone was silky. "Do you not a little exceed your instructions, Mr. Maitland?"

"Do I, sir?"

"Perhaps I am confused again by professional etiquette. I was under the impression that Bellerby had made my intentions quite clear when he retained you."

Antony got up. He was angry; and too angry to care that he was displaying it. "In the c-conduct of the case, sir, I'm afraid you will find my uncle is not open to d-direction."

"As to that, we shall see!" There was no doubt about the old man's anger now. "You've been talking to Paul and Timmy, but I've no doubt Sir Nicholas will have more wisdom than to listen to their nonsense."

"I'd better go." He had upset the impression of compliance, but for the moment cared nothing for that. "If you wish, I will recommend my uncle to see you at the first opportunity.''

''That will certainly be best.'' The old man's stiffness matched his own. ''I will speak to Bellerby.''

''Very well.'' He went to the door, but paused for a parting word. ''But don't be too sure about anything, Mr. Cassell. Then you won't be disappointed.''

CHAPTER 5

ANTONY ARRIVED home that evening much later than he had intended. When he let himself into the house in Kempenfeldt Square Sir Nicholas's quarters were in darkness, and he guessed (for once, without much pleasure) that he would find his uncle upstairs, awaiting his return.

He and Jenny had been married in the dark days of the war, and when Antony was out of the army again Sir Nicholas had given over to them the two top floors of his London house. It had proved to be a convenient arrangement, which none of them had ever wanted to change; and even now, when he was tired and disinclined for argument, Antony grinned to himself as he mounted the stairs. There were, after all, advantages in fighting on one's own ground. Sir Nicholas, when occupied with a brief, was as aggressive and quarrelsome as a dog with a bone; but it was not at these times, as his nephew well knew, that he was at his most dangerous. When he spoke you fair, and dealt most gently with the point at issue, then was the time for the prudent to retire to cover: to batten down the hatches, and make all secure.

He found Sir Nicholas in the living-room, prowling round the dinner table which had now been cleared so that one place only remained, and eyeing the remains of a salmon salad with every appearance of revulsion.

He transferred an unamiable stare from the fish to his nephew, and remarked bitterly, as Antony supplied himself with sherry, "I hope it chokes you."

"A fine, charitable sentiment! Am I to take it you've been talking to Bellerby?"

"He gibbered at me," complained Sir Nicholas. "He rang me up and gibbered at me. I couldn't stop him!"

38

"Well, I'm sorry about that," Antony admitted indifferently. His tone appeared to infuriate his uncle, who said with some heat:

"You forced me into this, against my better judgment; and now you have bungled the very first move in the game."

"If you'd seen him, sir—"

"I shall on Monday, so I understand. At least, I can promise you, I shan't brawl with him."

"I didn't exactly—"

"You lost your temper," Sir Nicholas was accusing.

"Well, really, sir, the old blighter was so smug—"

Jenny came in just then, with a plate of soup. "Come and eat, darling. I'm sure it's bad for you to quarrel with Uncle Nick on an empty stomach."

Antony took his sherry with him to the table. Sir Nicholas said in a crushing tone, "We were not quarrelling. I was merely protesting at the intolerable position in which your husband has placed me. A futile procedure, as I should know by now."

Antony pulled a face at his wife, and choked over his soup. As soon as he could, he said pacifically: "Well, sir, I'll admit it's very dreadful. What did Bellerby say?"

"I told you, he gibbered at me. I am not accustomed," said the older man, harking back to his original grievance, "to being gibbered at by my instructing solicitor."

"Well, you know Bellerby."

"To my misfortune. And if you tell me again," he added, seeing his nephew about to speak, "that it's an interesting case, I won't be answerable for the consequences."

Antony waved a deprecatory hand, and maintained a discreet silence. He addressed himself to his dinner. Jenny said, "It's not very warm this evening," and turned on one bar of the electric fire. Sir Nicholas sat and growled gently to himself. The silence lengthened.

After a while, Antony left the table, and moved to the circle of chairs near the fire. Jenny produced coffee, and placed cigars temptingly within the older man's reach. Sir Nicholas reached for one absent-mindedly, gave his nephew a look which was anything but affectionate, and remarked testily:

"Well? I suppose you have done something with your time since I saw you?"

Antony, about to indulge in a little more baiting of his uncle, caught Jenny's eye, and said meekly, "Nothing very startling, I'm afraid. But I've made a beginning by seeing some of the family."

"You'd better tell me first about your interview with Cassell."

"Yes, sir." This was dangerous ground, and he started out without any intention of dwelling unduly upon the details. "We began well enough, though he appeared put out not to be seeing you. He seemed to think the matter was settled, an open and shut case, no need for anything but for you to tell the court that Paul was mad. I enlightened him, tactfully." Sir Nicholas snorted. "Yes, really, sir. He then gave me the family history, in brief. Not much more than we know, and no value as evidence. And he couldn't give me any better reason for supposing Paul odd than the fact that he was quiet and moody as a child." Sir Nicholas looked up quickly, but made no comment. "I asked him, of course, about William Cassell's private affairs; I think that was fair enough, Uncle Nick."

"It's a point that must be covered, certainly."

"Well, that was what started the fireworks. He got very stiff with me, and we didn't get any further with that subject. It led us to his evidence about the murder, though."

"Which is—?"

"He heard the shot; he followed Timmy from the house; he saw Paul with the gun in his hand. For good measure, Paul said he thought he'd killed *him*. Well, even as Timmy tells it, his words could bear that construction."

"That fact is to be regretted, but is only too obvious. I still don't see why you deliberately—"

"It wasn't deliberate, sir. He wouldn't admit any other possibility than that Paul hated him and had tried to kill him."

"Couldn't you have left it at that?"

"I could have done. I should have done. I didn't." He sounded suddenly weary. "Shall we let it go at that, Uncle Nick?"

"You'd better tell me."

"He said I exceeded my instructions; that he thought Bellerby had made *his* intentions quite clear. I said the conduct of the case was your affair, and you weren't open to direction. That was all, really. Only the atmosphere was a bit heated, you know."

Sir Nicholas smiled suddenly. "Well, we'll take it he's a trying old gentleman. After all, there's no great harm done."

"But we agreed—"

"I'd like some more coffee, Jenny. Is there some?" Antony eyed his uncle suspiciously for a moment, and then got up and collected his empty cup. Returning it, refilled, he remarked in a troubled way:

"I'd better elaborate, all the same. His evidence that Paul shot Great-uncle William, but meant to kill his grandfather, is convincing. His statement that Paul is mad carries no conviction at all. Standing alone, his evidence would hang his grandson. What I can't decide is whether he knows it."

"Now that," said his uncle, with some enthusiasm, "is what I call a really nice point. I'm beginning to look forward to meeting our client."

"You're welcome to him."

"But meanwhile, I gather your interview was not prolonged beyond this point?"

"I retired in as good order as I could, and asked if Gregory Cassell was in. And I may as well say straight out, I saw him, but it was a waste of time."

Jenny, who had unearthed some knitting from underneath a cushion, looked up and said, "I wish you'd explain, darling. I'm getting dreadfully confused by all these Cassells."

"Oh, there are more to come. Wait till I get to the aunts; not to mention Brent."

Jenny looked appealingly at Sir Nicholas, who explained, "Ambrose and William Cassell were brothers. William (so far as we know) died without issue. Ambrose is a widower, with one unmarried daughter—"

"Aunt Marian," interpolated Antony.

"—and one married son, the Gregory Cassell of whom we are now speaking."

"Uncle Gregory is married to Aunt Agnes," Antony again broke in. "And Brent is their son."

Jenny put a hand to her head. Sir Nicholas smiled at her encouragingly. "Another daughter of Ambrose Cassell, Ruth (now deceased) married Matthew Herron, and was the mother of Paul and Timothy. Did they do it purposely, by the way?"

"Did who do what on purpose?"

"The Herron family."

"Oh, the names. I should think so, wouldn't you?"

"Is that clear now, Jenny?"

Jenny said, "Yes," but she sounded doubtful. After a moment she went on, "I think if you left out the surnames, and just called them Aunt and Uncle, it might help a bit."

"All right. But you'll have to remember that 'Uncle William' is really 'Great-uncle', from the twins' point of view, that is."

"And that being decided," said Sir Nicholas, with sudden impatience, "perhaps we may return to Uncle Gregory?"

Antony laughed. Jenny asked quickly, "What is he like?"

"He's the sort of man who snaps at his servants, and bullies his typist. You know."

"I think I do."

"Physically, he's a bad reproduction of his father: hair darker, clothes not so tidy, manner not nearly so precise. A fussy little man. Opinions, his father's watered down. Of course Paul had done it, he was quite insane, poor lad. It had been a great shock to his father, he was still greatly upset. Of course, they shouldn't have been so surprised, knowing Paul's family history and how strange he had always been."

"I am getting a little tired of that phrase," said Sir Nicholas. "Could *he* give any examples of this alleged strangeness?"

"He said the twins both had a great deal to thank their grandfather for, and were both ungrateful. Paul was quiet: sullen, according to Gregory; but Timmy didn't fare much better, though he admitted he was more lively. And that, Uncle Nick, was as near as I could get to a reason for his statement: you might as well try to cross-examine a jellyfish."

"Shall I have to?"

"No. He's as empty of information as he is of original opinions. All he could tell me about the evening in question was hearsay, though he gave quite a vivid account of Uncle William's arrival, and Timmy's rudeness, and how Paul ought to have been there. Not very useful. He was in the bath when the shot was fired, which somehow seems typical. He didn't hear anything until he came out of the bathroom, and by that time the commotion was in full swing."

"How delightfully vague."

"I asked him about the rifle. He said it belonged to Paul (it would!) and was only in town because it had been brought up for repairs. I'll remember to cover it with the others, though I don't expect it will help us much."

"How long had it been in the Wimbledon house? And who knew it was there?"

"That wasn't the sort of thing Uncle Greg would know. Both the twins keep guns at his country place for use when on holiday; he thinks Brent found it was faulty, and brought it up to town about a month ago; he doesn't know how long the gunsmith took over repairing it; and he thinks 'everybody' would know it was there."

"I hope," said Sir Nicholas, with more than a touch of sarcasm in his tone, "that you fared better with your next witness."

"Well, sir, not so's you'd notice it."

"However, you'd better let me know the worst."

"Just as I was going to leave Uncle Greg, Brent Cassell came in, and with him his betrothed, a lass called Audrey Barton, whom Timmy mentioned, if you recall."

"What were they like?" said Jenny; and "What had they to say?" said Sir Nicholas, almost simultaneously. Antony grinned.

"Brent is a good-looking chap, if you like the Clark Gable type. He sports a moustache, too; no doubt to foster the illusion. The girl is a red-head; not a beauty, but well-dressed and well-groomed, so that it takes a second, or even third look before you realise she is really rather plain."

Sir Nicholas glared at Jenny, who showed no signs of repentance, and remarked sourly to his nephew, "All this is quite fascinating. I take it Brent Cassell is one of the main witnesses for the prosecution. Did you spend all your time admiring his appearance; or are you about to tell me that his resemblance to a man who is, I believe, a cinema star, is relevant to his evidence?''

''It hadn't occurred to me, and there isn't any evidence, not yet. They seemed to be in a hurry, so we confined ourselves to polite nothings, and arranged to meet tomorrow.''

''Something attempted, something done!'' remarked Sir Nicholas, to nobody in particular. ''I'm sure you must feel remarkably satisfied with your day's work.''

Antony thought best to ignore his thrust. ''That wasn't quite all, I went out to Wimbledon again after that.''

Jenny said, ''Zeal, all zeal, Mr. Easy,'' but did not look up from her knitting. Sir Nicholas gave her a cold look, and then said, ''Well?'' in a tone that was just as chilling.

''Well, sir, first I saw Mrs. Cassell, Aunt Agnes, Uncle Gregory's wife.''

''Is that one person, or three?''

''One, sir. I'm trying to be clear—''

''Then pray continue trying. Heaven defend me from a more obscure statement than you are giving me.''

Jenny was moved to protest. ''Families are awfully difficult, don't you think, Uncle Nick?''

''I thought we had gone into this at quite sufficient length.'' He was still very much on his dignity. ''It should be possible to be a little more lucid.'' Antony caught Jenny's eye, and grimaced.

''Timmy gave me the word for Aunt Agnes,'' he continued. ''She's a querulous woman, mainly concerned with the lack of consideration shown to her by her family, her friends, even by circumstances. She takes the same line as her husband, as far as her professed beliefs are concerned: she thinks Paul has been very thoughtless!''

''Interesting, but irrelevant. Facts, Antony, facts!''

''None to be had, sir. She was in bed and asleep, and didn't know anything until Uncle Greg came back to their room to dress, after he had been down to find out what all the noise was about.''

''And about the weapon?''

''She knows *nothing* about guns, Uncle Nick. I can well believe it.''

''I see. And what else—?''

"I had a talk with Aunt Marian. Fortunately Aunt Agnes had a spasm, or something, about that time, and left us alone. So we had a nice cosy chat, all about the family."

"Is she nice?" said Jenny, hopefully.

"Very nice indeed."

"Was she helpful?"

"Yes, I think so. She gave me the background pretty well. She's well-disposed, but not an easy witness. A comfortable sort of person, with a mind like an amiable, pink blancmange."

Sir Nicholas shuddered, and put a hand over his eyes. Jenny giggled, and then looked unnaturally solemn. Antony said, "I don't see what's so funny."

"For once, I am in agreement with you. I ask for witnesses, and you offer me a film star, a blancmange, and a—a jellyfish. I see *nothing* humorous in the situation."

"I'm sorry, Uncle Nick, truly I am. But it *is* f-funny."

"I had better," said Antony quickly, forestalling his uncle who was looking outraged, and might be expected to bring his heavy guns to bear at any moment, "I'd better give you my talk with her in a little more detail." He slid down into a more comfortable position in his chair, and gazed at the ceiling for inspiration. "We were sitting in a small room, which I gathered is very much Aunt Marian's own domain—"

Miss Marian Cassell seemed glad when her sister-in-law left them, though her only comment was, "Poor Agnes. She feels all this very much."

"I'm sure," said Antony, "that it is a very sad time for all of you."

"Yes, indeed; poor Uncle William. Of course, he hadn't been home for years; but we had his letters, and I have such happy memories of him when I was younger."

"It was eighteen years since he was last at home, I believe."

"Yes, quite eighteen. I remember very well, because the day he left was the day we heard about . . . about Ruth and Matt. So you see, I couldn't possibly forget. That was so dreadful, I didn't think we'd ever have to go through anything so dreadful again."

"I want you to tell me what happened then, Miss Cassell. Will you do that?"

She looked at him in silence for a moment. She said, slowly, "I'll tell you about it, Mr. Maitland, because you said you wanted to help Paul. And I suppose he is mad, and you must know about his father. But it isn't easy."

Antony was silent. She went on, after a moment, "Ruth was my sister, you know. She was younger than I, very pretty and gay. We were very fond of each other, and I was so happy when she married Matt. They were quite a devoted couple, and then there were the twins, such dear little boys; it seemed as if they had everything."

"And Matthew Herron's brother?"

"Mark? They were twins too, you know, and so much alike you could never tell them, if you saw them apart. Ruth used to laugh, and say she didn't understand how anyone could mistake them. But, of course, she wouldn't be likely to do that. And then, without any warning, we heard they were dead."

"You had seen no trouble—"

"Oh, no, Mr. Maitland, there was nothing. I can assure you there was nothing. I know what they said afterwards, and I know my father, even, believed that Matt had been jealous of his brother. But we had seen no sign of that, and I am sure that there was nothing to see."

"There must have been some reason—"

"They said he was mad; and that must have been true, I know, because there was *no* reason. Do people need one, when they go out of their minds?"

He made no attempt to answer that. Instead, he asked: "Was there any history of insanity in the Herron family?"

"There was an uncle." She sounded doubtful. "But I don't think he was *very* mad, only he did like rabbits so much, some people do. But I think most families have some-one like him."

"Just gently crazy? Yes, I think so, too. Could you tell me what happened? I'm sorry to distress you—"

"It's so long ago. Eighteen years. A bit longer than that, because it was June. Uncle William was staying with us, you know, and we were all busy because he was catching an early train the next morning. Ruth came to tea, I remember,

and the twins were with her; she had to go home to get the
children to bed, and Uncle William went with them. I remember he made a mystery about a big parcel in the boot of
her car, I couldn't forget that because there were two big
teddy-bears in it, and Timmy told me about them. He said
they were sitting on the sideboard, and Mummy and Daddy
and Uncle Mark had all gone to sleep. He used to talk about
it a lot, you know, only he didn't really know what he was
saying, poor child. And that is what made me wonder
whether Father was right. Because Paul never said one word
about his parents after it happened, and they say it is bad for
you to repress things, don't they?''

"Did Timmy know what had happened that night?"

"Not really. He said—but I was telling you about the
evening. Uncle William stayed until nearly nine o'clock. He
had dinner with Ruth, because Matt was going to be late;
when he came Mark was with him, and after talking for a
while he left the three of them together. And nobody saw
them after that. Uncle William left as arranged next morning, and it was turned ten o'clock before we heard what had
happened.''

"He wasn't asked to come back for the inquest?"

"Oh, no, it was all so obvious, it wouldn't have done any
good. He wrote, of course, and told us about the evening;
and he hadn't any idea that anything was wrong when he left
them.''

"Have you his letter, Miss Cassell?"

"Well, he wrote to my father, you know. I could ask him
if he kept the letter.''

"I should be grateful.''

"And you wanted to know if Timmy could tell us anything. I think they went into the room in the morning, he and
Paul; but he said they were 'sleeping' and I never knew what
he really thought; or even when he became old enough to
realise that he had seen them dead.''

"Did nobody hear the shots?"

"That seemed so strange, in a block of flats, on a June
night, and nobody knew when it had happened. Afterwards,
you know, several people said they had heard sounds that
must have been the shooting. But they all gave quite differ-

ent times, and it wasn't helpful. And it wouldn't really have helped to have known.''

"To come back to more recent events, then, Miss Cassell, do you know anything about Paul's rifle being here?''

"I do indeed. I was so cross with Brent, because he knows I hate guns.''

"He brought it here, did he?''

"Yes, about a month ago. It made a great deal of trouble, because I was cross about it—there must be plenty of people who could have mended it in Midhurst—and then Paul was angry, too, because Brent had borrowed it, and that was how he knew it needed repairing.''

"Paul and Brent are not the best of friends, I gather?''

"I'm afraid not.'' She sounded apologetic. "They are so very different,'' she explained.

"I met Brent for a moment to-day. And Miss Barton.''

"Audrey? Yes, she is a dear girl. Ann's cousin, and they have spent a great deal of time with us, one way and another.'' It was obvious that this subject was being seized on as being more pleasant than the previous subject of their conversation. "You know, since Ann's mother died I have never felt that John Barclay was quite capable of looking after two young girls.''

"I haven't met Mr. Barclay. Is he a close friend?''

"Oh, yes. He is an artist, a charming man, but not, I fear, very successful. They live quite near, a studio apartment he calls it, not very convenient, I'm afraid. They have played together—the girls have played with the twins—since they were all quite small. It was quite a surprise to me, you know, Mr. Maitland, when Brent told me he was going to marry Audrey.''

"About the rifle—?'' Antony was apologetic in his turn. "Did it go to be repaired? And when was it brought back to this house again?''

"Timmy took it, I believe. You see, Brent wouldn't, after what Paul said. And Paul wouldn't, because he said it was Brent's fault. So when Timmy brought it back again, about a fortnight ago, I made him put it away in the cupboard in the downstairs cloakroom. Nobody ever goes there, so I knew—I thought it would be safe.''

"Miss Cassell, who knew it was there?''

"Well, Timmy, of course. And I am sure he would tell Paul. Yes, I know he did, because Paul told Brent at dinner that night. It was a week ago last Monday, and Brent has been staying with us a good deal since his engagement was announced, because of seeing Audrey."

"Who was there that night, when Paul told Brent about the rifle?"

"Father, of course. Not Gregory or Agnes. Audrey was there, I'm sure; and Ann, I think. And Bob Wayne, because Brent was teasing Paul, and he said something that changed the subject. And I thought he was being tactful, but I wasn't sure."

"Wayne?"

"He is Matt's cousin, but a much younger man. He was another frequent visitor at their home; and since they died he has been here almost as much. I think he felt their loss very keenly."

"Will you give me his address, Miss Cassell? Mr. Cassell said he would be a good person for me to see."

"He lives in Barnes, I'll write it down for you." Aunt Marian looked round a little wildly, and Antony produced a note-book and pencil. "There now . . . I hope you can read what I've written."

Antony removed his gaze from the ceiling, and looked across at his uncle. "And that was that, really, only I asked her about Uncle William's household in Portugal, and whether he spoke in his letters of his own affairs. For some reason that seemed to fluster her; she started talking about 'her dear father' again, so I came away. Timmy rang up just as I was leaving, to say he'd be later than expected. I had a word with him, and arranged to see him again to-morrow morning. I can go to the house at Wimbledon, Grandfather always goes to the office on Saturday morning, and the other members of the family are supposed to put in an appearance, too, but Timmy promised to play truant."

Sir Nicholas smiled at him amiably. "Rather a rigmarole. I don't envy you the task of writing a coherent report for Bellerby. However, her evidence has its points, which I see from your air of suppressed triumph have occurred to you, as well."

"I must say, I wish Grandfather would come across with that letter."

"I should think it extremely unlikely, you know. Why should he have kept it?"

"I can't imagine." Antony sounded despondent.

"And if he has kept it, and does produce it, I don't see that you'll be a halfpenny the better off." Sir Nicholas eyed the stub of his cigar regretfully, decided that they had come to the parting of the ways, and deposited it carefully in the ash-tray.

"What I like about you, Uncle Nick," said Antony with an air of great candour, "is: you're always so encouraging."

"Well, I think he's in a horrid mood," said Jenny, coming to life suddenly, and putting down her knitting. "You wouldn't know how to get on without Antony, Uncle Nick, and you know it."

The older man smiled sedately at her vehemence. "Peace, perfect peace, with loved ones far away. It would be so odd," he remarked, gently, "to discover for once the meaning of that eminently sensible remark."

CHAPTER 6

THE NEXT MORNING was sunny, one of September's better efforts. Antony took his way to Wimbledon in leisurely fashion, and walked warily up the drive of The Laurels until he saw that the doors of the double garage were open, and the only occupant was a showy little sports car. Whatever conveyed Ambrose Cassell to his place of business, it was something much less frivolous, so it seemed a fairly safe bet that the coast was clear.

Timmy had evidently been watching for him, and opened the front door before he had time to ring. He was looking more harassed than he had seemed at their previous meeting, and though he smiled as he asked, "What on earth did you do to upset my revered grandfather?" it was with no real amusement.

"Didn't he tell you?"

Timmy said precisely, "He told me what he thought of you; he didn't say why."

"Then I shall have to explain."

"Come in here." Timmy was leading the way towards a door at the right of the hall, when they were interrupted by a placid voice, and turned to see Aunt Marian coming down the stairs.

"Timmy dear, it's so *late!* You should be at the office. Whatever will your grandfather say?"

"He'll probably remember that my father was late for his wedding, and put it down to heredity."

"But, my dear, I remember perfectly: nothing like that happened, I assure you."

Timmy had the grace to look a little abashed. "Sorry,

Aunt Marian, I was only joking. Not very good taste, I'm afraid.''

She continued to look at him in a puzzled way. Timmy moved uneasily under her scrutiny. Antony was about to speak, when they were again interrupted, this time by Brent Cassell, who came out of the room behind Timmy and said in a voice that was speciously agreeable:

''No, indeed. But don't worry, Aunt Marian. He's showing no real signs of insanity just yet.'' He laid a hand on Timmy's shoulder as he spoke, a gesture to which the younger man reacted with rather exaggerated violence, squirming out of his cousin's grasp, and spinning round to face him with a look of such ferocity that Antony took two steps forward and grabbed Timmy's arm above the elbow with no especial gentleness. He spoke directly to Brent, and his tone was deceptively mild:

''You promised to answer some questions for me, Mr. Cassell. This seems as good a time as any.''

Brent's eyes travelled downwards, so that he took in, rather pointedly, Antony's restraining grip on Timmy's arm. He said, ''By all means, Mr. Maitland. If you have enough influence with my young cousin here to prevent him from doing me a violence.''

Antony heard Timmy catch his breath, and kept his own voice even with something of an effort. ''I have some business with him myself, but I'm sure he'll wait until we have finished.''

Timmy said sullenly, ''I'm staying with you. I want to hear what he says.''

''By all means.'' Brent was cordial. ''Shall we go back into the drawing-room? May we have its use for the next half-hour, Aunt Marian?''

''Of course you may. Mr. Maitland—'' She still had her look of confusion, and Antony smiled at her reassuringly. She shook her head at him. ''I'm afraid you upset my father very badly; he is really angry.''

''I'm not always very tactful, Miss Cassell.'' He relaxed his grip on Timmy's arm (though not without some doubts of the wisdom of this procedure) and allowed himself to be shepherded into the drawing-room, a much larger apartment than the one he had seen yesterday, but with the same air of rather shabby comfort.

Brent looked at him with every appearance of amusement, and let his glance pass to his cousin, where his smile became openly malicious. "Not the most suitable setting for our conference, I'm afraid. Are you sensitive to atmosphere, Mr. Maitland? We all fight rather shy of the study, just now; a useless sentiment, but natural in the circumstances."

"I find this a charming room," said Antony, avoiding the question. Timmy remarked, irritably:

"Stop playing the fool, Brent. Nobody wants to listen to you making flowery speeches."

Brent eyed him consideringly. "Do you know, Timmy, I think after all you're a little *de trop*. I'm sure we'd get on quicker without you."

Timmy looked mulish, and made no move to go. He looked at Antony. "I want to hear what he says," he said again.

"I don't think, to be honest, that your presence is likely to be much help." Antony spoke carefully, and was conscious of Brent's grin. Timmy looked from one to the other of them in silence for a moment, and then turned on his heel. At the door he paused, and said without turning his head, "I'll wait." He went out and closed the door quietly.

Brent laughed, and flung himself into a chair. "Spoiled brat!" he remarked. "Sit down, Maitland, and let's get down to it."

Antony ignored the invitation, and came to stand on the hearthrug before the empty grate. Finding the mantle of a comfortable height to accommodate him, he leaned a shoulder against it and looked down at his companion. "I shouldn't have thought that was a very fair description of your cousin," he said, mildly.

"He makes me tired."

"That's a pity. Do you think you could bear up long enough to tell me what happened the night your great-uncle was shot?"

For a moment, Brent did not reply. He said, at last, "Grandfather tells me you've got some bee in your bonnet about Paul."

"I don't think he's mad," said Antony, bluntly. "Do you?"

The other shrugged. "I don't, of course. But I don't see what this has to do with the problem."

"A good deal, I should have thought."

"Do you honestly think you'll be doing him a favour by maintaining his sanity, and seeing him hang? Not to mention, of course, our feelings as a family." He was sneering again, and Antony (remembering his importance as a witness) took a firm hold on his temper before he replied.

"There is an alternative."

"To prove him innocent? Don't you think that may be a little difficult?"

"I expect so."

"But look here." Brent abandoned his lounging pose, and sat up straight with a look of urgency. "If Paul didn't do it—"

"Someone else did. I had got that far." Antony's tone was dry.

"Well, I don't believe it. But it's going to cause the hell of a stink if you proceed on those lines." Brend was recovering his poise, but was still shaken. "May I ask if Sir Nicholas Harding agrees with you in this?"

"He hasn't seen Paul yet. Nor has he had the opportunity of studying the doctor's report," said Antony, with some care. "He agrees with me this far, however, that we have to cover every angle."

"No matter who gets hurt in the process? I'm beginning to appreciate my grandfather's point of view rather more vividly than I did at first."

"I'm sorry about that," said Antony, with truth.

"I'm afraid, anyway, you're in for a disappointment. I don't see what anyone can make of the evidence except Paul's guilt."

"May I hear it then, your evidence?"

"That's soon told: I took Audrey home, that's Miss Barton whom you met yesterday. I put the car away when I got back, and was just shutting the garage doors when I heard a shot. I ran down the path between the garage and the house, and round the corner to the back. Paul was there, with a rifle in his hand. He was staring up at the study window, which was lighted, and he didn't seem to see me. I called out to him, I think I told him to drop the rifle, because I didn't think it looked safe, I can tell you. And then Timmy came up, and Grandfather behind him. And we all looked through the study window, and there was Uncle William."

"May I ask you a few questions?"

"If you like." His tone was ungracious.

"How long was it after you heard the shot, that you arrived outside the study window?"

"I can't answer that precisely. Not more than a few moments, I should say."

"You realised immediately that a shot had been fired, and there must be something wrong?"

"Well, not quite immediately perhaps. But after all, in Wimbledon—"

"I see." This was a delicate point, and better not to press it now. "And when you first saw Paul how was he standing?"

"Near the shrubbery. He was staring at the study window. And he had the rifle in his hands."

"But he might have picked it up, just before you turned the corner?"

"That wasn't my impression."

"But you took it for granted that he had fired the shot?"

"Well, what would you have thought?"

"That doesn't arise. What did *you* think when you looked in at the study window?"

Brent seemed a little bewildered by this shift of ground. "Why—why I saw Uncle William, lying dead across the desk."

"You knew immediately that it was not your grandfather?"

"Yes, I did. Of course I did. I'd met him you know, not like Paul."

"And besides," said Antony, not without malice, "your grandfather had just joined you in the garden."

"I didn't know he was there until he spoke. They were alike, I admit, but I couldn't have mistaken them."

"Could Paul?"

"He'd never seen Uncle William, I tell you."

"What happened then?"

"Oh, Grandfather spoke to Paul, and Paul looked at him

as if he'd seen a ghost. So I took the chance, and took the rifle from him.''

''Did he resist?''

''Oh, no. He seemed dazed.''

''What was said?''

''I don't remember exactly. Grandfather shouted something, that Paul had meant to kill *him*, I think. And Paul said, 'I thought it was you, in there.' And then he gave me the gun.

When Antony went into the hall a few minutes later he found it deserted, and hesitated a moment wondering where to look for Timmy. Before he could make up his mind a door at the back of the hall swung open, and the young man came through bearing a cup of coffee. He seemed to have recovered himself somewhat, and tried to speak normally, though he did not look at Antony as he spoke.

''Would you like this? Cook's gone to the shops, so Aunt Marian and I have been foraging. This is quite a good cup of coffee, she made it.''

''Then, if Cook's out, may I come into the kitchen to drink it? I have a weakness for kitchens.'' He did not add, though he might have done, that he had also a weakness for knowing as much as possible about the terrain.

Timmy turned obligingly back through the swing door. He said, ''Aunt Marian's there. She's been telling me I mustn't embarrass your efforts on Paul's behalf. Did I?''

''You aunt is a very sensible woman.'' Antony made mental apology for his strictures of the evening before. ''I shouldn't like to seem to contradict her.''

Timmy paused at the kitchen door. ''Well, then, I'm sorry. But he does make me wild.''

''That,'' said Antony, ''is only too obvious.'' Timmy gave him a hurt look, and pushed open the kitchen door. ''If it is any consolation to you,'' Antony added, following him, ''I only kept my temper myself by considering the fact that Uncle Nick would have an apoplexy if I antagonised another witness.''

They went into a warm, bright room, full of morning sunshine. Aunt Marian was sitting at a table in the centre, with a cup in her hand. She greeted Antony placidly, and did not

seem at all put out by this rather unorthodox way of enter-
taining a stranger.

She provided them with more coffee, and produced a tin
of home-made biscuits. At the end of a quarter of an hour in
that friendly atmosphere Timmy had lost his sulks. Antony
found his respect for Aunt Marian increasing when she
drove them from the house with stern instructions to walk on
the common this lovely morning, and have their talk there.
"For I'd no real desire," he confided as they turned out of
the drive, "to encounter your cousin again."

"How did you get on with him?" Timmy sounded hesitant. "Or shouldn't I ask?"

"I made him sweat a little," said Antony with some satisfaction. "He's quite intelligent enough to realise he's the
obvious suspect, once you get round to questioning Paul's
guilt."

"But, are you? I mean, I thought—"

"I saw Paul yesterday morning, as I believe you know.
My uncle has accepted the brief (it isn't prepared yet, of
course, but that's beside the point). For your information,
your brother will plead 'Not Guilty'."

"And what then? I'm glad, of course," he added politely,
"that Sir Nicholas will be defending him."

"Then," replied Antony, "we shall do our best to sub-
stantiate the plea."

"By proving that he's mad." He was obviously making
an effort to speak without bitterness.

"No," said Antony.

Timmy turned quickly. "Then, you really don't believe
he's guilty?"

"Hell and damnation!" Antony's tone was explosive. "I
don't know what I believe. Your brother had more sense: he
didn't ask me that question."

"Well, I'm sorry." Timmy sounded subdued. "But I
don't quite see," he added with more spirit, "why it's such
a stupid thing to ask."

"Because a good solid belief would be helpful; all this
doubt is very unsettling." In his turn, Antony sounded apologetic. But he went on after a moment, with a return of his
former manner: "Don't you see, to plead insanity would be

playing it safe, in a way? The straight plea is difficult, and dangerous perhaps. Do you still want to back us?''

They had been standing still as they spoke, but now Timmy turned away and went on down the road. Antony fell into step beside him. It was some time before either of them spoke, and then Timmy said firmly, ''Yes, I'll back you. I think I would anyway, but even if I thought you were wrong I couldn't let Paul down.''

''I'm glad that's how you feel. But you won't like my questions, I'm afraid. I want you to tell me what you can remember about your parents' death.''

''I don't understand. I didn't think you'd want to know about that now. Only if you were going to say Paul was mad.''

''Get it out of your head that I'm doing this for fun. I don't know what I'm looking for, so I have to look at everything. I've got to know every least thing about your family, and not care (or act as if I don't) who gets hurt in the process.''

''I see. At least, I don't, but I'll take your word for it.''

''Then I want you to tell me what you, yourself, remember. Not what you've heard since.''

They crossed the road, and turned on to a path across the common. Timmy said, after a while, ''Where do you want me to start?''

''Anywhere. Anything you remember. Anything at all.''

''Well, I do remember Uncle William. And I remember being in a car with him, and we were excited about something.''

''You were going to your own home after visiting The Laurels?''

''Well, I *know* that, but I don't remember it. I don't remember things in—in sequence, at all, you know. Only odd pictures—but I know now, of course, pretty well how they fit together. So then I remember we were at home, and I was sitting on a stool near the fire; that's funny, I'm sure there was a fire, but it was June, wasn't it? Anyway, I was waiting for my father to come home because I wanted to show him something. But he didn't come, and I remember when we went to bed my mother said Uncle William was going away, and I had a sort of embarrassed feeling about saying good-bye.''

''And after that—''

''I went to sleep. I woke up once during the evening—at least, I don't know how late it was—and heard voices.''

''Whose voices?''

''My father's, I suppose, and Uncle Mark's.''

''Men's voices, anyway?''

Timmy pondered. ''Oh, I don't know. I think so. I don't really know.''

''And then—?''

''We must have been awake quite a long time in the morning before things began to seem . . . well, not as usual. But all I remember, really, is a feeling . . . cold . . . frightened . . . lost? I don't know.''

''But you went into the sitting-room, you and Paul?''

''I suppose so.''

''Surely—''

''I don't know, I tell you. I can remember, afterwards, that I thought I'd seen them asleep. But I don't really know what we did.''

''Have you ever discussed what happened with Paul?''

''No, he never would. It was some time, you know, before we . . . before I understood at all what had happened. When I began to, I used to listen all I could when people were talking; they do, you know, they never think children know anything. But Paul just used to disappear when that happened, and he never wanted to know, afterwards, what had been said.''

''You were curious, yourself?''

''I . . . yes, of course I was. I hated it, but I did want to know.'' He was on the defensive.

Antony said, ''I think it was very natural.'' He sounded absent, and in fact was thinking that Timmy (who believed Paul to be sane) would have made a better witness for the opposite view than the rest of his relations who so stoutly maintained his madness. This, however, was hardly a profitable reflection at this stage. He put it from him, and started again to question his companion.

An hour later, when they had returned, more or less, to their point of embarkation, Timmy had reached a stage of considerable agitation and Antony slackened his pace a little and changed the trend of his converse.

"I thought we might get some lunch, and afterwards you could introduce me to the Barclay household."

"All right," said Timmy; but he said it without enthusiasm. Antony wondered, briefly, which part of the outlined programme his companion found the most distasteful.

CHAPTER 7

THE BARCLAY apartment was large and untidy, and John Barclay himself was a large untidy man. The studio was half workshop, half living-room, and they found the artist sprawled comfortably on a sofa, eyeing a large canvas which he had propped up on an easy-chair in front of him. He did not look up when his visitors walked in, but continued his scrutiny, remarking after a moment, "What is wrong with this picture? I don't like it, but I'm blessed if I know what's wrong."

Timmy appeared a little dashed by this greeting, and gave his companion a sidelong, apologetic look. Antony, however, rising to the occasion, appeared in no degree taken aback, but remarked with feeling, "I don't know anything about art, I'm afraid; but I do know what I like."

That brought Jim Barclay's mind and eyes to his visitors without any delay at all. He frowned a moment, as though doubtful whether he had seen Antony before, and then threw back his head and laughed. "Fair enough. I thought for a moment you meant it."

Antony, abandoning his pose a trifle regretfully, grinned back at him. "I hope we didn't take you unawares. Timmy said it was all right just to walk in."

"Oh, it's you, Timmy. Come and sit down, my boy." He looked round vaguely, and swung his legs to the floor. "There should be some chairs."

Timmy took possession of the canvas (a landscape which appeared, at a glance, to possess a good deal of the rather vague charm of its creator), and removed it to the other end of the studio. "If you kept your belongings in their own place, you'd have somewhere for your visitors to sit down,"

61

he remarked. Antony took the vacated chair, and Timmy brought back a stool with carved legs and a shabby grospoint cover. "This is Antony Maitland, John. He's one of Paul's counsel."

John Barclay, who had been burrowing among the sofa cushions to find his pipe, turned now with it in his hand and gave Antony a look which was not vague at all, but shrewdly intelligent. "I'm glad to know you, Maitland," he said. "You've seen Paul?"

"Yesterday morning."

The artist looked away, and started to fill his pipe. He said slowly, "Old Mr. Cassell says he's mad. (I'm sorry, Timmy.) Do you think he's right?"

Timmy started to speak, and encountered a look which startled him into silence. Antony said, "Not my province, Mr. Barclay. That's something for the doctors to fight out between them."

Barclay gave him one swift look, and returned to the contemplation of his pipe. "Very well," he said. "I see questions are not in order. Though I suppose you have some to ask. You won't forget, when you see my daughter, that she's very personally concerned in this?"

"I won't forget."

"Ann would want to help," said Timmy. "Where are the girls, anyway? Don't tell me they've gone out."

"They're washing up. Or so I suppose. Give them a call, if you like."

"No, wait a minute. I'd rather talk to you first, if I may."

Timmy got up rather quickly. "I'll go and find them, anyway." He went out, and John Barclay turned his attention to Antony with no trace now of the cheerfulness which had characterised the first moments of their acquaintance.

"Well?" he inquired.

"You were a friend of Timmy's parents?"

"I was."

"Then you can help me."

"I wonder. You're taking that line, are you? Well, at least, you can tell me what Paul says."

"He says he isn't mad. He says he didn't do it." Antony allowed no comment to be implicit in his tone.

"But you're willing to prove insanity, if you can?"

"This isn't helping matters, you know. But since you've brought up the subject: do you think Paul is mad?"

That brought a silence. Barclay puffed at his pipe and then said, grimly, "I didn't. If you asked me on oath if he'd ever given me reason to think so, I'd have to answer 'no'. But what can one think, in view of the evidence?"

"Heaven give me strength," said Antony, crossly. "The evidence is a matter for us to argue about—the lawyers; not for every idiot of a layman who thinks he understands what it's all about."

His host gave him a puzzled look, and laughed a little, but rather uneasily. "I don't understand you," he complained.

"With respect, sir, that doesn't worry me unduly. All I want is a few facts, if I can get 'em; and I'd rather you left the interpretation of them to my uncle." Barclay looked an inquiry. "Sir Nicholas Harding; he's leading for the defence."

"So Cassell brought that off? All right, Maitland, I'll endeavour to suppress my natural curiosity. What do you want to know?"

"I still want to know about Matthew and Ruth Herron."

"There's nothing I can tell you. They were a charming and devoted couple. I saw no evidence of madness in Matt; and certainly no signs of anything that would have warranted his thinking that Ruth and Mark—"

"What happened was unexpected, then?"

"Completely so. I can't put it strongly enough."

"And you saw them regularly?"

"Two or three times a week. At least that, during the last year. That was immediately after my wife died; Ann was a baby, and not then in need of companionship; I got friendship from them, and affection, which I needed very badly."

"And yet you saw nothing?"

"Nothing whatever. Good heavens, I saw them only the day before. Mark, too. Everything was completely normal."

"You mean that on that occasion—the last time you saw them—they were all three together?"

"Mark was there when I arrived, but left after about half an hour to go to his tennis club. After he had gone we sat and talked, and Bob Wayne came round. We left together, about eleven o'clock. Matt was a little quiet, but nothing unusual in that. We can't all be in good spirits all the time.''

"You thought him depressed?"

"No, nothing as definite as that. A little thoughtful, perhaps." He added irritably, as Antony was about to speak, "Of course, I've thought about this, and it's a wonder I haven't magnified it into something, considering what happened next day. But there *was* nothing out of the ordinary, certainly nothing between him and Ruth."

"Between Matthew and his brother, then?"

"I tell you, nothing." He paused a moment, and then added as though unwillingly, "He did say, as Mark was leaving, 'You'll let me know to-morrow, then?' Mark said, 'I'll phone you.' That was all."

"Matthew didn't explain what they were talking about?"

"He did not. There was no need. It was nothing."

"But Mr. Wayne—I haven't seen him yet, but I'm told he thought—"

"Bob was being wise after the event." Barclay was emphatic.

"An imaginative gentleman, Mr. Wayne?"

Barclay laughed. "Anything but. Quite a prosaic fellow. All the same, he never mentioned this queerness of Matt's until afterwards, when it was easy enough to imagine—"

The door at the far end of the studio opened, and Audrey Barton came in, followed more slowly by a slight, brown-haired girl, whose hesitating manner was a sharp contrast to her more forceful cousin. "We heard you laughing," Audrey said accusingly, "so we thought you must have finished." She did not wait for confirmation, but came to sit on the sofa beside her uncle. Her air was determined. She looked directly at Antony and said, "Timmy says you're going to help Paul. And we're not to ask questions. Well, that's all right with me, if it helps at all. But Grandfather Cassell says you're an interfering young nincompoop. Are you?"

Antony said mildly, "I do admire Mr. Cassell's choice of epithets. I'm afraid you'll have to make up your own mind about my mental attainments, however. You wouldn't be very likely to accept my own estimate, after all."

Audrey looked a little taken aback. Barclay laughed at her

doubtful expression, and remarked, "I shouldn't worry too much about Mr. Maitland's ability. He's the only man, if it interests you, who ever got a rise out of me before even we were introduced."

"Which ought to remind you," said Antony to Audrey Barton, "that we met yesterday, but I haven't yet—"

"Oh, Ann, I'm sorry. This is Mr. Maitland. My cousin, Ann Barclay."

Ann came forward. She kept close to Timmy, but looked at Antony with a good deal of interest. She said, "Timmy says you've seen Paul. Is he well?"

"He is perfectly well, and in fairly good spirits."

Timmy pushed her towards the stool, and provided himself with a cushion from the pile behind John Barclay on the sofa. He said, "Had you finished?"

"I think so. Unless—?" He looked at the artist, who shook his head. He was looking at his daughter, and his expression was sombre. Antony went on, "I didn't have a chance to talk to you yesterday, Miss Barton—"

"Can I help? I didn't think—"

"You went to dinner at The Laurels on Tuesday."

"Oh, yes, I did. But I didn't see Paul. And if I had, and he'd *gibbered* at me," she added, with a sudden spurt of anger, "I wouldn't tell you about it."

"Well, as the question doesn't arise, let's not worry about it. Tell me about the evening, though. What time did you get there?"

"About half past seven, I think. Brent came for me, and I know I was ready at a quarter past, and I had to wait a few minutes before he came."

"And then—"

"Well, it was just the usual family party, you know. Only a little more formal than usual, because of Uncle William. Not that he was at all stuffy, I thought he was a dear, but he had a sort of old-fashioned air of courtesy which put everyone on their best behaviour."

John Barclay looked at her, a little impatiently. "Come now, my dear, you never had anything but 'old-fashioned courtesy' from Ambrose."

"But, John, he's such an iceberg!" protested Audrey. "And that night he gave a first-class exhibition of chilly politeness." She looked across at Timmy, who was sitting on the floor, hugging his knees. "Didn't he?" she appealed.

"Sticky, definitely sticky." Timmy's tone was hollow. "Not one of our more hilarious evenings."

"Not really. Still, there was no open unpleasantness; just atmosphere."

"But the atmosphere was connected in your mind with Mr. Ambrose Cassell's mood?"

"Oh, yes, but then you see it wasn't the first time—"

"And, of course, your fiancé had told you what had happened earlier in the day?"

"Well, he said—he said Grandfather had found out about Paul and Ann. And that there had been a row."

"And did Brent also tell you who told Grandfather?" inquired Timmy, with sudden belligerence.

"No, I thought—" Audrey looked bewildered. "Didn't Paul tell him?"

"You could put it that way if you like." Timmy's voice was contemptuous. "Brent congratulated him, so of course Grandfather asked what it was about. Paul told him then . . . naturally."

"I didn't know. It wasn't very tactful." Timmy snorted, and she added with more vigour. "That's all very well, Timmy Herron. You didn't do anything to make things better."

"Well, how could I? Grandfather was all worked up, if I'd spoken at all there'd have been trouble."

"You're not always so poor-spirited."

Ann spoke into the silence that followed. "That's not fair, Audrey. You know what Timmy means." She flushed a little, as they all looked at her, but went on with determination. "It was very sensible of him—"

"Oh, sensible!" Audrey was impatient. "If you call it sensible to sit like an image and not say a word—"

"What Ann means, my good idiot," said Timmy, with an air of great politeness, "is that Grandfather was in the mood to throw the past in my teeth, on the slightest provocation; or even on no provocation at all. And regardless of the fact that we were not alone. You might have enjoyed the resultant row; Brent would have enjoyed it, I'm sure; I shouldn't."

Audrey looked at him. "Don't be a beast, Timmy," she said. "You're not very fair to Brent, are you?"

"Fair!" said Timmy. "No, I suppose I'm not fair."

"And just as well!" said Ann. The unexpected severity of her tone startled her cousin, who looked at her quickly and then gave an uneasy laugh:

"I'm sorry, darling! Don't let's quarrel. Not now, when we ought to be thinking about Paul." She turned back to Antony again, and did not see Ann's sudden look of distress, or the fierce look that Timmy gave her. "I'm not being helpful, am I? I should like to be, but I don't see—"

"I must ask you again whether anything unusual occurred that evening?"

"There wasn't anything. There was Grandfather's mood, I told you. And everyone else seemed just as usual. I wish I could say something different."

"Do you, indeed?" said Timmy, whose belligerence seemed undiminished. "And which of us would you choose to hang, my girl, if you don't think it should be Paul?"

Antony said, sharply, "Be quiet, Timmy!" Audrey flushed scarlet, and Ann began, very quietly, to cry. John Barclay, apparently tiring of his role of passive spectator, spoke with authority. "That's quite enough from you, my children. We've enough trouble without your squabbles. And you won't help matters by crying, Ann. You'd better stop."

Ann sniffed a little, but dried her eyes obediently. She put a hand out to touch Timmy's shoulder, and he turned to look at her. "I'm sorry, Ann." His look was hidden from the two on the sofa, but from where he sat Antony could see his expression well enough. The words were the simplest kind of apology, but the look that accompanied them was one of such unconcealed devotion as to end for ever any doubts he might have had about Timmy's feelings for his brother's betrothed. He said, into the silence:

"Well, it seems you can't help us, Miss Barton," and his tone was as flat as the words. "Can you, Miss Barclay?"

"I don't know. I wasn't there . . . that night."

"Did you see Paul? I've wondered about that; whether he came to you when he left his own home, I mean."

"No; no, he didn't. I didn't see him all that day."

"He said he'd been walking on the common," Timmy volunteered.

"Well, I was at the office till five, of course. But I didn't expect to see him, because of Uncle William."

"When did you last see him?"

"Not since Monday evening. You see—" She stopped, and looked at Antony in a helpless way. Again Timmy interrupted her.

"They arrested Paul on Tuesday night; well, it was Wednesday morning, actually, but we hadn't been to bed."

Audrey got up, with a quick, uncontrolled movement, that lacked altogether her usual grace. She said, abruptly, "I'm going out." And added from the doorway, with a look over her shoulder that did its best to be casual, "I've got to meet Brent."

As the door closed John Barclay looked at his daughter, and his expression was troubled. Ann looked at Timmy, and did not speak for a moment. Then she said, "He seemed just as usual. That's what you wanted to know, isn't it?"

"Precisely," said Antony, at his driest.

She looked at him then. She said, as though the words were hard to find, "He talked about telling Grandfather about us, only not just then, you know. He thought perhaps Uncle William might help us, if he had any influence with his brother. We were rather disposed to like Uncle William, because Aunt Marian had talked about him."

"But in the event," said John Barclay, "Paul never met him."

"You sound like Brent." Timmy was still truculent.

"I'm sorry, Timmy. But there's one thing I feel we can't afford not to have clearly stated: I gather from what you told us that old Ambrose had gone over your family history rather thoroughly in the course of his row with Paul. That would have upset him . . . wouldn't it?"

Timmy looked at him. He seemed to have come to the end of his anger. "It wasn't the first time," he said.

"You could take that either way." The artist looked at his daughter again. "It has got to be said, Ann. In fairness to Paul—"

"Paul isn't mad." Ann spoke clearly, and in tones that were commendably matter-of-fact.

"But your father's right, my dear," said a deep voice from the doorway. Antony turned and found himself looking straight at the ugliest man he had ever seen.

He realised a moment later that his ugliness was not of nature, but the result of a disfigurement which had affected all the left side of the man's face, and seemed to have put the whole out of shape. In spite of this, there could be no denying that the newcomer brought with him a friendly feeling, a charm of manner that made his rather shocking appearance seem of little moment. He went on speaking, without allowing the silence his interruption had occasioned to lengthen unduly.

"Even if he doesn't go out and out for an insanity plea, there's no harm in stressing anything that might be considered a mitigating circumstance. I'm sure you'll agree with me," he added, with a nod to Antony. And explained to his host, "I met Audrey in the hall, so she told me—"

"This is Bob Wayne, Maitland," John Barclay put in. "Timmy's cousin."

Wayne smiled at the others for a moment, before turning his attention to Antony again. "Don't you agree with me?" he insisted.

"With limitations," said Antony, cautiously. "Mitigating circumstances would be mighty tricky ground in the case of a man accused of shooting his great-uncle. I gather, however, that you have something in mind in the nature of a temporary loss of control, so that lack of responsibility might be argued. It's a point, certainly." He caught sight of Timmy, who was looking mutinous, and frowned at him. Wayne saw the look, and turned the subject smoothly.

"I came with a purpose, John. Greg phoned me that his father was anxious to see us this evening. Can you and Ann go round there? I've promised to go."

"Well, I expect . . . what on earth is Ambrose up to?" said Barclay, a trifle fretfully. "We'll go if he makes a point of it."

"Greg seemed quite anxious. I don't know what the old boy wants, though."

Antony took the opportunity of the continuing talk between the two older men to say to Timmy, "Will you do something for me?"

"Of course. Anything."

"Don't be so rash. Though the first part's pleasant enough. Like Brent, I'd prefer your room to your company for a while. I suggest you take Miss Barclay with you; there's a good film at the Empire, I think. It would do you both good."

"Well . . . all right."

Ann said doubtfully, "Do you think we should?"

"I'm quite sure of it." Antony smiled at her. "If you've any scruples, dismiss them. And then this evening—"

"We shall give The Laurels a wide berth," said Timmy, firmly.

"Oh, no, you won't. That's the second part of my programme. I'm sorry, Timmy, but I want you there."

"I don't understand—"

"Just general principles. You can tell me about it tomorrow. And, Timmy—" he added, as the two young people turned towards the door , "relax if you can, and don't be so suspicious. I won't double-cross you . . . or Paul."

"No, I know." He looked rueful, and his smile was half-hearted. Antony watched him follow the girl from the room, and knew some misgivings.

Barclay and Wayne fell silent as he turned back to look at them. In both he now sensed a certain caution, a reserve, which might be difficult to overcome. But Wayne smiled at him, and said in his pleasant way, "Having got rid of the youngsters, what now?"

"It isn't easy to discuss this affair before young Herron," Antony remarked; and heard, with surprise, a defensive note in his voice. "And as you reminded me, Mr. Barclay, it can't make pleasant hearing for your daughter."

"And must we discuss it?" Wayne asked. His tone was casual.

"If you will bear with me. Mr. Cassell intimated that you might be in a position to help me."

"I don't see how. I never met 'Uncle William' you know."

"I didn't. But it may not be material. What I had in mind—"

"Maitland wants details of the Herron family, Bob."

Barclay interrupted without ceremony. "I've known topics that pleased me better, but I can see the point, of course."

"Of course. Well: Matthew and Mark were my cousins, though older than I was. I suppose I knew them as well as anybody."

"When did you last see them?"

"The night before . . . wasn't it, John?"

"That's right." Barclay had picked up his pipe again, and was stuffing tobacco into it with an air of rather fierce abstraction.

"Well, that's all there was to it. I went round about nine o'clock; and, come to think of it, Mark wasn't there. It must have been the previous Sunday I saw him."

"But that night . . . the night before they died—"

Wayne frowned. "There was nothing. I had thought for some time that Matt was off-colour, but he was no different that night. Ruth complained of a headache, and went to bed a little before we left. And that wasn't very late, was it, John?"

"Eleven, or thereabouts."

"Well . . . that was all."

"And you never saw them again." Antony's tone was reflective, and his remark a statement rather than a question, but Wayne took him up with sudden sharpness.

"I told you . . . that was the last time. When I heard . . . do we *have* to talk about this?"

"I should like you to tell me how you felt when you heard what had happened."

"Well," said Wayne again. "I couldn't believe it. Only when I thought about it, Matt had seemed strange before."

"Stuff and nonsense!" said John Barclay, erupting into the conversation in a way that seemed quite foreign to his nature. "You know you were being wise after the event, Bob."

"But why should you think so? Do you deny Matt was mad? A sane man could never have suspected—"

"No, I agree. But I still say he seemed sane."

"Well, it's no good arguing over matters of opinion. I don't see that what we *thought* can be helpful, anyway."

Antony grinned at him. "Why not?"

"You're collecting evidence. Would my opinion, say, be admissable?"

"What touching innocence! There are more things presented to a jury for consideration than ever get into the court record."

"I see." He sounded doubtful. "Do I take it that I'm a prospective witness?"

"I'm afraid so. You, and Mr. Barclay. You must have realised that the death of Paul's parents is likely to be considered important. And you seem to have been their most intimate friends. Miss Cassell has also been most helpful."

"Marian . . . well I never!" Wayne sounded startled, but Barclay replied with a return to his former serenity:

"Well, of course. After all, she and Ruth were very close." He turned to Antony again. "Do you feel your case progresses?"

"I suppose so." He sounded doubtful, but added a moment later in more hopeful tones, "There is also the question of Uncle William, about whom I gather you cannot help me, Mr. Wayne. But Miss Cassell has promised—"

"You know your own business, of course," said Wayne (and his tone made nonsense of the words). "But I don't quite see—"

"Does that matter?" Antony's tone had suddenly a dangerous sweetness, so that the man addressed looked at him sharply, and John Barclay laughed aloud.

"I should have warned you, Bob: Maitland sees no reason why he should make us party to his affairs. I've been warned off already."

"I see." Again his tone gave the lie to his words. "But William Cassell—"

"Is, after all, dead. Surely that entitles him to a little consideration?"

"But if Paul meant to kill Ambrose—"

"Then William's very innocuousness must be of moment. Don't you see?"

"Yes . . . well—"

"It doesn't really matter to you, anyway, Bob," the artist interrupted. "You didn't know him, so I gather Marian and I share the doubtful honour of being regarded as possible sources of information. And Greg, I suppose . . . but I bet he'd have nothing to tell you."

"Well, as you knew Uncle William, suppose you and Maitland consider him together." Wayne's tone was still as pleasant as ever, but in his expression Antony discerned the faintest echo of Timmy's mutinous look. Barclay grinned.

"Come to that, I'm a broken reed, I'm afraid," he said, ruefully. "I'd help and willing, but most of what I know of him is what Marian has told me from time to time."

"But you knew him when he was in England before?"

"Oh, yes. But what does one really know of one's contemporaries' elderly relatives?"

"Quite a lot, sometimes," said Antony. And Wayne grinned, and added:

"Altogether too much!" with a sudden reversal of mood.

"Well . . . if you like. But not," Barclay insisted, "if they spend most of their time abroad."

"I suppose," remarked Wayne, with sudden diffidence, "that fact might have its own importance. Is that what you meant?" he added, turning to Antony; who suppressed his renewed irritation at this passion for explanations and replied briefly:

"Uncle William's inoffensiveness. Precisely!"

"And do you also wish to inquire into our knowledge of the intended victim?" Barclay sounded amused. "Or will you make your own researches into the character and habits of Ambrose Cassell?"

"Preferably, both." Antony's answering smile was a trifle half-hearted. "It's a tricky business, at best, asking for opinions of a man who's still very much alive."

"In case they prove libellous? That might well be the way with old Ambrose?"

"Surely not, John. I admit he's a holy terror; but not so bad, really."

"If you consider his treatment of the twins 'not so bad', Bob, all I can say is you're easily satisfied," Barclay retorted.

"Well, he's inclined to squash them, I know. Don't you think they sometimes ask for it?"

"Perhaps. But not that he should remind them—"

They were still wrangling when Antony left ten minutes

later. He did not feel he had added very much to his store of knowledge, but after all, you never knew what might prove to be useful. He went home and spent half an hour over his notes. Jenny, coming in with a teapot, found him scowling at a half-filled sheet of writing paper and interrupted firmly:

"That's quite enough of the Cassells for to-day, darling. Won't they wait till Monday?"

"I expect so. All the same—" He left the desk, and came across to stare down absently at the tea-tray. After a while he looked up and said with amusement, "I've been usurping your prerogative, my love, and indulging in a little match-making."

"Oh, Antony!" Jenny was reproachful. "Who?" she added a moment later, as her curiosity got the better of her.

"Young Timmy and Ann Barclay." Antony was both smug and apologetic.

"But she's engaged to Paul."

"She's in love with Timmy. And he with her."

"Oh, well, that's different. But will Paul mind?"

"That I can't tell you." He was serious now, and sounded tired. "But I do know I don't like this affair . . . not one little bit."

"Are you sorry you asked Uncle Nick to take the brief?"

"Oh, no, that's one thing I am sure about: I'm very glad indeed. But I only wish I could see a happy outcome."

"Poor Paul," said Jenny.

"It isn't only Paul, you know," added her husband sombrely.

CHAPTER 8

At about eleven-thirty next morning Antony was engaged in demonstrating to his uncle the validity of the title of an obscure Lancashire landowner to a piece of unreclaimed moorland, ("which I cannot conceive that anybody in his senses would want," said Sir Nicholas, in a bored way). He was doing this with the aid of a dilapidated and rapidly disintegrating Abstract of Title, and both men were leaning over the desk in the study considering it when they heard the door open and Jenny said, without preamble, "Timmy Herron just phoned."

Something in her tone made Sir Nicholas look up quickly, but Antony was absorbed in his argument and straightened up in a leisurely way, saying as he did so, "That's good. Is he coming here? I'm hoping—" He broke off abruptly as he caught sight of Jenny's worried look. "What is it, love?"

Jenny came into the room. She said, "I told him to come. He's very upset. He says someone has poisoned Aunt Marian."

Antony said, "Damn!" and then, ridiculously, "that's really too bad!" Sir Nicholas asked, more pertinently:

"Is she dead?"

"No, but they don't think she'll get better. They've taken her to hospital."

That was all Jenny knew, and she went upstairs again presently, leaving the two men to await Timmy's arrival. "I'd better see him," said Sir Nicholas. "I'll give you a few minutes, and then join you."

When Timmy came, Antony was shocked by his appearance and fetched brandy from the dining-room before he allowed the younger man to talk. His hand was shaking, and

75

the glass rattled against his teeth as he drank. After a moment he said, "Thank you," and put down the glass and closed his eyes. Antony said:

"You'd better tell me."

"Yes, I know." He opened his eyes again and gave his companion a look of apology. "I'm sorry to make such a fuss. They don't think she'll live, you know."

"Tell me about it," said Antony again.

"Rose found her—the housemaid—she takes her tea at eight o'clock on Sundays. So then there was the doctor, and a fearful panic all round. And after that, the police. Dr. Hearn said we must, but he thought she'd taken something herself, you know. We all thought that. She felt it dreadfully, about Paul."

"But the police didn't agree?"

"The police," said Timmy flatly, "think it was me." He appeared stimulated, rather than depressed by this statement, and eyed Antony challengingly.

"Surely not! After all—"

"Let the witness tell his story his own way," said Sir Nicholas quietly from the door. Timmy shied like a startled horse at the sound of his voice, and looked rather wildly at Antony, who explained:

"My uncle. Sir Nicholas Harding. This is Timmy Herron, sir. He's telling me—"

"Yes, I heard." Sir Nicholas crossed the room to take the chair opposite the visitor. "I'd like to hear why you think the police suspect you," he remarked.

"Well, they practically accused me." As he talked, Timmy was regaining something of his former belligerence. "You see, first the doctor told them she'd tried to kill herself; then later on they said it couldn't have been that, because it was the wrong medicine. That was after *their* doctor came."

"The wrong medicine?" said Sir Nicholas. "What do you mean by that?"

"Her sleeping stuff. She used to take some tablets called 'Drowse'—not every night, I mean, just when she couldn't sleep. But last week when she was upset the doctor gave her a prescription, so she used that instead."

"And it was one of these two preparations—?"

"We none of us thought about it at first. Only later on, when we were talking, I remembered there were only three of the 'Drowse' tablets left when the prescription came. I knew because I took the bottle up to Aunt Marian, and she said something about it being a waste; so she opened the box, and there were just three tablets there, and she put them away in the drawer of her bedside table." Timmy paused for breath, but went on without prompting, "We thought it must have been the doctor's stuff she'd taken, but Dr. Hearn said it couldn't have been that, because she had it on Wednesday, and there were just four doses gone, as there should have been, and the prescription hadn't been renewed. So that made us wonder, you know. Then the other doctor came, the police chap—I don't remember his name. And he asked Dr. Hearn about the prescription, and the ingredients (whatever they were) were quite different from what's supposed to be in 'Drowse', so he was sure the tablets were what she had taken."

"Even so," said Sir Nicholas, thoughtfully, "it could be argued that your aunt had herself replenished the supply."

"Well . . . not very plausibly." Timmy was apologetic. "I mean, why should she? It would have been so easy for her just to take enough of the medicine, or what she thought was enough."

"It will, however, have to be looked into." Sir Nicholas looked across at his nephew, who was scribbling industriously on the back of an envelope. "However, granted the police have decided they are dealing with a case of attempted murder . . . you haven't explained to us why they should think you guilty."

"I don't believe they think I really meant her to die. Only you see, it seemed obvious that there wouldn't be two people killing off the family, and as Paul was out of this . . . I don't know if I'm being very clear?"

"Admirably so." Sir Nicholas had been occupying himself at unnecessary length with the lighting of a cigar, and carefully refraining from looking at the visitor. Now he turned to face him, but his air was still casual. "You are saying that as your brother had an alibi for this second crime, a strong presumption is created of his innocence of the first."

"That's it. I said that to Brent . . . something like it, anyway. And I think they must have heard us talking. They hinted that I'd thought of that before, and done it to try and prove Paul couldn't be guilty.''

Sir Nicholas made an abrupt movement, and fixed his eyes on Timmy with a look that was now anything but casual. ''And they had grounds for this suspicion?'' he asked.

''I . . . no, of course not.'' Timmy was clearly taken aback by the question. He glanced across at Antony, and then looked down at the hearth-rug, and added, ''I didn't think—I suppose it was stupid—I didn't think that perhaps you wouldn't believe me.''

Sir Nicholas gave an exasperated growl, and Antony said hastily, ''I warned you before about jumping to conclusions.''

''Well, I can see . . . I mean, you don't really *know*, even about Paul, do you?''

''That,'' said Sir Nicholas with an air of patience, ''is beside the point. What else have you to tell us?''

''That was all, really.''

''I hardly think—'' began Sir Nicholas, but Antony interrupted him.

''What's on your mind, Timmy?''

Timmy looked uneasy. He said, after an appreciable hesitation, ''I can't help but realise that they've only my word for the fact that there were no more than three tablets. Aunt Marian knows, of course, but it doesn't look as if she will be able to tell anyone.''

''Well?''

''Well . . .'' Timmy swallowed, and looked from Antony to Sir Nicholas, and back again. ''This isn't going to help you believe me,'' he said plaintively.

''Never mind that!'' Hearing the sharpness in his nephew's tone, Sir Nicholas sat back in his chair with an amused look to wait upon events.

Timmy did not answer immediately. All the fight seemed to have gone out of him now; he looked uncertain, and very unhappy. After a moment he squared his shoulders, rather with the air of one who faced a firing squad. ''Well,'' he said again. ''They haven't got round to it yet, but when they do . . . they're going to find my fingerprints on the pill-box in Aunt Marian's bedside drawer.'' He looked again from

Antony to Sir Nicholas, and added gloomily, "I think that's bound to give them ideas . . . don't you?"

"You haven't yet explained to us how it came about," said Sir Nicholas, quietly. "I presume you are able to explain?"

"I can do that all right," said Timmy. "But I don't know whether you'll think it convincing or not. And as the police already—"

"Let's leave the police out of it for the moment. We're concerned now to know the strength of the case against you."

"Well, you see," said Timmy, "it wasn't exactly a jolly evening. Aunt Marian got upset, what with one thing and another, and about ten o'clock I got the idea she couldn't stand very much more, so I persuaded her to go to bed. I went with her—I mean, we left the drawing-room together—and I told her I'd bring her some hot milk." At this point Sir Nicholas got up, walked across to the window and back, and stood on the hearth-rug looking down in an intent way at the speaker. Timmy eyed him warily, but did not interrupt his tale. "Cook had gone to bed, and it was Rose's night out, so I warmed the milk and took it up to her. I was about ten minutes, I suppose."

"Do the police know this?"

"Yes, because they asked about what she'd had. So I told them about the milk. That was quite early on, they didn't mention it again."

"I see. So you took the glass upstairs—"

"She was in the bathroom when I got to her room, but the door was slightly ajar. She called out to me to go in, so I went across and put the milk down on the bedside table. She said 'thank you', and after a moment she said, 'I must have a book. And someone seems to have taken the one I was reading.' So, of course, I went to look."

"And how far afield did your search take you?"

"I went down to her sitting-room, because of course I knew she must have left the book somewhere herself. And there it was."

Sir Nicholas frowned. Antony said, "That's the small sitting-room near the side door, isn't it?" He turned to his uncle as Timmy nodded. "You go through a swing door from the front hall, sir, and down a passage. It would be quite possible for someone to go up the main staircase in the time it took, though I admit it doesn't leave much time for manœuvre.''

The older man did not comment, but said only, ''How long were you away from your aunt's room, Mr. Herron?''

''About . . . about ten minutes, I should think. I know it seems a long time,'' he said, into the silence that followed this admission. ''Ann was in the hall when I went down, and she went with me, and we talked for a few minutes. Then I took the book upstairs again, and she was going home.''

''Did you see anyone else while you were downstairs?''

''Only her father, he was waiting for her when we got back to the hall.'' He paused a moment, but as no further inquiry came went on slowly, ''Aunt Marian was still in the bathroom when I got back. I called out to her to hurry, or the milk would be cold, and she switched out the light almost immediately, and came out. I wanted her to take something, because I didn't think she'd sleep if she didn't; and I opened the drawer without thinking, and took hold of the box. It's one of those shiny, red pill-boxes,'' he added, in gloomy parenthesis, ''and I should think the surface would be just about perfect for fingerprints. Anyway, she remembered the stuff the doctor had given her (though I think she really preferred the 'Drowse', and only took the other because she felt it would be somehow discourteous not to); so she went back into the bathroom again to take it.''

''Could you see her?''

''Yes, I . . . she didn't close the door. The bottle was in a cupboard over the wash-basin. She took it down, and she shook it . . . rather thoroughly . . . rather like performing some magic rite; and then she poured some into a medicine glass, and pulled a face as she drank it.'' He stopped, and shifted a little, restlessly, in his chair. ''Then she rinsed the glass, and I suppose she put it down but I didn't see where, and came out into the bedroom again. Do you think—''

''I think that if the police find traces of a drug in the glass your aunt drank milk from last night (or even in the medicine glass, though that seems less likely), you must realise that your position is a very serious one,'' said Sir Nicholas.

"I should not be doing you a kindness by attempting to minimise the gravity of the situation."

Timmy looked at him a little blankly. He said, slowly, "I can't help feeling that if I'm accused of murder—or even attempted murder—it will make things rather worse for Paul than they are already."

"That is also true. What concerns us at the moment, however, is the possibility of such a charge being brought."

"Concerns us?" said Timmy. "Does that mean—?"

Sir Nicholas smiled at him suddenly. "It means my nephew is 'interested'," he said. "As I seem likely to be involved willy-nilly, I may as well give in gracefully."

"I see," said Timmy. He sounded doubtful, and looked across at Antony with an air of uncertainty. "I don't understand why you should believe me, though. It isn't as if my story is at all convincing."

"Probably the incorrigible perversity of my disposition," said Sir Nicholas gravely. And Antony, who had been listening to this exchange with some anxiety, relaxed again and began to feel in his pockets for another envelope.

"You were telling us that Aunt Marian took a dose of the doctor's sleeping draught," he prompted. "What happened then?"

"She went to bed. I showed her the book, and she said it was the right one, and she was just starting to drink her milk when I left her."

Antony had abandoned the search for an envelope, and wandered across to the desk in search of a writing-pad. He said without turning, "Do you remember, was there any skin on the milk?"

"I don't know. I didn't notice. But I don't think there can have been," he added slowly. "She was just sipping it, but I'm sure she'd have moved the skin first if there'd been any, or at least pulled a face when she found it was there. Do you think that means it *was* in the milk . . . whatever she took?"

"I think there should have been a skin on it; after all, you say it had been standing there for ten minutes. If something had been put into the glass, and stirred to dissolve it—well, it's only a guess, after all."

"And not a specially helpful one," Sir Nicholas put in.

"We shall know soon enough what the police have discovered."

Probably too soon, thought Antony, eyeing their visitor with sudden compassion. He had come back to stand on the hearth-rug, and the note-book he had brought with him had gone into his pocket unused. "And that was the last you saw of Aunt Marian?" he added aloud.

"Only this morning, and of course she wasn't conscious." He looked down at the rug again, and said as though the words were difficult, "They wouldn't let me go to the hospital; she may be dead now, I just don't know."

"You can telephone presently," Sir Nicholas offered. "But it won't be much use until they have had time to get her settled, and see what can be done."

"And meanwhile," said Antony, "I want to hear about last night. Remember?"

Timmy looked up at him. He shivered, as though he were cold, and closed his hands together and put them between his knees. He said, in an expressionless tone, "I remember."

Antony was firm, though sympathetic. "I'm sorry if it was a bad evening. But I do want to know what your grandfather was up to."

"That's easily told." He didn't sound as though he found the recollection either easy or pleasant. "He wanted to know what questions you'd been asking; and what had been told you as well."

"I see." Antony was thoughtful. Sir Nicholas, who had again been observing the visitor closely, interrupted before he could go on.

"I should like to emphasise, Mr. Herron, that—painful as all these questions may be—they are of the utmost importance to your brother."

"I . . . well . . . that was all there was to it, really. Except that he tried to persuade them (in the most delicate manner imaginable) that there was no doubt at all of Paul's guilt; and that it would be foolish, and cause unnecessary trouble, to encourage you in the belief that it might be possible to prove him innocent."

"And what was the reaction to that?"

"I don't think any of them had had any doubts—about

Paul, I mean. Bob Wayne and John Barclay, at least, had no idea you contemplated anything else; but he soon disabused them of that idea. And I've told you the rest."

"Except the arguments Grandfather used."

"Well, he just went over the reasons for thinking Paul mad. And he did try to get rid of me first, I will say that. I told you it was a jolly evening." He paused a moment, and added apologetically, "I've learned to live with the idea of what my father did. But I don't much care for having it thrown up in my face, you know."

"I'm sorry," said Antony again. He turned to his uncle, who took no notice of his look of inquiry, but asked quietly:

"It is a point which has exercised my mind, Mr. Herron: whether or not your brother also learned to live with that idea?"

Timmy took his time over this, but answered without protest. "I don't think he did. But we're very different, you know; we don't react the same way to things at all."

"Very well. We'll leave it at that. Have you any more questions, Antony?"

"Not at the moment. I'd like to go to Wimbledon with you after lunch, Timmy. Jenny'll give us some lunch," he added, as the other got up, and looked around uncertainly.

Sir Nicholas roused himself from a fit of abstraction. "I think it likely that the police will want to see Mr. Herron again before long," he said. "I needn't warn you to be careful."

"No," Antony was thoughtful again. "You mean that as soon as we make use of this 'laws of averages' argument to help Paul Herron, we provide—*ipso facto*—a motive for Timmy?"

"Precisely. The police, of course, are perfectly well aware of the points you made to your cousin," Sir Nicholas added to Timmy, who was looking bewildered. "But we don't want to give them a chance of getting them from you in the form of a statement."

"Of course not." Timmy sounded blank. Sir Nicholas gave him an encouraging smile, and turned back to his nephew.

"Who is in charge of the case?"

"Superintendent Forrester. And the inspector's called Conway."

"Hm! Well . . . I've encountered Forrester in court on several occasions. He isn't a man to trifle with, I can tell you that. He's bland on the surface, and hard as nails underneath it, I should say."

"Sounds ominous," said Antony, gloomily.

"I will leave it to your ingenuity," Sir Nicholas informed him, with the glimmer of a smile, "to extract from the police any information that may be going."

Antony turned towards the door, shepherding Timmy before him. He said, over his shoulder, "Of course, you aren't *really* interested," and Sir Nicholas grinned at him briefly, before he replied with a return of solemnity:

"I have, after all, a duty to my client."

"Fiddlesticks," said Antony, crossly. And shut the door firmly upon any possible retort his uncle might be contemplating.

CHAPTER 9

THERE WAS no news of Aunt Marian, either bad or good; the impersonal voice from the hospital said only that her condition was unchanged. Timmy was quiet as they made their way to Wimbledon when lunch was over, rousing himself only once to remark gloomily, "They'd have told us (wouldn't they?) if she was any better." There seemed to be no answer to this, and Antony did not attempt reassurance. Having suffered himself, on occasion, from the careless optimism of friends, he did not feel any desire to subject his companion to the same treatment.

It was three o'clock when they arrived at The Laurels and the party might have been drawn up to Antony's own specifications. John Barclay and his household had arrived in force, and Bob Wayne also had come in search of news. And Ambrose Cassell wasn't there.

As he had been rather doubtful of his reception, Antony was well enough pleased by this, but Timmy's look of strain deepened when he heard that his grandfather had been sent for to the hospital. He did not comment, however, but went across the drawing-room, where the family were assembled, and joined Ann and Audrey who were sitting together on a sofa under one of the long windows. Antony, from the doorway, watched Ann's expression lighten; and saw Audrey's quick look at her cousin as she moved to make room for the newcomer.

Uncle Greg had got up, and came forward fussily. He seemed a little taken aback at the sight of a stranger, but unprepared (in his father's absence) for actual rudeness. Antony produced his most persuasive manner, and after a moment was waved to a chair and made free of the gathering. "You see us all waiting, Mr. Maitland. My father has promised to telephone when there is any news."

John Barclay spoke up from a chair across the hearth. "It seems from what we heard last night that when you visited us we were a little misled as to your intentions." He had returned momentarily to his air of vagueness, but there was nothing vague in the look which Antony encountered when he turned to reply.

"I'm sorry you should feel that," he replied mildly.

"Well . . . no need to apologise," said Barclay.

"He didn't, actually," Timmy put in. He spoke absently, with no effect of rudeness, but subsided hastily when he found the attention of the company fixed on him.

"You might say, 'a wolf in sheep's clothing'." Robert Wayne's tone was gently malicious. And Barclay answered him with unexpected asperity:

"I might, of course, if I wanted to be trite. And if I had observed anything at all sheep-like in Maitland's attitude yesterday."

Wayne grinned. "Yes, an unfortunate remark. However," he turned to the newcomer, "we were interested to learn that you feel there is some doubt, not only about Paul's insanity, but even about his guilt."

"To be accurate, I informed Mr. Cassell only that we must consider all possibilities. And to match platitude with platitude, we are still 'exploring avenues'," said Antony.

"But you can't deny you would like to prove Paul innocent?" said Brent, suddenly joining the conversation.

"I see no reason to deny it. Would you have any objection to his being acquitted?"

"Why no, of course not. I'd be very glad if I thought. . ." Brent sounded, for the moment, most uncharacteristically unsure of himself. From the corner of his eye, Antony was conscious that one of the girls in the window had moved abruptly. "But I don't think you've a hope," Brent went on more firmly. "And that being so, I think it's a mistaken kindness to try to prove him sane."

Audrey spoke suddenly, "But, he isn't mad," she said flatly. "You don't think so . . . really, Brent?"

"No, I don't, my dear." He looked at her for a moment, and then added with deliberation, "But I don't think he's innocent, either.'' The girl looked at him without speaking, and something in her expression made him add, irritably, ''Well, I'm sorry; but you did ask me, you know.''

''Of course,'' said Audrey, tonelessly. ''And you have to say what you think.'' She looked at her uncle, and added coaxingly, ''John, *you* don't—''

''I think, for Paul's sake, his counsel must be very careful before they decide not to use so obvious a line of defence,'' he replied. ''I told Ann this yesterday, and Timmy too, after you went out. I don't think they agree with me, but Bob does. Don't you, Bob?''

Wayne hesitated. ''I would have agreed with you yesterday,'' he said at length. ''But I've been thinking since then, and if there's any chance at all of getting a straight 'not guilty' verdict, I feel Maitland is in the right of it.''

''I think you're mistaken,'' said Barclay, hotly. ''And after all—'' He stopped, looking at Ann, and his expression changed. ''Well, it's no use quarrelling; it is, when all's said and done, a matter between Paul and his counsel, who will no doubt advise him to the best of their ability.''

Wayne smiled at him. ''We'll agree to differ, then.''

''The question really is,'' said Audrey, with a suddenness and clarity that brought every eye on her, ''what Mr. Maitland thinks he can do for Paul.'' She looked at Antony. ''Will you tell us that?'' she demanded.

''No,'' said Antony. He spoke quietly enough, and succeeded fairly well in hiding his irritation. ''It's not a question I could answer at this stage, even if I wanted to.''

''And you don't want to?'' insisted Audrey.

''I do not. It would be most improper—'' He was speaking primly, and Audrey suddenly grinned at him.

''Pax,'' she said. ''I spoke out of turn; I often do.'' She turned to her cousin, as Ann put a hand on her arm. ''I know, darling, you're more concerned than I am. Only I did want to know—''

''It will be all right, Audrey; truly it will.'' The reassurance sounded oddly, coming from the younger girl.

''Do you really think so?'' Audrey's voice was bitter. Ann's hand dropped back into her lap again, and she looked for the moment very much as though she were going to be sick; then she said steadily, without taking her eyes from her cousin's face, "Paul isn't mad, and he didn't kill Uncle William. So nobody can prove he did."

"And the moral of that is: somebody else is guilty." Brent's voice was at its most mocking. Antony saw Timmy stiffen and wished a little ruefully that he had thought to warn him again to avoid any further clashes with his cousin. But Ann said, "Well, of course!" in a matter-of-fact tone, so that Brent eyed her doubtfully, obviously wondering what she would say next. As she had relapsed into silence, however, he continued after a pause, though with something less than his usual assurance:

"Well, even granted all that—and I disagree with you one hundred per cent, you know—even granted that Paul is as innocent as a lamb, there's still last night's little affair to be explained away, I'm afraid."

"You can't blame Paul for that," said Audrey quickly.

"No, my dear. I don't want to 'blame' anybody. But the police seem to have their own ideas on the subject."

Timmy said, "Did you suggest to them that I might have poisoned Aunt Marian, Brent?" He spoke quietly, but he had taken out a cigarette a few minutes before, and Antony saw that his hand was shaking.

Both Barclay and Wayne, who had been listening in silence to these exchanges, were moved to speech by this remark. Wayne said, "It seems on the face of it an odd suggestion," and looked round the company inquiringly, as though awaiting enlightenment. Barclay said, "But why should he have done that, Timmy? And what earthly reason could anybody have for thinking you wanted to kill Mariam?"

"The idea is," Timmy replied, but he did not take his eyes from his cousin's face as he spoke, "the idea is I did it because Paul couldn't be blamed for it anyway. So the police would think 'if someone else poisoned Aunt Marian, that same person probably killed Uncle William, too'."

"But, of course, you didn't do anything of the kind," said Brent.

"No," said Timmy, still very gently. "But you haven't told me yet whether it was you who put the idea into the heads of the police."

"Well, I didn't."

"But you did tell Grandfather," said Ann, who had turned very pale, but retained her air of serenity. "I thought you were only joking."

"In this instance I'm afraid the joke—such as it was—was Timmy's."

"I didn't . . . I wouldn't." Timmy was indignant. He sounded, also, much younger than his years; so that Antony was reminded of childhood squabbles, and realised that the cousins' relationship had never proceeded beyond that stage. "You know I wouldn't have done anything to hurt Aunt Marian."

"Well, who then? Who would have wanted to hurt her? And after all, I'm only saying," said Brent with a show of reasonableness, "that you meant to give her a slight overdose, and something went wrong."

"Do you think," said Ann, "do you think the police will say Timmy did it?" She turned to Antony with an air of appeal; and again he was unable to offer her reassurance.

"I can't tell you that, Miss Barclay. But I can say that my uncle will be unwilling to let the matter rest, whether or not an accusation is formally laid." He paused, and looked round the group of people. "It has its importance in planning Paul Herron's defence."

Brent Cassell said, "What did I tell you!" and his father added petulantly:

"Well, I must say, I cannot help but agree that you will do far more harm than good with all these inquiries."

"Whom do you suggest I shall harm? If you mean you'd rather see your nephew hang than have the family inconvenienced," said Antony bluntly, "I can only say, I don't think much of your sense of values."

"I mean," said Uncle Greg, with a sudden awkward assumption of dignity, "I mean I think Paul is guilty; and that you will serve his best interests by demonstrating his madness, of which we are all perfectly well aware, rather than by trying to prove his innocence."

Barclay said regretfully, "I agree with you there, though I'm sorry to say it." He sounded troubled, and looked across anxiously at his daughter. Ann looked down at her hands, and said nothing in reply. Audrey started to speak, but thought better of it, though she turned quite pink with what Antony took to be suppressed indignation.

Brent looked at her in silence for a moment, and then allowed his eyes to travel slowly from her to Ann, to Timmy. Finally he turned back to Antony again, saying with a show of helpfulness that he did not trouble to make convincing:

"We've been side-tracking you, I'm afraid. You were talking about last night's affair. What do you want to know about that?"

"Quite a lot, if you'll help me."

"I'm sure," said Brent—still with his air of spurious politeness—"we shall all be very willing."

"What do you want to know?" Wayne's tone was brusque, and he cast a look of irritation in Brent's direction; of irritation, or perhaps of angry dislike? Antony couldn't decide, and he didn't have time to ponder the question. He said to Wayne:

"Anything, and everything. I'm not fussy."

"Well—" said Wayne, with a return of his habitual look of amusement. "That's a tall order."

"Not really. Start by telling me what you think really happened." There was a small stir among the people present as he spoke, but he resisted the temptation to look round at them, and kept his attention on Wayne, his look inquiring. (They'd be going round in circles all afternoon if he didn't watch it, and nothing learned at the end of it all.)

"I think it was an accident." Wayne was definite. "But I seem to be a minority of one—nobody agrees with me."

"But if Miss Cassell only had three of the 'Drowse' tablets left, and they seem to think it was those she took—?"

"Well, I think we've to grant the second point, from what Greg and Brent have told me. But about the number of the tablets . . . you could have been mistaken, Timmy, surely you can't be certain?"

"I am certain," said Timmy. "In some ways I wish I weren't."

"But accidents do happen," Robert Wayne persisted. "The strangest things, and you never can explain them."

"Unfortunately, the police have a habit of looking for explanations," said Antony. "And I must admit, I'm partial to them myself."

Wayne shrugged. "But anything else is unthinkable. Marian would never—"

"I understood that the first reaction to that idea—in the family at any rate—was not one of disbelief." Antony transferred his look of inquiry to Gregory Cassell.

"Because we could think of nothing else." He gave his customary quick look round the company, and added more firmly, "One just doesn't think of a thing like murder . . . not till it's beyond all doubt."

And that, thought Antony, is true enough. "But you must have got used to the idea by now," he said aloud, deliberately clumsy.

"You forget. Paul is safely in prison," remarked Brent. "And, as Timmy pointed out, two murderers in one family is rather an excessive allowance. Not that I think," he added, "that Timmy really meant to kill Aunt Marian."

"Obliging of you!" said Timmy, explosively. Antony caught Brent's eye and said quietly:

"It seems a little early to reach a conclusion—"

"What else can I think?" His air of candour was a little overdone.

"I could suggest several other possibilities to you, without, I think, straining your credulity."

"No doubt you could." Suddenly his tone was spiteful. "I only hope you won't be given the opportunity of exercising your ingenuity in this connection in court."

There was a silence. Into it, Wayne remarked, with an air of false heartiness, "Well, we all hope that, don't we, John?" And John Barclay, without ceasing his contemplation of the ceiling, said seriously:

"I sincerely trust—"

As he spoke Ann turned back to the room. She looked at her father doubtfully, and then said, "You don't believe it, John? Not you?"

Barclay said uneasily, "I can't help remembering what Ambrose said last night." And he looked at Timmy as he spoke.

"He said a lot of silly things," Ann remarked flatly.

"He said I was 'quite irresponsible'," Timmy put in. "Was that what you meant, John? Does poisoning one's aunt come under the heading of irresponsibility, would you say?''

"Well, if I'm being unfair, I'm sorry," said Barclay. He was still looking at Timmy Herron, who in his turn was looking at Ann. He said over his shoulder:

"I shouldn't worry about it. What's a little thing like an accusation of murder . . . among friends?'' His voice was expressionless, and did not echo the bitterness of the words. Barclay looked distressed, but made no further comment.

Antony said, into the silence, "If we could, perhaps, leave these matters of opinion and turn to those of fact?''

They looked at him then, he could feel the antagonism in the room, as palpable as a spoken threat. Brent said, "What do you want to know?'' and his tone was dangerous.

"About last night. What happened after Miss Cassell retired?''

Gregory said, in a worried way, "It seems rather a strange request, Mr. Maitland.''

"I think it is not unreasonable, in the circumstances.''

"Meaning . . . ?'' said Brent. And Antony met the challenge in his tone with some bluntness.

"Meaning, I want to know who had the opportunity to poison Miss Cassell,'' he said. And again was aware of the bitter antagonism of some, at least, of his audience.

Barclay said, after a moment, "The party began to break up. Not quite immediately, perhaps five or ten minutes after Marian went. It wasn't the most comfortable kind of social gathering, you know.''

"I can well imagine it." But the trouble was, as he realised later, that it had not been in any sense a formal party. Composed as it was of family and familiar friends, there had been no reason why it should remain static; in fact, if they had been deliberately trying to confuse matters, they couldn't have made a better job of it. Any one of them could have slipped up to Aunt Marian's room while Timmy was downstairs looking for her library book. On the question of opportunity alone, there was nothing to indicate one as being more likely than the others.

He persevered, of course (even, as Sir Nicholas pointed out when the matter was reported to him, beyond the point of usefulness), and it was nearly half an hour later when he recognised, regretfully, the futility of further questions, and got to his feet. "Well, I'm very grateful for your patience, particularly under such distressing circumstances." He looked at Timmy, trying to catch his eye. "I think I should—"

Timmy wasn't listening. He said, "I just heard the phone ring," and then went across the room and opened the door, and stood there. Everyone in the room was listening, too; they heard the small sound of the receiver being replaced, and then the voice of Rose, the housemaid, a little flustered, more than a little worried:

"That was the police, Master Timmy. They asked if you were home, and then said would I tell you that they'd like you to go to Scotland Yard straight away to make a statement." She paused, and added in a puzzled voice, "They didn't wait for me to ask you; they seemed to take it for granted that you'd go."

Timmy looked at her blankly, and turned away without acknowledging the message. He said to the room at large, "I thought, perhaps, it was from the hospital." And then, taking a grip on the present that was visibly an effort, he added, to Antony, "You heard what she said. Will you come?"

"Of course."

Gregory Cassell said, with an attempt at an air of authority, "Your grandfather would wish me to telephone to Bellerby."

"Well, I don't want him," said Timmy, flatly. His air of abstraction robbed the words of too much rudeness. "Maitland promised—"

"You should have more thought for your grandfather's wishes. Really, Timmy, you are a most thoughtless boy." This was Aunt Agnes, at her most querulous. Timmy took no notice. He was looking at Ann.

John Barclay also was looking at his daughter. He said, after a moment, "Perhaps we should go home, my dear. I'm sure they'll ring us as soon as there's news of Marian."

Ann got up. She said, without expression, "Yes, of course. Are you coming, Audrey?" But she didn't look at her father as she crossed the room. She turned briefly at the door, and said, "I hope it's good news." She did not speak to Timmy as she passed him.

Antony contented himself with the briefest of farewells, and added briskly, "We'll go now, Timmy. I don't expect it will take long." Timmy turned without another word, and crossed the hall and went out of the front door. As he followed, Antony heard the outburst of talk in the room behind him; and from the back of the hall Ann Barclay, talking to the housemaid. Her voice was as gentle and unperturbed as usual.

"You'll telephone, Rose, won't you, when there's any news? You see, they might be too worried to think about me."

"I'll ring you, Miss Ann. Don't you worry." And Antony reflected, as he followed Timmy down the drive, that he wouldn't have taken a bet on whether it was Aunt Marian's health, or Timmy's return from jeopardy that was to be the subject of the communication. Most likely both. And Rose—not a doubt of it—would repay a little attention.

CHAPTER 10

THEY WERE RECEIVED at Scotland Yard with the intelligence that Superintendent Forrester was awaiting them. Antony walked in the rear of a small procession down a long, dark corridor, and wondered as he did so whether his companion was going to emerge from his present trance-like state in time to deal competently with the police interrogation. Timmy had been vague and distant in his manner ever since they left the Wimbledon house.

Superintendent Forrester was a big man, and appeared even larger in the confines of his own room than in the wider spaces of a court. He received them with an air of sleepy good-nature which Antony (remembering his uncle's remarks) decided it would be unwise to accept at face value. He had in support Detective-Inspector Conway, a thin-faced man with a square jaw, a waspish air, and (they soon discovered) an acid tongue.

Timmy ignored their greetings, saying only, "We haven't heard from the hospital yet. Have you?"

Forrester said in his quiet way, "I'm sorry, we have no news of Miss Cassell." While Conway, who had established himself a little way from the desk, as though to dissociate himself from the proceedings, remarked, "We can appreciate your anxiety, Mr. Herron." His tone was sarcastic and Antony looked at him with interest. Timmy, however, did not seem to suspect him of a double meaning. He sat down rather heavily in the chair which Forrester had indicated, and said with an air of inconsequence:

"This is Mr. Maitland."

"Your solicitor?" said Conway, giving Antony a sharp look.

"My . . . my legal adviser," said Timmy. He appeared to be pleased with the phrase, and grinned at Antony over his shoulder; even the small effort involved in choosing a reply seemed to have had a tonic effect on him. The dazed look became less marked, and he did not drop his eyes when Inspector Conway eyed him with an air of calculated curiosity.

Forrester said, "I've encountered your uncle in court, Mr. Maitland; and seen you in his company, I believe."

"On several occasions," Antony agreed.

"And you're one of Paul Herron's counsel?" His tone was mild, but Antony recognised the quality of insistence of which Sir Nicholas had warned him.

"I am, indeed. But at the moment, I understand, we are to concern ourselves with what happened to Miss Cassell; and, as Timothy Herron has told you, I am here in his interests."

Forrester looked amused. He did not reply directly, however, but glanced at his colleague and said merely: "Inspector Conway has some questions for your client, I believe."

Antony pulled up a chair, a little behind and to the left of the one Timmy had taken. He said, as he sat down, "I don't know yet whether we're answering any questions. Perhaps Inspector Conway will explain why we should do so?"

Again Forrester glanced at his colleague, and again his expression was one of gentle amusement. Conway tightened his lips, and said brusquely, "That shouldn't be difficult, I think. We are investigating a case of attempted murder."

"But, are we?" He sounded innocent; but the superintendent's look of amusement vanished as he spoke, and was replaced by a penetrating stare which Antony sustained with equanimity.

"I have no doubt of it," said Conway, sharply.

"I'm afraid I haven't sufficient data to form an opinion," said Antony, apologetically. His deprecatory air was purely illusory. "Perhaps you can convince me?"

Conway looked at his superior officer; he was obviously beginning to lose his temper. Forrester shrugged and spread his hands in an eloquent gesture, and the inspector turned back again with an attempt at patience too obvious to achieve its object. "Miss Cassell was not drugged with the medicine her doctor prescribed," he said. "A quantity of

'Drowse' sleeping tablets, probably about a dozen, had been dissolved in a glass of milk she drank after she retired.''

''And so—?'' said Antony. His attention was on Timmy, who had stiffened at the inspector's words; but he achieved the air of one who did not intend to concede one point without full explanation, and Conway's look spoke his exasperation.

''You are aware that Mr. Herron—*this* Mr. Herron—has stated that only three 'Drowse' tablets remained when the doctor's prescription was delivered from the chemist?'' Antony nodded, and the detective continued, ''Very well, then: to establish attempted suicide you must also explain why Miss Cassell should have troubled to replenish her supply of sleeping tablets, when she had a whole bottle of the doctor's prescription ready to her hand. An accident is even more unlikely . . . in view of your client's statement.''

Forrester broke in at this point. ''I don't think we need labour the point, Conway. Mr. Maitland has discovered, I think, what he wanted to know: namely, the drug used and the medium through which it was administered. You can't expect him to admit the validity of your arguments; but I'm sure,'' he added, turning to Antony, ''that enough has been said to convince you of the propriety of allowing Mr. Herron to answer a few questions?''

''We are, of course, aware of our duty as citizens,'' Antony replied, solemnly. And grinned, as Conway frowned at him. ''Wasn't that coming next?'' he asked. ''I wanted to get in first with it. But as for these questions: you don't propose to caution us?''

''For the moment, no.'' Forrester had regained his look of amusement, but his tone was wary.

''Then you won't have much recourse, will you, if we don't feel inclined to answer you?''

''We should draw our own conclusions,'' said Forrester. His pompous tone parodied Antony's solemnity of a moment before. Conway, who had for some minutes been only too obviously on the brink of impatient speech, interrupted:

''If I may say so, sir, this is only wasting time.''

''Not if we have convinced Mr. Maitland,'' said Forrester.

"Well," said Antony, "at least we'll see what these questions of yours are."

Timmy had turned sideways in his chair, to follow this exchange. He looked now at the big man behind the desk and said composedly, "As a matter of fact, I *do* want to help you. Only not to prove I doped her, because I didn't."

"Very well, we'll see what you have to tell us." Again he turned to his colleague. "Inspector Conway—"

"Yes, sir." He sounded grim; obviously he did not mean to be conciliated by the belated offering as a favour of what he considered should have been his by right. "To begin with, Mr. Herron: you told us that at first you thought Miss Cassell had tried to kill herself."

"Yes," said Timmy.

"Can you explain why you thought that?"

"Because of Paul."

"But later you abandoned this theory?"

"I had to. I mean, I began to wonder when Dr. Hearn said there wasn't much of the medicine gone; you see, I took it for granted it must have been that because I knew there were only three of the other tablets, and I knew (or thought I did) that there was nothing in the milk."

"You took her the milk, and watched her drink it?"

"She'd started to drink it when I left her. But we thought—"

"You'd better explain," said Antony, "just what happened after you took the milk to your aunt's room."

Timmy explained. "So you say the milk was standing on the bedside table for ten minutes or more while Miss Cassell was in the bathroom and you were downstairs?"

"Yes."

"And did you encounter anybody on this excursion of yours?"

"No; that is, if you mean upstairs. I told you I was talking to Miss Barclay in the little drawing-room."

"That is the young lady who is engaged to your brother?"

"Yes." Timmy flushed, and looked round at Antony with sudden anxiety. "Do you mean—?"

"Never ask a policeman what he means," Antony advised him. "He might tell you!"

"Well, as you say you changed your mind about what had

happened—about whether your aunt had tried to kill herself—what conclusion did you reach in its place?''

Antony opened his mouth to speak, but closed it again without further interruption. Timmy said carefully, ''I didn't really think it out . . . not at first.''

''Didn't you, Mr. Herron?''

''No. You don't, you know. You *know* things, but you don't believe them.''

''What did you know?''

''That's just about enough of that, Inspector,'' said Antony, pleasantly. ''Facts, yes. Opinions, no.''

''But Mr. Herron expressed an opinion to certain members of his family which seems—to say the least of it—relevant to this matter.''

Antony smiled, and shook his head. Timmy said quickly, ''Who told you what I said? Was it my cousin, Brent?''

Conway said, ''No,'' and snapped his mouth shut almost before the word was uttered. ''I'm not here to give information, Mr. Herron,'' he added.

Timmy ignored this. He looked round again at Antony and said positively, ''Then it must have been Grandfather. I had wondered about that.''

''Well, be that as it may,'' said Antony, ''let us return to our matters of fact.''

''Very well.'' Inspector Conway looked, momentarily, at a loss; and Antony smiled sedately at him, and then at the superintendent.

''For the purpose of your questions only, Inspector, we'll grant your assumption that a deliberate attempt was made on Miss Cassell's life. Without prejudice, of course. Let's go on from there.''

''On the assumption, then, that such an attempt was made, what would you suggest the motive to have been?'' Conway was watching his words now, but he gave no sign that the effort gave him pleasure.

''I don't know. I thought perhaps—''

Antony caught Forrester's eye, which was fixed on him with a quizzical expression, and burst out laughing. ''We are flattered, of course, by this interest in our opinions, but—'' He turned to Conway, who was looking outraged.

"I'm sorry, Inspector, really I am. But I did mention 'facts', you know."

"After all," said Forrester, "Mr. Herron knows much more about his family affairs than we do. He could be very helpful."

"I think not." Antony was definite.

"I appreciate your dilemma." Forrester was sympathetic, but the amusement in his voice was not quite hidden.

"So we'd really get on much quicker," said Antony, ignoring this, "if Inspector Conway could bring himself to stick to the 'matters of fact' we agreed on."

"Very well." Conway snapped the words, but continued a moment later, more calmly, "Perhaps Mr. Herron will give me the facts about Saturday evening. There was quite a gathering at your home, was there not?"

"Oh, yes," said Timmy. He sounded doubtful, and gave Antony a worried look. As he received no discouragement, however, he went on more confidently to enumerate the people who had been present. "They were all there when Miss Barclay and I got in, about nine o'clock. My aunt retired at ten o'clock, and I understand the party began to break up almost immediately."

"And the reason for this meeting? It was, after all, an odd time," remarked Forrester with a wary eye on Antony, "for a purely social gathering."

"It was my grandfather's idea. He wanted to talk things over."

"A council of war, in fact."

"That's a good enough description." Timmy's tone was not forthcoming. "And as to which of them had the opportunity of giving Aunt Marian poison," he added triumphantly, "I don't know. I wasn't there."

"No. You had gone out when Miss Cassell did, and about ten minutes later you went upstairs with a glass of hot milk for her."

"That's right."

"Can you describe what happened in a little more detail?"

Timmy did so; and resisted, well enough, the temptation to over-elaborate. "A very clear statement," commended Forrester, as he concluded. "Which brings me, Mr. Herron, to my next question: are you familiar with Miss Cassell's habits?''

"Well . . . of course.''

"Then you can tell us, I am sure, how she normally took the 'Drowse' tablets.''

"She didn't take them every night, you know.'' Timmy sounded anxious, but did not this time look for guidance. Inspector Conway said, dryly:

"So you already informed us.''

"I suppose you mean *how* she took them,'' said Timmy. "Like an aspirin . . . she swallowed them with a drink of water.''

"Or milk?'' Forrester was casual, and Antony felt his nerves tighten as he sensed the approach of a climax.

"Quite often. She liked hot milk in bed, last thing.''

"Some people dissolve aspirin before taking them.''

"Well, I wouldn't. They have a filthy taste if they start to dissolve in your mouth before you swallow them.''

"Have you ever tried 'Drowse,' Mr. Herron.''

"Good lord, no!'' Timmy was emphatic.

"Then perhaps you are not aware of certain useful properties it possesses?''

"It sends you to sleep, I suppose.'' Timmy was wary again. "I know Aunt Marian never took more than one tablet.''

"But somebody gave her twelve of them.''

"So you say.''

"You may take my word for it. But these properties I spoke of . . .'' Forrester paused, but went on with no change of expression, "The tablets dissolve quite easily, even in cold water, and are practically tasteless.''

"And did you know *that*, Mr. Herron?'' said Conway.

Timmy looked from one to other of them; and then twisted in his chair to look at Antony. After a moment he turned back to Forrester, and said, coolly enough, "I didn't, as a matter of fact. But I don't see that it signifies.''

"Don't you, Mr. Herron?'' Forrester was still deceptively bland, but something in his tone seemed to sting the man he was addressing, so that he retorted with sudden heat:

"No, I don't! Anybody could have experimented if they wanted to find out—'' He broke off, and Antony saw his left hand tighten suddenly on the arm of the chair. "Well, I know *I* could have done," he admitted. "But so could anyone else!"

"Of course they could," agreed Forrester, cordially. "But you see, Mr. Herron, *your* fingerprints were on the pill-box in Miss Cassell's bedside drawer."

Antony opened his mouth to intervene, but shut it again at a gesture from Timmy, who replied without hesitation, "Well, of course they were! What has that got to do with it?"

"Quite a lot, I should have thought." Conway seemed put out by this casual treatment of the police bombshell, and sounded aggressive. Antony reflected, and not for the first time, that Timmy appeared at his best under the stimulus of adverse circumstances. Most likely this thought had already occurred to the detectives, and it was no comfort to realise that it could be interpreted, without too much distortion, as confirmation of the police theory. He said mildly, into the silence which followed Conway's remark:

"At least, Superintendent, you appear to accept Mr. Herron's statement that there were only three sleeping pills left?"

Forrester smiled at him, and shook his head gently without replying. Timmy looked round again. "I don't get that," he complained.

"The police theory seems to be that the three tablets were used for the purposes of experiment, and a further supply purchased when it was seen to be feasible . . . you know, Superintendent, with the best will in the world, I can't help feeling you're assuming too much there."

"Do you think so, Mr. Maitland? I might say the same of your own assumption."

"About your theory?" The detective shook his head. "Well, then . . . look here, how many tablets did you find in the box this morning?"

"Three." Forrester seemed again to be amused by something that had been said.

"But—" said Timmy, and Antony interrupted him.

"The superintendent hasn't forgotten what you said: only he prefers to believe there were four, or perhaps five tablets put away when Aunt Marian changed to the doctor's prescription. And if you want to know *why* he wishes to believe this, it is because in that way his discovery of your finger-prints has a significance it would not otherwise possess.''

Conway said, ''That's very unfair—'' but Forrester broke in, saying placidly:

''You must admit, it's an attractive theory.''

''What theory?'' said Timmy, explosively. Forrester spread his hands apologetically; and Antony replied with his eyes on the detective's face:

''That there were—say—four tablets, one of which you abstracted for experimental purposes, leaving your prints on the pill-box. Having satisfied yourself of the suitability of 'Drowse' for your purpose you set about procuring a more plentiful supply.'' He added, with a smile, ''At least, Super-intendent, you're postulating a commendable degree of thrift on the part of my client.''

''I'm not wedded to the theory.'' Forrester's tone was as equable as ever. ''If you can explain—''

''Of course we can.'' Antony sounded expansive, but Timmy said, more cautiously:

''The fingerprints?''

''If you please, Mr. Herron.''

''I said it was quite simple,'' he protested, and went on to repeat what he had told Antony and Sir Nicholas earlier in the day. Forrester eyed him benevolently, Conway with ob-vious scepticism. But neither of them spoke, and Timmy's explanation faltered a little, and he moved uneasily under their combined scrutiny. ''That's all there was to it,'' he said at last. And added, truculently, ''I don't expect you to believe me.''

This remark, not unnaturally, evoked no response. Con-way said, ''Thank you, Mr. Herron,'' and looked at his su-perior officer. Forrester's air of affability was very marked as he replied to the unspoken question:

''I don't think, Mr. Herron, we need trouble you any fur-ther for the present.''

Timmy got up. He looked uncertainly at Antony, who met the superintendent's regard with one equally urbane, and asked gently, ''And the meaning of that is—?''

''Just what I say, Mr. Maitland. You, of all people, will not expect me to be more explicit.''

"Fair enough." He shook his head at his client, who was obviously eager to be gone. "Sit down, Timmy. We haven't quite finished yet."

"But he said—" Timmy sounded mutinous, but he returned to his chair obediently enough. "I don't see what else they want," he muttered.

Antony ignored him. He said to the superintendent, "Now that we have satisfied you in this matter, perhaps you will be good enough to give me a little help." He smiled at Conway's look of indignation, and added, "I should have said, of course, 'satisfied you for the present'."

Forrester took no pains to hide his amusement. "That makes a difference, of course. What do you want of us, anyway?"

"A little advance information. I shall see what you make available to Bellerby, of course (if it comes to that), as I have already seen the statements concerning Paul Herron. But it might save time if you told me now." He gave the detective an amused look, and added disarmingly, "My time, I mean."

"Well," said Forrester. "That sounds reasonable enough. I can't help feeling, though, that I might more reasonably apply to you in this connection."

"Oh, no, Superintendent. That isn't at all what I had in mind."

"I thought as much. But I understand you spent some time at The Laurels this afternoon."

"So I did." Antony's tone gave nothing away.

"In any event, there's nothing I can tell you. The analysis won't interest you at this stage, though I have no doubt it would be most interesting and instructive to hear you try to pull it apart in court."

"You understand me so well, Superintendent. We'll let the analysis pass for the moment."

Conway, who had been thumbing through a file he had taken from the desk, looked up at that and said, "I should have thought it would have been of considerable concern to you."

"Not at present. As the superintendent so rightly surmises, we should question it if it suited our book, regardless of the content." He turned back to the senior of the two officers, and added sadly, "You know, I think we're shocking Inspector Conway."

Forrester, who had no desire to see his subordinate baited beyond a certain limit, shook his head reprovingly. "We're away from the point, Mr. Maitland."

"So we are. What else can you tell me?" said Antony, promptly.

"We are looking for the chemist who sold 'Drowse' recently to a member of the family, or a close connection. If there is such a chemist, of course. But we can't do much till to-morrow."

"We have been to the shop that usually served Miss Cassell," Conway put in, "and seen the two assistants as well, the ones, I mean, who don't live (like the owner) over the shop. They have no knowledge of any of the tablets being bought for her recently."

"Which doesn't look like suicide," Antony agreed. "She'd have no reason to go farther afield herself. So that takes us to the next point: how do your inquiries progress into William Cassell's private affairs?" He looked from one to other of the detectives. Forrester's face was suddenly blank; Conway looked disapproving, but that was nothing new. "Now don't," he added gently, "pray don't tell me you've made no inquiries. I wouldn't believe you, you know."

Forrester said slowly, "We have no statements in this connection which you could properly ask to see. And surely Mr. Cassell has given you particulars of his brother's affairs?"

Antony grinned. "Our client is reticent on the subject," he admitted. "We have got Bellerby on to him about it, of course, so we'll get the information sooner or later. I'm only asking you to save me a little time."

Forrester appeared to find this reasonable enough. "Now I wouldn't have thought that old Mr. Cassell would have jibbed at a thing like that," he said incomprehensibly. Antony looked inquiring, and he continued after a moment of seemingly pleasurable contemplation, "Your Mr. Bellerby will have the information soon enough. I understand the bulk of William Cassell's property is abroad, but he has some interests in this country also. His will, naturally enough, is in Portugal; we've no details yet, but I learned by cable from Lisbon that the main beneficiary is his son.''

''But he wasn't married!'' Timmy entered the conversation abruptly, and Forrester turned towards him a face that was again politely blank.

''No,'' he agreed.

Timmy gave a yelp of laughter, hastily suppressed. He said apologetically, with an eye on Conway who was looking outraged, ''But it is funny, Inspector, if only you knew my grandfather.''

''I have met Mr. Cassell.'' Conway's tone was repressive. Antony, who would have preferred to take a few moments to digest this piece of information, said at random:

''That's interesting, Superintendent. Do I take it this son is in Portugal?''

''He is. His name is Manuel da Costa Calleya.'' Forrester reached for a scrap pad. ''I'll write down the address for you,'' he offered, ''rather than try to pronounce it.''

Antony accepted the scrap of paper gratefully. ''Not that I expect it will help you,'' said Forrester, with a note of satisfaction in his voice.

''Probably not.'' He stood up as he spoke, and Timmy followed his example with considerable alacrity. ''Then I won't trouble you further, gentlemen. I'm extremely grateful for your patience.'' Forrester's farewells were amiable as ever; and if Conway's tone retained something of reserve, that was only, Antony felt, what he had expected.

The shadows were lengthening when they came out into Whitehall again, though the streets were still hot after the day's sunshine. Antony turned homewards, and Timmy fell into step beside him without comment. He said, when they had negotiated the crossing successfully, ''That wasn't too bad. Was it?''

''Not bad at all.''

''When will you see Paul again?''

''To-morrow, I expect. Or Tuesday.''

The silence lengthened. After a while Timmy said, ''Lord, what a mess!'' And added, awkwardly, ''I think Ann would like you to tell him that she . . . that we don't believe it, you know.''

"I'll tell him," Antony promised. And forbore to question his companion further about this rather ambiguous message.

In the event, Timmy spent the evening in Kempenfeldt Square, and did not need over-much persuasion to do so. The hospital bulletin had changed slightly, and he was now informed that Miss Cassell was 'as well as could be expected.' Taking what comfort he could from this obscure pronouncement, Timmy murmured an apology and dialled the Barclays' number. Antony left him to it, and went out to join Jenny in the contemplation of her larder.

Before very long Timmy wandered out to join them. "Ann thinks that might mean she's a little better," he said. "Do you suppose—?"

"Hospitals are always very careful what they tell you," said Jenny. Her tone was reassuring, but she looked anxiously at her husband as she spoke, and Timmy did not pursue the subject.

CHAPTER 11

SIR NICHOLAS, regaled next morning with the story of his nephew's visit to Wimbledon, and later to Scotland Yard, was amused by the account of the interview with the police. "But it won't do to underestimate Forrester," he warned, when Antony had finished.

"I assure you, sir, I have the greatest respect for him; and for Conway too, though he must find his temper a handicap."

"I don't imagine you did anything to help him keep it," said Sir Nicholas, dryly.

"Well, no. It was really irresistible—"

"The things you find irresistible will be getting you into trouble one of these days. Now, if you could be irresistibly compelled to be polite to our client this morning it might be of some help." He did not sound hopeful, and Antony grinned.

"I'll do my best, but I expect the old boy will be out for blood. I'm sorry about that, you know."

"Don't disturb yourself unduly. I've no doubt we shall survive the meeting, and I must admit to a certain curiosity—"

"I'm pretty sure he suggested to the police that Timmy drugged Aunt Marian," Antony interrupted. "What bothers me is whether he did it in good faith."

"From your account of the people you saw at Wimbledon, it seems he isn't the only one with that idea."

"No, but the others got it from him. Even Brent . . . now there's a tough customer, Uncle Nick."

"I rather gathered you weren't soul-mates. To return to your young friend Timmy Herron for a moment—"

"Well, sir?"

"He seems to have a head on his shoulders." Sir Nicholas sounded approving. "I think I must make a point of seeing the brother before long."

"We'll ask Bellerby. Would to-morrow morning suit you?"

"Admirably. We'll fix that, if we can."

They had gone down to chambers in good time that Monday morning, as Ambrose Cassell was due at ten o'clock. Antony, having finished his narrative, had got up to wander round the room, and come to rest again, as he usually did, leaning against the bookcase near the window, and looking down idly into the court below. It was a grey morning, but no cooler, with a feeling of thunder in the air. He said now, without turning his head:

"There's one thing, sir. Try and get a bit more out of Grandfather about Uncle William's affairs."

Sir Nicholas frowned. "I will, of course. But I don't quite understand your interest."

"I'd have liked Uncle William's evidence. After all, he knew Matthew Herron. As I can't have that, I'd like to talk to someone who knew him well."

"You're not coming back to the insanity theory, are you?" The older man's tone was suspicious, and Antony grinned.

"Far from it; though if things get any more involved than they are at the moment I shall begin to wish I *could* believe it."

"Then what—?"

Antony turned at last from the window. "Here they are now. Bellerby looks harassed, so I hope you're feeling strong this morning."

"I gather conciliatory tactics will be in order. You might bear it in mind."

"The best line of soothing syrup. I get you," agreed Antony. And went on, as his uncle scowled at him, "As to what I'm thinking, I'm not so sure myself. It will keep, anyway."

"I shall look for further enlightenment, if you survive the conference," said Sir Nicholas, without sympathy.

Antony retreated towards the window again. "I shall rely on you to draw his fire," he said.

As old Mr. Cassell came into the room, closely followed by his solicitor, his expression gave no clue to his feelings; but his reply to Sir Nicholas's greeting lacked cordiality. Mr. Mallory, who had himself escorted the visitors, retreated without delay and shut the door firmly. Bellerby muttered an introduction, Sir Nicholas indicated a chair, and the old man seated himself. The solicitor, after one expressive glance in Antony's direction, collapsed into a chair some distance from the others, and fell to mopping his brow.

"I hope you have good news of Miss Cassell, sir?" Antony moved from the window to his usual chair at the corner of his uncle's desk.

"She is still alive." He did not volunteer anything further and his tone was not encouraging. Sir Nicholas permitted himself a faint, deliberate, look of surprise, but said amiably:

"I am glad Bellerby arranged this meeting. One or two points have arisen—"

"I had hoped Bellerby had made it quite plain to you, Sir Nicholas. I am here to satisfy myself as to your intentions in this matter."

"I have accepted the brief. Surely you were aware of that?"

"So I have been informed. I wish to know, however, whether this young man spoke for you when he told me that you had rejected the idea of pleading insanity on my grandson's behalf."

"My dear sir, I am quite in your hands, and Bellerby's." The stiffness had melted from Sir Nicholas's voice, and Antony realised he was enjoying himself. "I must make my case according to the information with which I am provided by my instructing solicitor, and I cannot possibly say at this stage what line it will be best to follow."

Ambrose Cassell sat back in his chair. He seemed to be taking his time about his next remark. Antony said, "My words were, if you recall, that we must look at all possibilities," and received in reply a look so chilling that he thought with some amusement that perhaps he would have been safer, after all, in his favourite vantage point by the window.

"You also said, 'Sir Nicholas is not open to direction,' as I remember very well," the old man retorted. "Isn't that correct?"

"So far as the conduct of the case is concerned, perfectly correct," said Sir Nicholas blandly. "Did you expect anything else?"

"But I tell you, the boy is mad!" Ambrose Cassell's voice had risen, and his manner showed his agitation. Sir Nicholas said:

"If that can be demonstrated, I in turn can demonstrate it to the court. You must realise, Mr. Cassell, that I have to rely on the information with which I am provided."

"I cannot see why you should need to be convinced of what I tell you. It isn't only Paul—there is what happened to my daughter to consider."

"I don't quite understand you, I'm afraid."

"I think you understand me very well, Sir Nicholas. I should prefer that we spoke together without evasions."

Antony noted the danger signals; the tightening of his uncle's lips, the slight pause before he answered at his most dulcet, "I am relieved to hear it. Very well. You are trying to tell me, I collect, that Timothy Herron was responsible for this new tragedy?"

"I am, indeed. And if that doesn't prove there is insanity in the family my poor Ruth married into, I don't know what will."

"He seems to me, however, to be a singularly level-headed young man."

"Cold blooded," said Ambrose Cassell. "You must allow me to know better than you, Sir Nicholas. After all, he has been a member of my household for eighteen years now."

"Well, perhaps we should leave this question for the moment, and turn to your reason for believing that Paul Herron shot your brother."

The old man had recovered himself during this exchange, and his answer came sharply, "I found him with the gun in his hand: reason enough, I think. He said he meant to kill me. And as for Timmy—"

"Well, Mr. Cassell?"

"As for Timmy, at least you will admit he had every opportunity; and was quick enough to make the point he must have thought was to his brother's advantage.''

"But you said, I think, that you had observed no previous signs of madness in him?''

"All this should hardly be necessary. Is the family history not sufficient proof?''

"That is one of the things my nephew has been endeavouring to inquire into. But he has not (forgive me) met with very much co-operation.''

Old Mr. Cassell scowled. "He also wished to pry into my brother's private affairs. And those, you must admit, cannot be relevant.''

"On the contrary. I have myself a very lively interest in them.''

"But from what I myself told Maitland—and I understand he spoke also to my daughter, and to certain family friends—you must surely know enough to believe that both these boys could have inherited their father's insanity.''

"The operative word there is 'could,' Mr. Cassell. I must tell you that what we have learned so far by no means supports your contention. I cannot go into court with a case based on suppositions.''

"But, Matthew Herron—''

"A man who shoots his wife in certain circumstances—imaginary, or not—would not necessarily pass on to his sons a taint of insanity. Cases of that sort were only too familiar during the war years. If I come to believe the boy mad, I shall make use of it, of course. At the moment, I have no evidence that he is insane.'' Sir Nicholas's tone was still gentle, but he was not mincing his words, and Antony watched the growing anger in Ambrose Cassell's face.

"I tell you, I am not—we are none of us safe while Timmy is at liberty. And if Paul is freed—''

"Good heavens, man, they are your grandsons,'' Sir Nicholas expostulated. "Can you not think for a moment what you are doing to them, if they should be innocent?''

"Paul wanted to kill me. He admitted that, and anyway was caught red-handed. And who but his brother could have had a motive for giving Marian an overdose of that stuff she takes at night?''

"That is what I want the chance to find out.'' Antony

realised that his uncle's control was hard held, and began to speculate on the outcome of the interview.

"Well, you won't do it by asking questions about my brother William." Ambrose Cassell was positive. "So I hope you realise that!"

"Far from it." Sir Nicholas came to his feet as he spoke, and he made no attempt now to hide the anger he felt. "I would remind you, Mr. Cassell, that *I* am responsible for the conduct of the case."

"I seem to remember a saying," retorted the older man, "to the effect that he who paid the piper could therefore call the tune."

"I'm afraid that wouldn't hold in court," said Antony, apologetically. "I don't recall a precedent—" But his uncle swept aside this interruption, saying caustically:

"Allow me to tell you, sir, that if I throw up the case, there isn't a counsel in England would touch it . . . at your dictation!"

"Is that a threat, Sir Nicholas?"

"A fact, Mr. Cassell. I have a great respect for facts; I earn my living by them."

"And if I will not tolerate this . . . this defiance of my wishes—?" Ambrose Cassell was shaking with anger. For the first time Antony saw him as an old man, but saw him thus without pity.

"I'm afraid you have no alternative," said Sir Nicholas, with a note of satisfaction in his voice.

"May I remind you that you were briefed on my instructions?"

"That can be remedied." Sir Nicholas picked up from his desk a long blue document, tied impressively with red tape. "So much for your brief," he remarked, and tore the paper across and across. Antony heard the beginnings of a protest, hastily suppressed, from Mr. Bellerby; his uncle dropped the fragments of the document into his waste-paper basket, and dusted the tips of his fingers together with a slightly self-conscious air of drama. "So much for your brief," he repeated, and eyed the old man challengingly. After a moment he went on, and though his voice was gentle now he still retained his air of satisfaction, "Now, Mr. Cassell, you may do as you please; but perhaps I should remind you that

Paul Herron is under no obligation to accept the representation of a counsel of your choosing.''

''As to that, we shall see!'' In his turn, Ambrose Cassell got up and glared across the desk.

''Indeed we shall. As for me, I shall defend your grandson on a dock brief, if necessary. And I do not think we shall plead insanity.''

''I warn you, sir—''

''Well, sir?''

''This can have no end but disaster.'' He spoke stiffly, and there was no effort at conciliation in his tone.

''I think not.''

Poor Mr. Bellerby, who had been (as Antony later described it) hopping about in an agitated way on the brink of the conflict, was moved to expostulate. ''But, Sir Nicholas—'' His client turned on him a look of basilisk intensity.

''There is nothing more to be said.'' He showed now very little sign of emotion, but his voice shook a little as he turned back to address counsel. ''I will bid you good day, sir.'' Bellerby shrugged, gave a last, helpless look from uncle to nephew, and followed him out of the room.

Antony closed the door softly, and turned an amused face to his uncle. ''I've heard some smooth performances in my time, but for sheer nerve—''

''You do not, I hope, imagine that I was trifling with our visitor. I meant every word I said.''

''Oh, come off it, Uncle Nick!'' He ignored the older man's look of outrage, but considered it politic to conceal the amusement he was feeling. ''I'd have found your performance much more convincing if you really had torn up the Herron brief.''

Sir Nicholas continued to eye him stonily for a moment, and then began to laugh. ''I wonder what I *did* destroy,'' he said, looking vaguely in the direction of the waste basket.

''Never mind that now,'' said Antony. ''I suppose I'd better see if Bellerby is coming back.''

He encountered the solicitor in the outer office, and led him back with honeyed words to his uncle's room. Sir Nicholas allowed him a few minutes uninterrupted speech, and then cut short his lamentations briskly, ''Yes, it's a great pity, but it can't be remedied now. I need your help, Bellerby.''

"But, Sir Nicholas, it is quite out of the question! A man of your standing—''

"Forget my uncle's dramatics for a moment,'' said Antony. "We couldn't work on a dock brief, anyway, in a case like this: if that's what is worrying you? What we want is a nice, young solicitor; one you can persuade into believing that the publicity will be almost as useful as getting paid for what he does.''

"Quite right,'' approved Sir Nicholas. "It's asking a lot of you, Bellerby, but I take it you don't feel free to represent Paul Herron yourself?''

"I'm afraid not.'' Bellerby paused a moment to adjust his ideas, but was commendably quick in reaching a decision. "I realise you feel it is in Paul Herron's best interests . . . well, of course you do. I think I know the man you want.''

"Good for you,'' said Antony. Sir Nicholas commenced a more orthodox expression of his gratitude, and Bellerby laughed.

"I'm a fool, I suppose. I'm sure young Maitland will be persuading me next that it's my duty to see Paul and talk him into consulting my rival.''

"Well, I really don't see who else can do it.'' Antony's tone was solemn, and the solicitor laughed again.

"But I wouldn't agree,'' he added in a scolding tone, "if the man I have in mind didn't seem likely to become my son-in-law.''

By four o'clock Bellerby had telephoned to say that he had been to the prison to see Paul Herron, who had proved more than willing to hand his affairs over to a solicitor who was not his grandfather's choice. Geoffrey Horton, who had been qualified for some five years, was still the very junior partner in his father's firm. He greeted Antony, who arrived on his doorstep at about four-thirty, with a show of enthusiasm; and admitted, when the preliminaries were politely over, that he was doing his best to work up a criminal practice. "Though so far I've lived mostly on conveyancing,'' he added, ruefully.

Antony, weighing him up covertly, thought that Bellerby's choice was good. Horton was a square-built young man, with hair that had more than a hint of red in it (and more than a tendency to curl); he had also a hearteningly cheerful way with him, and a pugnacious set to his jaw. He showed no sign of being put out by the rather unusual nature of the approach which had been made to him, but returned look for look with unabashed friendliness. Antony relaxed, and grinned at him. "It's good of you to take it on," he said.

"I must admit I'm not quite clear what it's all about," said Horton, shuffling papers on his desk. "But I'm sure you're going to explain it all to me."

Antony obliged, reflecting as he did so that it was an amusing reversal of the common order that he should be briefing, if only verbally, the instructing solicitor. He took time to go into some detail in the matter, and Horton made copious notes to implement the sheaf of reports that Bellerby had handed over to him. The account of the meeting that morning obviously delighted him, and he was grinning as Antony finished speaking. He then straightened the papers in front of him, laid down his pencil and picked it up again, and gave his companion a look of inquiry. "Well, now—" he said.

"I think that's all," said Antony. "All the facts, that is."

"Am I to understand that you are convinced both of Paul Herron's sanity and his innocence of this murder?"

"It's nowhere near so simple. I think he's sane; I don't think he killed William Cassell. If he did do it, I don't think he knows it."

"That would bring us back to the insanity plea."

"Oh, yes, we can't rule it out yet. And if you're wondering, in that case, what's all the fuss about?—I can only tell you you'll know when you meet old Mr. Cassell."

"I can hardly wait," murmured Horton. "Have you any suggestions about our next step?"

"To see Paul Herron. To-morrow morning, if you're free. Sir Nicholas hasn't seen him yet."

"To-morrow will suit me," said Horton. Antony gave him credit for not making play with a diary. "And then—?"

"Well, there are one or two things: you'll forgive me, I know, but you haven't had the chance to think it out yet. One is to meet Timmy Herron; as you'll have gathered, he may need your services before we're through. If you can manage lunch to-morrow, after we've been to Brixton, I'll ask him to come along, too.''

"Good idea.''

"Then, I'd like you to get in touch with Manuel—William's son. It's possible he may be coming over here to look into his affairs. Bellerby can help you there, I expect. If he isn't coming, I'll have to fly over to see him; at his convenience, of course.''

"Right,'' said Geoffrey Horton, scribbling industriously.

"And the other thing is, we need a private inquiry agent; do you know one who isn't too obsessed by divorce? If you don't, Cobbold's are quite good: respectable and trustworthy, to the best of my knowledge.''

"And what are they to do?''

"Dig into the past: eighteen years and more ago. Matthew Herron's affairs, of course; and all the people we've been talking about to-day.''

Horton put down his pencil. "That's a tall order, you know. I take it you're covering the insanity angle in case of need?''

Antony did not reply for a moment. Before he did he got to his feet, and began to prowl quietly about the rather narrow room. "No, that isn't the idea at all,'' he said at last. "I'm probably making a fool of myself . . . I've very little to go on. But what I'd like to establish is a motive for the murder of those three people, all that time ago.''

The other man whistled. "You mean, you think some outside person killed them all: *not* Matthew Herron?''

"I don't know what I think,'' said Antony, irritably. "Yes, I do . . . I think it's a possibility. And that's all.''

"Well, all I can say is, this opens up a new train of thought,'' said Geoffrey Horton. And the look he gave his companion was a compound of respect and no little alarm.

CHAPTER 12

ANTONY LEFT the solicitor's office not long after that, after promising to spend as much time as possible during the next few days in talking again to possible witnesses, so that their proofs could be prepared. He came down into Bucklersbury and found that it had started to rain; it certainly felt fresher, and they seemed to have got away without a storm. He started to look round for a taxi, conscious of a sudden feeling of depression that the long vacation was now well past, so that he had left behind for the present the sweet air of the country and the smell of the earth after rain. In which thought he was rather less than honest, as he would have repudiated with horror any suggestion that he should earn his living other than at the bar.

"And not so much earning our living about *this* business," he said to himself. And found comfort in the reflection that this, at least, no one could blame him.

He was not, however, to enjoy this delusion for long. Jenny greeted him with the news that Sir Nicholas had come home early from chambers and been up to drink tea with her. "He only went five minutes ago," she said. "Halloran is dining with him. But he said to remind you that none of this would have happened if *you* hadn't lost your temper when first you saw Mr. Cassell."

"The . . . the old serpent!"

Jenny giggled. "Well, he had to say something," she pointed out. "I would have loved to be there this morning!"

"It had its points," Antony conceded. "Did he tell you all about it?"

"Well . . . I think so."

"Did he tell you that he formally repudiated Ambrose Cassell, and all his works—?"

"Yes," said Jenny.

"And that he underlined his action by dramatically tearing up his brief?"

"He didn't tell me *that*," said Jenny. "Did he really?"

"Well, in the interests of accuracy, what he tore up was a request for his opinion on a rather tricky point of company law. (And what Harting's will say when we break it to them that we need a duplicate, I cannot think.) But the effect was everything he could have wished."

Jenny laughed again. "Well, I do wish I'd been there," she repeated. "I always seem to miss the best things."

"I don't think, you know," said Antony, suddenly sober, "that you'd have enjoyed it much, really."

"No, I don't suppose so. He sounds a horrid old man; and really, darling, it's a wonder if Paul *didn't* try to kill him."

"And that, my love, is sheer exaggeration—and you know it." Antony collapsed on to the sofa and stretched luxuriously. "At least," he added, "I hope it is. I wouldn't like to feel there might be strychnine in the soup one evening, if you were feeling annoyed about something."

"Soup!" said Jenny, in accents quite as dramatic as any Sir Nicholas had indulged himself in earlier in the day. She disappeared at a run in the direction of the kitchen, and as soon as she had gone the telephone rang.

It didn't seem likely that Jenny's culinary activities could at this moment conveniently be combined with taking the call. Antony got up reluctantly.

The telephone asked for Mr. Maitland, and announced itself as Superintendent Forrester when he admitted his identity.

"Hallo, Superintendent. And what can I do for you?"

"I hear," said Forrester, carefully casual, "that Paul Herron has got a new solicitor."

"Why, yes, since this afternoon only. Did Bellerby tell you?"

"He advised me he had passed on the papers. And I'll not deny, Mr. Maitland, that I've been puzzling over the reason. Mr. Bellerby wasn't exactly forthcoming on the subject."

Antony chuckled. "I'm sorry to disappoint you if you're expecting startling revelations, but it's really quite simple. Young Herron decided he'd rather have his own legal representative: Bellerby is his grandfather's solicitor, you know."

"I see." Forrester sounded doubtful. "That rather goes to confirm the story that there's bad blood between him and old Mr. Cassell . . . don't you think?"

"Not necessarily. But I'm quite happy for you to indulge in whatever flights of fancy you wish. I don't see how you could make a point like that in court; do you?"

"Perhaps not." Forrester sounded amused now, though his tone held also a shadow of regret. "He's got a good man in Geoffrey Horton," he added, with an air of expansiveness (so that Antony pulled a face at the telephone and wondered what was coming next). "Bellerby has more experience, of course. Still, Horton should do well, very well."

"I think so, Superintendent. How is Miss Cassell, have you heard?"

"Not much change. If you want my opinion, though—"

"What do you think?"

"She's held her own for a good time now. It may be a good sign. I—" He broke off, and there was a silence. Antony prompted:

"Yes, Superintendent?"

"It's not an expert opinion, of course. She was a pleasant lady, I hope I'm right."

"And so do I. The doctors haven't given you any idea when she'll be able to talk?"

"They haven't reached the stage of admitting the possibility that she'll ever be able to do so," said Forrester. He added, "Why do you ask?" and his tone just missed being casual.

"Because . . . look here, Superintendent, have you got anyone at the hospital?"

"That won't arise until there's some chance of her regaining consciousness. Just now—"

"But you could put someone there," Antony insisted. "After all, someone tried to kill her once. Presumably the reason still exists."

"Do you think so?" The detective sounded sceptical, and Antony replied rather sharply.

"Yes, I do. And I think we should both be sorry if anything happened to prevent her getting well."

"We should, indeed. But I can't agree, Maitland. The facts—"

"Damn the facts!" said Antony explosively. "At least, facts are all right if you know them; but you *don't* know what happened."

"Now, there I must disagree with you."

"Well, if you mean Timmy, why haven't you arrested him?"

"Oh, come, Mr. Maitland! It's a far cry from suspicion to legal proof, as you very well know."

"Then you shouldn't refuse to look after Miss Cassell, if you only *suspect* what happened to her," retorted Antony.

Forrester's voice changed. "You're really serious about this, aren't you?" he asked.

"That is what I have been attempting to convey."

"Well, I can't do anything official; but I will have a word with the doctor, and the ward sister." For the first time, he sounded worried. But his tone changed again as he added the query, "I understood from Bellerby that the briefs have been returned to him?"

"Horton has asked us to carry on. We have to go through the forms, you know." He knew as he spoke that the detective was curious, and his reply merely tantalising.

"Yes, I see." Forrester would obviously have liked to pursue the subject; equally obviously, he could think of no further question that he could, with propriety, ask. "Well, Mr. Maitland—"

"There's one thing *you* could tell *me*," said Antony. "What do you think of our client, Superintendent?"

"In what way?"

"Do you think he's mad?"

"You've seen the doctor's report, I suppose?" His tone promised no enlightenment.

"And a lot of good it did me," Antony grumbled. "Who ever could tell what a doctor meant by reading his report?"

"These medical terms—"

"Oh, not that. Just a professional love of obscurity—"

"Such as is sometimes to be observed in members of the legal profession," remarked Forrester. Antony laughed.

"Well, fair enough," he admitted. "But, be a sport, Superintendent. What does he really think?"

Forrester hesitated. "He doesn't think your client mad," he said at last. Something in his tone made Antony ask quickly:

"And what do *you* think?"

"Now . . . what use can a layman's opinion be to you, Mr. Maitland."

"None at all, so you might just as well tell me." He thought but did not add aloud, that the jury, after all, would be laymen too.

"Well, Conway agrees with the doctor—"

"He would!"

"—and so do I, really."

"But—" Antony prompted.

"Well," said Forrester again. "I have to say he showed no sign of insanity. And I'm not without experience. All the same . . . you know this as well as I do, Mr. Maitland . . . there *is* the family history. And it *does* make you think!"

"And that's the whole trouble," said Antony dejectedly, as he related the conversation to his uncle next morning, while Sir Nicholas was still at the breakfast-table. "You could certainly convince the jury, if you wanted. And what if we don't find another line?"

"We'll worry about that when we have to." Sir Nicholas was placid. "I cannot believe in this particular type of hereditary madness, I'm afraid."

"Nor I. But the case against Paul is strong, Uncle Nick. And the possibility of insanity only makes it stronger."

"The prosecution won't mention it."

"Not directly. But they'll call their doctor to deny it; that'll make the jury think!"

"And you're afraid we shall have to display the family history in the course of the defence? Don't dither, Antony."

"No, sir. But I don't like it."

"It's an interesting case," said Sir Nicholas, with obvious intent to annoy. Antony grinned reluctantly. "But you haven't finished,'' his uncle pointed out. ''Did anything else transpire from this conversation?''

''I remembered to ask him about the letter Uncle William was writing when he died. I pointed out we should have had a copy, and he said we could if we liked, he'd send it to Horton; but there was only a fragment, he said, and it couldn't be relevant.''

''I see. And I expect he's right.'' Sir Nicholas pushed aside his coffee cup, and got up rather reluctantly. ''Do we go straight to the prison?''

''Yes, Horton will meet us there.'' Antony got up in his turn, and eyed his uncle gloomily. ''I've got the jitters,'' he said apologetically. ''Are we downhearted? Well . . . not very!''

They found Paul Herron in despondent mood, and disinclined for any discussion that went beyond the subject of costs. Obviously he had had time for reflection since Bellerby's visit, and his thoughts during the night watches had not been reassuring. Sir Nicholas listened patiently for some time, but broke in without ceremony when he felt his client had enjoyed sufficient liberty of expression. ''You must not worry unduly about this, Mr. Herron. I take it you have realised that this case is causing no little stir?''

''Why, yes, sir.'' Paul sounded startled. ''But I don't see—''

''It would be unkind in you to prevent us from reaping the advantages of the publicity involved,'' Sir Nicholas pointed out gently. Antony kept his countenance, but Geoffrey Horton's equanimity was not equal to this flight of fancy. Counsel turned on him a cold look, and demanded: ''Is that not so, Horton?'' in a tone that did not admit the possibility of contradiction.

''Indeed it is.'' His agreement was perhaps a shade too heart-felt; but, after all, the idea of Sir Nicholas Harding looking for a little free publicity was enough to stagger even a more experienced man. He turned to his client, and added reasonably, ''You have been good enough to accept my advice, Mr. Herron. So I hope you will be guided by me on this point, also—''

''I'm sorry.'' Paul smiled at him briefly, but his eyes

went back to his counsel's face before he went on. "It would be ungracious of me to refuse your help—"

"Then let us get down to business." Sir Nicholas seated himself, and after a moment's hesitation Paul Herron followed his example. He said:

"Is there any news of Aunt Marian? Bellerby said—"

"There is still nothing definite, I'm sorry to say. But she is holding her own, and that is hopeful, I think."

Paul looked down at the bare table. He said slowly: "Was it because . . . she thought I killed Uncle William?"

"I see Bellerby did not tell you the whole. It seems certain she did not take the overdose of her own wish." Sir Nicholas's tone was deliberately colourless. Paul looked up at him, and said in a startled tone:

"You mean it was an accident?" He looked from one to other of the three men, as Sir Nicholas shook his head. "Then . . . someone tried to kill her?"

"I believe so."

"But that . . . that's fantastic." He was taking his time to think the matter out, but asked after a moment, "What do the police think?"

"They think, if I understand rightly, that there has been a clumsy attempt (not intended to be fatal) to prejudice matters in your favour." Sir Nicholas made no effort to elucidate further, but sat back to watch his client grapple with this new idea. Paul frowned, and said slowly:

"I don't see . . . unless you mean . . . Timmy? Oh, no!"

"You don't feel they may have reason?"

"I do not. Surely, sir, you don't believe—?"

"As it happens, no."

"They . . . they haven't arrested him, have they?"

"Not as yet." He added, with quick sympathy for Paul's look of distress, "I do not believe they will take any action while your case is still *sub judice.*"

"I see." He turned to Antony, and added slowly, "How does Timmy feel about this?"

"He has been mainly concerned for your aunt. But—"

"There's one thing," said Paul, who had obviously not been listening. "Someone did it . . . not Timmy; and not me." He hesitated, but went on steadily, though he flushed as he spoke. "Not even in my sleep."

Sir Nicholas looked at his nephew, with a coldness whose source Antony had no difficulty in recognising. Well, admittedly he had realised when first he saw Paul Herron that the younger man (in spite of his protestations) knew some inward qualms as to his possible actions while he was sleep-walking; but it wouldn't have been good policy, at that stage, to mention the matter to his uncle. He returned the look with an unrepentant grin. Sir Nicholas frowned, but his irritation was not reflected in his voice as he turned back to Paul Herron.

"I have heard your story as you told it to my nephew. I should like to go over it with you."

"Yes, of course." He both looked and sounded nervous. "I've been thinking it over, of course, but there doesn't seem to be anything that would help."

"Well, you can leave us to worry about that. Tell me what happened that Tuesday; the day your uncle died."

"I never saw him, you know. Not till after he was dead." He looked inquiringly at Sir Nicholas, who nodded, but made no attempt to modify his demands. "I was home to lunch, Timmy and I came back from the office together, though we both thought the reception committee would have been better if it had been just the older ones. I mean, they knew him. Only after lunch I had the row with my grandfather, so I went out. I went on to the common, it would be about two-thirty, I suppose; and I walked right across, pretty quickly because I was angry; and then I came to Queen's Mere, and there was the traffic, so I stopped for a bit and thought what I'd do next."

"And what did you decide?"

"I went on across the heath, and into Roehampton. I'd cooled off a bit by that time, and went more slowly, and I had a cup of tea at a place in the High Street, and then I got a bus down to Putney Bridge and walked along a bit and looked at the river."

"And what were you thinking about all this time?"

Paul seemed disconcerted by this query. "I was angry," he said after a moment. "I didn't really think at all, clearly; just things going over and over in my mind. Then I tried to plan what to do, only I didn't seem to be able to think of anything."

"Why did you need a plan?"

"Because I didn't feel things could go on as they were; not after—"

"After what, Mr. Herron?"

"Well . . . I wanted to get married, you know?"

"But you were going to say: after what had been said. Were you not?" insisted Sir Nicholas.

Paul looked at him in silence. "Does it matter?" he said at last.

"I'm afraid it matters a great deal. I can understand your reluctance to discuss the subject, but I must know what passed between you and your grandfather."

"Hasn't he told you?" He sounded bitter; but added wearily, as Sir Nicholas shook his head, "I'll bet he told the police."

"That is precisely why I wish to hear from you what happened."

"Well, I wasn't surprised he was angry. Brent had been making mischief, that's not important; though how Audrey can think . . . but you don't want to hear about that. I decided while we were having lunch I'd keep my temper, just tell him what I wanted to do as if I'd meant to anyway, and see what he said."

"And did you adhere to this admirable resolution?"

Paul grinned at him unexpectedly. "Not so as you'd notice it," he admitted. "He let fly before I'd got fairly launched on what I wanted to say; and after that it wouldn't have done much good if I had kept calm . . . not that I did, of course."

"I'm still waiting to hear exactly what was said."

"Well, I had a chance of going in with a chap I know; he has two hundred acres, down in Hampshire, and he wants a bit more capital so we thought we might make a go of it between us. There's a good cottage, so I thought we might as well get married right away. Grandfather didn't agree."

"But in a year's time—"

"I didn't want to wait a year. It's a long time, you know, when you don't like the job you're doing; besides, Harry couldn't wait that long, and I might never have had another chance like that because I shan't have much capital, you know.'' He paused, and his look was challenging. ''Not really helpful, is it?''

''I don't think you quite realise yet, Mr. Herron,'' said Sir Nicholas quietly, ''exactly what will happen when you come to trial.''

''Do you think I haven't thought about it?'' Paul sounded defiant. Sir Nicholas went on without noticing the interruption.

''On this particular point what will happen is this. Your grandfather will give his evidence; he will go into some detail about the interview we are discussing (I'm afraid you must face that as a fact).'' Paul, who had been very pale, coloured up as he spoke, but his eyes were steady. ''Counsel for the Prosecution will, therefore, be well armed with information on this subject; and if you take the stand I think it very unlikely that he will let you go without eliciting your version of what happened. What you tell him will not be very important, the court will already have heard the facts from Ambrose Cassell, but the impression you make on the jury is very important indeed: they must not think you less than candid on any point.''

Paul Herron looked at his solicitor, who returned his regard gravely and gave a nod which he hoped was encouraging. ''I suppose I have to give evidence,'' he said; but he was obviously not thinking what he was saying, and his voice trailed away and his eyes shifted and met those of his junior counsel.

''That isn't quite the point,'' said Antony.

''No, I know.'' He looked back at Sir Nicholas, and said in a rush, ''He said I'd no right to think about marriage, ever. Because of what my father did, and because he was mad.'' He put up a hand for a moment to cover his eyes, and added in a strained tone, ''He said a lot more, of course; but it all came to that.''

Antony, who was watching his uncle, saw the sudden bleakness of the older man's expression. Sir Nicholas said only, ''What was your reaction to this suggestion?'' and his tone gave no clue to what he was feeling.

''I . . . I hadn't thought about it before. I suppose I should have done. That's what I was thinking about: I knew

I'd have to tell Ann, only it wasn't easy. And I didn't think I could stay at Wimbledon.''

"But what did you say to your grandfather? Did you use threats?'' Sir Nicholas was insistent. Paul looked at him blankly.

"I don't think so. I don't remember really. I know I was furiously angry; and that's why I've wondered sometimes . . . but I didn't try to hurt him knowingly, sir, I swear I didn't.''

"We'll come to that in a minute. Let us return to the river at Putney. What time was it when you left there?''

"Oh, about six o'clock, I should think. I still didn't know what to do, and I didn't want to see Ann. I thought I could have talked to Audrey first, but she was going to dinner at home, so that was no good. Finally, I got on a bus and went up to the West End, and had a meal of sorts at a corner house. Then I went home; it was about nine o'clock; I went in by the side door, and straight up to my room. I didn't know I was tired, but I thought I'd read in bed; and I must have gone straight to sleep.''

"And then—''

"I woke up in the garden.'' Paul was leaning forward now, his arms on the table, his voice earnest. "I've thought since that I must have heard the shot, but then I was just bewildered. I was standing on the grass, because I remember how it felt to my bare feet, and I was facing the shrubbery and I went in among the bushes, but I don't know why I did that. And I didn't know then, either, so I turned back towards the house again; at least, I suppose that's why, only everything was confusing. It wasn't very dark, and there was the light from the study window, and my .22 was lying on the grass. So I picked it up, and I looked in at the study window, and there was Uncle William; only I thought then it was Grandfather who was lying there. And then I heard someone shout.''

"Just a minute. Are you quite sure of the sequence here? You picked up the rifle, you looked in at the study window, and *then* you heard the shout?''

"Yes, I'm sure that's how it was. Only there was no time at all, really, between my picking up the gun and hearing

Brent; it only took a second or so, I suppose, to look up and think Grandfather was dead.''

''Are you quite sure, Mr. Herron, that these things happened precisely as you have told us?''

Paul looked at him steadily. ''I've told you the truth so far as I remember it, sir. But I *could* have dropped the gun in the instant before I woke; I've thought and thought about it, and I just don't know.''

''That isn't what you said before,'' Antony put in. ''You said you'd have known if your sleep-walking had been different from other times.''

''Well, that's what I thought then. But how can you be certain of anything?''

''You're doing too much thinking, my boy,'' said Sir Nicholas. ''If you could just relax and leave the worrying to us—''

''Can *you* believe I didn't do it?'' Paul turned to him eagerly. ''You see, I can't help going over things, and after all . . . my father—''

''Listen to me!'' said Sir Nicholas, at his most peremptory. ''What happened to your parents was unfortunate, but in no way concerns you or your brother. Hereditary insanity, where it exists, has other symptoms than sudden murderous outbreaks by men who have previously shown no signs of madness. And I do not think you would seriously have considered the possibility that you killed your uncle while you were asleep, if it had not previously been suggested to you that you were insane.''

''No . . . no, I don't think I should. But after all, my father was mad; he must have been.''

''You have no doubt heard the phrase 'insane with jealousy'?'' queried Sir Nicholas. ''It is a hackneyed and clumsy phrase in which there may be, on occasion, a certain amount of truth. But no doctor would recognise its validity, and certainly it could not be inherited.''

''Then all that about my getting married—''

''Was so much nonsense,'' said the older man flatly. ''I tell you straight, Mr. Herron, I don't see my way yet in this case. But the sooner you get all this rubbish out of your head the better. I can't put up an adequate defence for a client who's wondering all the time if he really is innocent.''

"I—" said Paul. He looked at Antony appealingly, and then back at Sir Nicholas. "Could you tell that to Timmy, sir?"

"Your brother has more sense than to be worrying his head about things like that," said Sir Nicholas crushingly.

"Still—" said Paul, with an effect of stubbornness.

"I'll tell him," Antony volunteered. "I had a message for you by the way. From your brother, and Miss Barclay. They wanted you to know they believed in you."

"Thank you." He was quiet for a while, and then went on: "I know they'd *say* that anyway, but I think perhaps it's true. Only I've wondered about Audrey; whether Brent—"

"Miss Barton, I believe, is just as convinced of your innocence," said Antony. And added, with a smile: "And even more vociferous on the subject."

"She would be," nodded Paul. He sounded genuinely amused, and Sir Nicholas eyed him with interest. Paul turned back to him with an apology. "I'm really grateful, sir. And I'll think about what you've said—"

"We haven't quite finished, I'm afraid." He looked at his nephew, who nodded in reply to an unspoken question. "I must ask you," said Sir Nicholas, turning back to his client, "to tell us what you remember of the night of your parents' death."

Paul made no reply for a moment. He was obviously shaken, and clenched his hands together on the table in front of him in an attempt to steady them. When he spoke his tone was flat, and he no longer looked at his questioner: "It's a long time ago. I'm afraid I don't remember."

"You were six years old. Do you remember your father and mother?"

"Yes, but—"

"And your Uncle Mark?"

"Yes."

"But nothing of what happened when they died, and you went to live at Wimbledon?"

"Nothing at all. Really! Nothing!" He sounded desperate now. He said accusingly, "You said it had nothing to do with us; with Timmy and me."

"It might have to do with William Cassell's murder,"

said Antony. "And with what happened to your Aunt Marian."

"I don't understand."

"I don't expect you do. But I wish you'd try to remember."

Paul shook his head. "How can I? It's so long ago. I've never thought about it."

"Well, think about it now." Antony spoke with all the emphasis he could command. "And don't ask why. Not just yet; because I couldn't tell you."

Sir Nicholas got up. "You realise we are by no means at the end of our questions," he said regretfully. "There is this matter my nephew has raised—and I do ask you to treat it with all seriousness. And the things that happened on the day your uncle was killed . . . they must be gone over and over until we are all heartily sick of them. But it has to be done."

Paul looked up at him. "I'll do my best," he said; and scrambled belatedly to his feet. "But about . . . that night," he went on. "Other people must know what happened; I mean, they were grown-up, they wouldn't have to make themselves not think of it: Bob Wayne, perhaps, or John Barclay. Or even Uncle Greg."

"We shall ask them, of course. But, after all, you were there." Sir Nicholas spoke idly enough, and was astonished to see the effect of his words. Paul sat down again abruptly, and looked for the moment as though he were going to faint. He said, at last, speaking with difficulty:

"Yes . . . I was there." He did not seem to hear their farewells, but roused himself a little when Antony, lingering, said rather loudly:

"Don't forget, I shall be back in a day or two."

Paul smiled back at him. But there was no warmth in the smile; and no amusement, now, in his eyes.

CHAPTER 13

SIR NICHOLAS was going straight back to chambers, while the two younger men were to meet Timmy Herron at a restaurant near the Strand which was busy enough to offer them a reasonable hope of privacy. Antony returned from seeing his uncle into a taxi, to find Geoffrey Horton unlocking his car. He seemed preoccupied, and the solicitor eyed him questioningly. "Sir Nicholas seems put out," he hazarded after a moment.

The car slid into the stream of traffic, and tucked itself in comfortably behind a stout, red bus. It was sunny again today, but the oppressive feeling of the last few days had given way to freshness after last night's rain. Antony watched idly while a thin lady hesitated on the brink of self-immolation, and then grinned at his companion. "He's raising hell because I didn't tell him Paul Herron had doubts himself about whether he shot his uncle," he admitted. "I'm not in a position to argue; he knows well enough I wouldn't have told him anything to discourage him from taking the case."

"You don't seem unduly worried."

"Well, no. That isn't what he's angry about really."

"Isn't it?"

"His sense of justice is outraged, that's his trouble. Old Mr. Cassell is *not* a sympathetic character," he added, "but Uncle Nick wouldn't admit, of course, that his emotions are in any way engaged in the matter." He paused, while Horton—seizing his opportunity—swept past the bus; joining the queue again, by way of change, behind a lorry generously laden with beer barrels. "However, to get back to cases, what do you think of your client?"

"Well!" said Geoffrey Horton. He drove for a moment in silence, and his expression became a trifle dogged. "If I'd met him in the ordinary way—on a matter of business, or at a party—I'd have thought him a pleasant chap, one I wouldn't mind knowing better. Seeing him in the present circumstances, I couldn't help but wonder—"

"I know," agreed Antony, and sighed. "That's what I felt the first time I saw him; and what's bothering me is how much my dislike of old Cassell is influencing me now."

"Do you think Sir Nicholas would let that weigh with him?" Horton's tone was bracing.

"No, but he's looking at it from a different angle. He's quite sure Paul is sane, so if he had any doubts they would be as to whether he might be not guilty, after all. I'm pretty sure he didn't do it; not 'of his malice aforethought', you know. But I wouldn't altogether rule out the possibility that he did it without knowing."

"I see." Horton seemed to be giving his thoughts exclusively to his driving, but added after a moment, "I thought Sir Nicholas was pretty convincing on the insanity angle, you know."

"Oh, so did I. And so did Paul, I hope. It may encourage him when we really get down to our researches into the past."

"It may," said Geoffrey, doubtfully. Antony sighed again, and slid down a little further in his seat.

"Know any good psycho-analysts?" he inquired. "It sounds like a job for one, and I never did fancy myself as having a good bedside manner."

Timmy Herron joined them soon after they had got settled in a corner of the long room. Antony thought as he watched him picking his way among the tables that his rather Byronic appearance was even more marked than usual. Now that he had come to know the younger man he was used to discount his rather stormy good looks; but he wondered what Geoffrey Horton was thinking, seeing him for the first time.

The newcomer acknowledged the introduction politely, but his manner was subdued and a little withdrawn as he seated himself. Antony (once the important business of ordering their meal was accomplished) allowed Horton to take up the conversation, which he did without encouragement: giving Timmy a brief account of how he had become associated with the affair, and passing to the events of that morning and counsel's opinion of the inadvisability of an insanity plea with so much good sense and so little dramatics that by the time the soup was served the younger man had relaxed his wariness, and was sufficiently himself to enter into an argument with the wine waiter over the relative merits of two different vintages of Sauternes. The waiter, used to an easy victory, retired discomfited before what was obviously superior knowledge, and Timmy grinned apologetically at his companions.

"Thank you," said Antony gravely. "I usually forget your association with the trade."

"Not any longer," said Timmy. The momentary animation left him. "I couldn't stick it at home, so I've got myself a room in Earl's Court."

"Have you—?" said Antony; and "Do the police—?" commenced Geoffrey Horton at the same moment. Antony stopped, and said encouragingly to the solicitor, "Your client, I believe."

"Have you told the police where you are living?" said Geoffrey.

"No, I—"

"You should have done. However, I'll phone them after lunch, with your agreement."

"Well, of course. Thank you." Timmy seemed a little bewildered, but grateful enough. He turned back to Antony. "When I rang the hospital this morning they said Aunt Marian was 'comfortable'," he said. He sounded anxious, and Antony said quickly:

"Isn't that better? It sounds to me—"

"Well, I'd have thought so. But they won't let me see her." He stopped, and frowned. "They won't let anybody see her," he added in an aggrieved tone.

"And that's a good thing," said Antony; and did not hide altogether the relief in his voice.

The waiter intervened at this point, and there was a changing of dishes, so that Timmy was able to relapse into rather moody meditation again. He roused himself when they were alone, saying to Antony, "From what Mr. Horton tells me, I've reason to thank Sir Nicholas for his kindness to Paul, as well as to me.''

''Well, I shouldn't try at the moment. He's in one of his moods,'' said Antony undutifully. ''By the way, is Miss Barclay staying in her job, or is she leaving Cassell's too?''

''I thought she might want to, but she said—'' Timmy stopped short, and looked from one to other of his companions, as though whatever it was that Ann Barclay had said, the full import of her words had only just struck him. He put down his knife and fork, and abandoned even the pretence of eating. ''Look here,'' he said earnestly, ''just how much chance is there really of Paul getting off?'' And added, as Antony hesitated over his reply, ''I'm sorry, I know you dislike that sort of question. But if he doesn't—' He shook his head, as though he was trying to clear it of uncomfortable thoughts.

Antony ignored the apology. ''I want to see Barclay again,'' he remarked. ''Have you any suggestions about time?''

''I don't think it matters. He's likely to be home during the day, because mostly he's working.'' He added, despondently, ''But I don't think he'll be able to help you, now he's made up his mind—''

''On the contrary, it may be all for the best.'' Antony went on quickly, without involving himself in explanation, ''There's Wayne too. What does he do, and when could I best see him?''

''He's a stockbroker. I think his working hours are pretty orthodox, so evening would be best if you want to see him at home.''

''Aunt Marian gave me the address. In Barnes, if I remember—''

''That's right. He has a flat—I think it's what they call a maisonette, really—the ground floor of an old house: rather pleasant, and he has the garden which he likes messing about with.''

''Is he married?''

''No. I think he's a bit self-conscious, about his face you know.''

Geoffrey Horton looked inquiring, and Antony explained, ''Burns, I think. Was it the war?''

"Oh, no. Before that."

"What happened, then? It's a shocking disfigurement, poor chap."

"Well, I don't know much about it, because he's been like that as long as I remember. But he had a business of some sort, and there was a fire, or an explosion, or something."

"Bad luck. Can you think of anyone else, Timmy, who knew your parents and is still connected with your family?"

Timmy reflected. "No, I can't. There are some aunts, my father's sisters; but they live up north somewhere, and I've never even seen them. And I hear from my godparents, but they're in Kenya; and Paul's are dead. I don't know anyone else."

"I see."

"I expect Aunt Marian could help you most, after John and Bob Wayne. If she gets better—"

"And your uncle?"

"Uncle Greg? Well, of course. I always think of him as being much older, but he isn't really. But I think he and Aunt Agnes had their own friends."

"Well, I'll try." Antony turned to look for the waiter, who was not far to seek. Timmy said, as the man went away to fetch their coffee:

"I wish I understood—"

"What was Barclay's wife's name?" asked Antony, who was in no mood for explanations. "Do you know?"

"Well, I do as a matter of fact." Timmy seemed a little startled, but left his grievance obediently enough. "She was Ann, too, and her maiden name was Foster. And she was at school with Aunt Marian, that's how I know, because she still talks about her; and that's why she's so fond of Ann, I suppose—and Audrey, too, though her mother was an older sister and she didn't know her so well."

The coffee arrived, and Timmy drank thirstily. Antony, feeling a little foolish in the role of nursemaid, tried to persuade him into taking some cheese. Geoffrey Horton took out a note-book and wrote down the address in Nevern Square where Timmy was staying for the time being.

They parted on the pavement some ten minutes later; or rather, Horton left them to retrieve his car and return to his office, but Timmy lingered after he had gone, and said at last:

"I'm rather at a loose end, you know. I suppose there isn't anything I can do?"

"Not really. Unless . . . can you drive?" he added, on an impulse.

"Yes, of course I can." Timmy sounded eager.

"Then I can save a taxi fare," said Antony lightly. "We'll go home and collect the car. But it'll mean a lot of waiting about," he warned.

"I don't mind that. Don't you drive yourself, then?"

"Not now. Not if I can help it."

"It's your arm, isn't it?" Timmy sounded diffident.

"Is it so obvious?" He tried to keep his voice casual, but it was a sore point, and he didn't quite succeed.

"It isn't at all." His companion seemed eager to make amends for a possible blunder. "John Barclay mentioned it, I expect he's more observant than most people. Was it the war?"

"It was." Antony was disinclined to elaborate. He suffered still a good deal of pain and inconvenience from his damaged shoulder; but it was the circumstances of the injury, rather than his present disability, of which he did not wish to be reminded. He was thinking as they walked that he could understand, only too well, how Paul, hating the facts of his parents' death, had turned so desperately from the recollection that now he could say, with truth, that he did not remember. He did not, therefore, realise how short his answer had been until he heard Timmy say, rather huffily:

"I'm sorry."

Antony roused himself. "No need to be. It doesn't worry me now, and I manage very well without driving. Jenny's an expert, anyway; she drove an ambulance during the war. But I don't care to leave her hanging about for hours, which is where you come in. Will you be bored?"

"Probably," said Timmy. "But I'm glad to have something to do."

They collected the car, and Antony left a note for Jenny. He was by no means resigned, in spite of what he had said, to being always a passenger, but he breathed a sigh of relief when he saw that Timmy had reasonable skill and an affectionate feeling for the car; he had made the suggestion on impulse, and realised that it was one he might well have regretted. "First," he said, settling himself comfortably, "we'll go and disturb Dr. Hearn's afternoon siesta." Timmy was concentrating, and gave only a grunt by way of reply. "After that, you can help me interview Rose."

"Rose? What on earth—"

"You really must," said Antony, in mild protest, "stop thinking everything I do has a significance. We'll none of us know what's important until we've got our case into some sort of shape; and we're a long way from that, yet."

"I know . . . exploring avenues," said Timmy, on whom the slight activity seemed to be having, as usual, a tonic effect. "Well, if you need a Watson, I'm your man."

Their luck was in, and Dr. Hearn was found at home. He was, in fact, in his garden, and as Timmy was able to identify him Antony walked straight down to where he was prodding rather ineffectually at his compost heap, and cornered him without offering him any chance of escape. The doctor blinked at him in a short-sighted way, pushed up his spectacles which had come to rest on the tip of his nose, said, "Of course, of course, only too glad my dear fellow," and led the way into the house by a side door.

It was a relief to find that, though Dr. Hearn's surgery shared with his person a certain comfortable untidiness, he gave no sign that his mental processes were other than clear and orderly. Antony explained himself, and the doctor put his fingertips together and eyed him benevolently. "Well, now, it will be a pleasure to help you if I can. But tell me, Mr.—Mr. Maitland, did you say?—will you be following this insanity theory?"

Antony entered into further explanation with what patience he could muster, and succeeded fairly well in keeping from his voice a note of long-suffering. "That is something we can only decide on the evidence. So far we are still collecting facts."

"I see."

"So that is why I have come to you, Doctor. You know Paul Herron well, no doubt, and his brother too."

"Oh, yes, indeed. Ever since they came to their grandfather's house, and a sad business that was to be sure."

"Will you tell me what you thought of them: then and later?" said Antony, and the doctor threw up his hands in a pretence of consternation.

"That seems to me to be casting your net pretty wide, Mr. Maitland. Still, in the circumstances, I must do my best." He paused to consider, and then went on, "They were six— seven?—years old when I first saw them; something like that. And a fine time we had with young Timmy. Tears and nightmares, and not to be wondered at, poor child."

"And Paul?"

"As different again. Not a word to be had from him, or any crying either. I thought at first he had realised nothing, only then about a month later he started the sleep-walking. Worried the family, I can tell you, and it was years before he grew out of it."

"You may be asked if it is possible he was malingering at that time."

"May I? Well, you know as well as I do that's impossible to prove. There are children who do, of course, but he was a bit young for that, and I certainly thought it was genuine."

"You know perhaps that Paul says he walked again in his sleep, on the night William Cassell died?"

"Yes, I have been told that."

"Do you believe him? No—that's the wrong question—is it likely, do you think?"

"In the circumstances that have been described to me," said Dr. Hearn dryly, "very likely."

"And, on the other hand, if you are asked your opinion of Paul's sanity, what will your answer be?"

"Well . . . now." The doctor pushed his glasses up his nose again, and looked at his visitor through them rather doubtfully. "I should say, I think, that I had never observed signs of madness in him. And I should add that I am not, after all, an expert."

"You saw him after the murder?"

"I did. He was certainly not normal at that time; but neither, I think, were the other members of the family. I was out when the message came, so the police were already in possession when I arrived, and young Paul had been taken into custody."

"Did you, yourself, Doctor, entertain any doubts as to his guilt?"

"It did not seem to be a matter admitting of any doubt. I was deeply grieved by what had happened, but I was told he had been seen—"

"With the gun in his hand . . . after the murder," said Antony quickly. "If you believe him guilty I must ask you (for my own information only) whether you also think him mad?"

The doctor looked harassed. "I should prefer to take refuge again in my ignorance," he said with a sigh. "Ambrose Cassell informed me that his grandson was mad, and at his request I recommended that he consult Charles Macintyre, who is an expert in the field of neurology and mental disorders."

"That was the chap Bellerby took to see Paul," Antony commented. "I've read his report."

"He is certainly not in disagreement with old Mr. Cassell's theory."

"Damn it all," said Antony, exploding suddenly, "he said there were 'suggestive symptoms'; and if you show me the man who doesn't display *some* signs of abnormality to the expert's eye, I'd expect him to be an oddity."

"You have a poor opinion of my profession, I fear." Dr. Hearn shook his head sadly, but did not appear to have taken offence. "I am sure, Dr. Macintyre gave a sincere opinion—"

"Of course he did. That's what I'm complaining of. He was looking for signs of madness—"

"Just as you, young man, are looking for signs of your client's innocence. Are you not?" the doctor pointed out blandly.

"You mean, I'm likely to see them whether they are there or not?" Antony sounded subdued.

"On your own thesis, it seems likely." He was firm, but apologetic. Antony smiled a little wryly.

"Then perhaps we could go on to the subject of Timmy Herron?" he suggested. "Do you think Dr. Macintyre would find suggestive symptoms in him, too?"

"No, I do not." The doctor was speaking emphatically now. "It is not within my province to speculate on the likelihood or otherwise of the police theory concerning the poisoning of Marian Cassell, but I am convinced that if it was done by Timmy Herron it was undertaken quite coolly in the mistaken belief that he was helping his brother."

"You think that possible?" Antony sounded dejected, and his companion took him up sharply.

"Possible, yes. I did not say I thought it likely."

"No, I see. About Miss Marian Cassell—"

"She was unconscious when I saw her. It was obvious she had taken something; I feared—I admit, I feared it had been deliberate. In the very unhappy circumstances—"

"But later you changed your mind?"

"She was taking the prescription I gave her, had obviously taken one dose each evening. For that matter," he added angrily, "if she had drunk the whole bottle it would have had no lasting ill effects. I know these women!"

"You don't think, then, that she may have suspected the innocuous nature of the mixture you gave her?"

"Certainly not. She has a proper confidence in me," said the doctor with some pride.

"Then I must content myself with what you have told me. I'm very grateful." Antony got up as he spoke.

"I'm afraid I haven't been helpful." Dr. Hearn shook his head regretfully. "You have asked me questions, and I have done my best to answer as accurately as possible; but the answers were not always what you wish to hear, nor what I would wish to tell you if I had any choice in the matter."

"But you do think Paul may have murdered his great-uncle; and Timmy tried to poison his aunt?" Antony was speaking almost to himself, but the doctor broke in angrily:

"I am a reasonable man, and I believe in facts. But I cannot judge . . . those unhappy young men—"

Antony looked at him with the glimmer of a smile. "Thank you, Doctor," he said again. "I asked your opinion, and you have given it to me honestly, I know. I can't grumble about that." He turned at the door, and found Dr. Hearn's eyes fixed on him, and their expression anxious. "Don't worry, sir," he said. "It's up to the lawyers now. So leave the headaches to us."

"I shall be glad to." His tone was emphatic. But he sat back in his chair as the door closed behind his visitor; and it was a long time before he again retrieved his glasses from his nose-tip and returned to his pleasant preoccupation with his compost heap.

Timmy took one look at Antony's face when he rejoined him, and drove off without saying a word. The drive to The Laurels was accomplished in silence, but Timmy said, as he parked the car at the back of the house, "I suppose . . . did Dr. Hearn say he thought Paul was mad?"

"He wouldn't commit himself, but he doesn't think that," replied Antony, shortly.

"I see." He spoke very quietly, but at his tone Antony twisted round to look at him.

"I'm sorry, Timmy," he said. He found it impossible to explain his depression; or to tell his companion that he could fight a hostile witness and be stimulated by the conflict, but that this passive acceptance by a sincere and friendly man of "facts" he believed to be false was something he found difficult to counter.

Cook was inclined to be difficult about leaving them alone; which caused Timmy to remark bitterly later that he had had plenty of opportunity of seducing Rose while he was still living in the house, without returning at four o'clock in the afternoon and bringing a witness! It was the housemaid herself who provided the solution of their problem by a handsome offer to prepare as well as serve Mrs. Gregory's afternoon tea, if Cook would go and have a nice lay down. Cook departed, prophesying woe; and Timmy, looking slightly less strained, sat down at the kitchen table, waving to his companions to join him.

Afterwards Antony was to wonder what he had really expected from the interview. Admittedly, it was reasonable to suppose that Aunt Marian must have had someone to talk to in this rather dreary household; he wasn't surprised to learn that she had confided, to some extent, in Rose . . . but the subject of the confidence was a facer, no doubt about that!

It took time, of course; time, and caution, and several false starts. Rose was a tall girl, with dark, straight hair and considerable composure of manner; he liked her none the less for being wary in her answers. But what he elicited at last was that Miss Cassell had asked her to look for an old letter when she was doing the study—". . . a letter with a funny stamp. She said it was very wrong of her to ask me, but one must be *ruthless* when people were in such trouble. And she gave me a little lecture about how dreadful it was, but just this once—''

There was an interruption here, because the letter had to be explained to Timmy. ''It was Uncle William's account of his visit to your parents just before he left England the last time.'' But, after all, Rose hadn't found the letter.

Antony thanked her. It was illogical, he knew, to be cast down because just for a moment he had begun to hope . . . through his gloomy reflections he became suddenly aware that Rose was still speaking. *''What* did you say?'' he demanded.

''—and she said, after all, she'd been thinking perhaps it would be at the office. Because Mr. William always had business things to write about—''

Antony got up. Of course it was foolish, and of course the letter might well be ashes long ago. But perhaps it was there, in the files at Cassell and Company's offices; and perhaps it would tell him . . .

''Thank you, Rose,'' he said again, and swept Timmy towards the door on a wave of gratitude, enthusiastically expressed. They were half-way to the car when he stopped in sudden consternation. ''Blast it, young Timmy, what did you want to go throwing up your job for, just when I need you at the office?'' he said.

''I'll go back,'' Timmy offered. He didn't sound eager, and Antony laughed, and took his arm, and went on towards the car.

''Now, don't start being noble. We'll think of something, don't worry,'' he said, reassuringly.

CHAPTER 14

THE NEXT on the list was John Barclay, and Antony was glad enough of a guide who knew the district. Having previously made his way to the apartment on foot, he had only the vaguest idea of where it was situated in relation to the Cassell house. Timmy, suddenly mulish, parked the car firmly in the next street and declined to proceed any farther. He gave minute directions for the completion of the journey, and Antony left him to his vigil.

He thought his luck was out, as there was no answer even when he forsook the old-fashioned bell-pull and resorted to pounding on the door. As he turned away, however, he found Barclay on the path behind him. The artist was more neatly clad than usual, and seemed to have abandoned for the time being his customary vagueness. It appeared to give him no pleasure to recognise his visitor; he scowled, and said sourly, "You here again? I didn't think—" This was hardly encouraging, even when he added grudgingly, "Oh, well, I suppose you'd better come in."

Antony followed him with no more than a murmur of acknowledgment; he felt his footing was too precarious to be jeopardised by incautious speech. The older man threw his hat into a chair near the door of the studio, removed his jacket and tossed it carelessly in the same direction, and crossed towards the living area of the big room tugging at his tie as he went. Antony closed the door carefully, and joined him; moving a pile of books and sitting down uninvited in the chair he had occupied on his last visit. Barclay, removing his tie altogether with a final tug, sat down heavily in his favourite place on the sofa and regarded him without friendliness.

"I've just come from the hospital," he announced. Antony endeavoured to look both sympathetic and inquiring. "They won't allow visitors," the artist went on. "They wouldn't let me in."

"Still, I heard the news was better." Antony decided that his visit, after all, would accomplish little if he didn't break his cautious silence. "Didn't they tell you—?"

"They *said* that 'her condition was improved'." Barclay adopted a prim, expressionless tone to deliver this quotation. He seemed to regard the pronouncement with suspicion, and added gloomily, "How can you believe that, when they won't let anyone see her?"

"Simple faith," said Antony, incautiously, "is more than Norman blood." The remark had at least the advantage of riveting his companion's attention. Barclay emerged from his fruitless contemplation of the iniquities of the medical profession, and started to feel about among the sofa cushions.

"It's on the table," said Antony, pointing. The artist looked, picked up his pipe without comment, eyed the younger man for a moment in silence, and inquired gruffly:

"Well? What do you want?"

"There are a few points—" said Antony deprecatingly. He did not find the other's expression encouraging.

"I seem to have done nothing for days but answer questions," said Barclay.

"I'm sorry you feel like that," said Antony, with truth. "What happened at The Laurels after I left on Saturday?"

Barclay seemed taken aback by the question, as indeed his companion had intended. "Nothing at all," he snapped after a moment. "We came away."

"Just like that," said Antony admiringly. "How I like people who don't linger over their farewells."

"Well, as to that, Greg was fussing and Agnes was lamenting. I left Bob Wayne there, and brought the girls home." He paused, meditating a grievance, and added a trifle querulously, "And a fine time I had with them. Anyone would think it was all my fault."

"You mustn't expect logic from girls," Antony pointed out. "Are you still backing your reason against their intuition? That's a silly thing to do."

"Oh, lord!" said Barclay. His brief flare of anger had burned out, leaving him momentarily adrift and purposeless. "If you must have it, I think old Ambrose is in the right of it when he says Paul should plead insanity. After all, whatever he has done, we none of us want the boy to hang."

"But if—just suppose it, sir—we could get him off on a straight 'not guilty' plea, would that satisfy you?" Antony's tone was casual, but he suddenly felt that the answer to this query might have some importance.

Barclay moved uneasily, and avoided the younger man's eye. "You do have the habit of asking the most damnable questions," he complained. "Very well: I don't want Ann to marry into that family."

Which was natural enough, Antony reflected, and a more straightforward answer than he had had a right to expect. He said slowly, "Thank you, sir. Now, there are still these few matters—"

"Yes?" He sounded wary now.

"I want you to go again over what you told me about Matthew and Ruth Herron."

Barclay looked at him as if he couldn't believe his ears. "But why?" he asked; and his voice rose on the question until it was absurdly like a squeak. "I don't mind, of course, but old Ambrose said . . . I mean, after what happened yesterday—"

"You heard about that, did you?" Antony sounded resigned. "I seem to have said so many times that nothing about the conduct of the case can be decided until we have all the facts . . . but nobody will believe me."

"You're not telling me Sir Nicholas will be making an insanity defence after all?" demanded Barclay, frankly incredulous. "If so, why all the fuss?"

"My uncle is not the most even-tempered of men," said Antony, with the air of one making a reluctant admission. "It's a pity he ever had to meet old Mr. Cassell."

"Well, it certainly seems to have led to a good deal of misunderstanding. Though, even before that, you yourself—"

"I only told him we had to look at the case from all angles," Antony protested. "Perhaps he's allergic to members of my family," he added.

"Perhaps he is." The artist's tone was dry. Antony felt a sudden surge of irritation, hastily suppressed. After all, annoying though it was, this cross-questioning suited his book well enough at the moment, and if Barclay jumped to the wrong conclusion that was all to the good.

He got up to leave about twenty minutes later, and did not feel that much had been accomplished. They had gone again over all that had been said on his previous visit, as well as the events of the day Marian Cassell had taken the overdose of sleeping tablets. Nothing had been added, nothing was forgotten. Antony was aware, however, that Barclay's attitude had hardened since they had spoken together. Whatever the cause, in so far as was in him he had now taken sides against the Herron twins.

Before he reached the door, however, there came the sound of footsteps in the passage outside, and Audrey Barton came in, closely followed by Brent Cassell. Antony had the impression that they had been arguing; the girl's colour was high, and the man had a look of irritation, faint but unmistakable.

Audrey said, "Oh," and stopped when she saw the visitor. Then, "Have you any news, Mr. Maitland?" she asked eagerly. But before he had time to reply Brent came up beside the girl, and spoke aggressively.

"Well, what is it this time? Were you waiting for us?"

"I was on the point of leaving," said Antony. "Of course, I'm always glad to see Miss Barton."

Barclay laughed suddenly, and sounded really amused. Audrey's flush deepened, and she looked anxiously at Brent, who was scowling. "Well, I must say, it's very nice if you don't want to ask any more questions," she said. She seemed to be talking at random, and in the same spirit John Barclay said, half seriously:

"I suppose nobody cares at all if I'm driven mad by them."

"Poor Uncle John." Audrey attempted a light tone, which did not conceal her nervousness. Brent said almost simultaneously:

"Not tactful, John. Insanity is a sore subject these days, I doubt if even Maitland sees the humour of it." And without waiting for comment he swung round to face Antony, adding sharply, "Have you heard anything of my young cousin? He has left home, and it is causing the family some concern."

Antony did not look at the girl, but was conscious of an added tension about her. "If you mean Timmy Herron, I don't expect he'll come to any harm," he said lightly. "No doubt you'll be hearing from him, and meanwhile I shouldn't worry . . . too much . . . if I were you."

Brent caught the sardonic inflection on the last words, and flushed angrily. "So you do know where he is," he said, accusingly.

Antony, thinking of his patient chauffeur, could not repress a flicker of amusement. The other caught the look, and said hotly, "Perhaps you won't think it so funny—" He broke off, closing his mouth firmly on what would evidently have been an indiscretion.

Audrey said quickly, "What were you going to say?"

"Nothing. Forget it!"

"I should like to know—" Antony began; but Brent, suddenly at ease again, interrupted him.

"Now that's where you're wrong, Maitland." His smile was openly malicious. "It would give you no pleasure at all."

"In that case, I must hope to be spared the knowledge." He spoke lightly, to hide the fact that he was perturbed by Brent's words, and still more by his manner.

Audrey, still looking at her betrothed, said, "Brent?" questioningly; and he was no longer smiling as he turned back to her.

"I said, forget it!" he snapped. And again Audrey flushed, and again she looked at Antony as though for help.

His smile was reassuring; his words, he felt, sadly inadequate to the occasion. "Don't worry, Miss Barton. That's my job, now." He was appalled to see that she was very near to tears. She moved nearer to him.

"You've seen Paul?" she asked.

"Don't worry," he said again. "He asked how you were taking it, and was cheered by what I told him."

Audrey's smile was suddenly radiant. "Timmy said last night—" she remarked, thoughtlessly, and was interrupted by Brent, who took two strides to her side, grabbed her arm, and said violently:

"So you *did* see him. Now if you know where the brat is, Audrey—" His grip tightened. Antony saw the tears in the girl's eyes (he thought they were of pain, but of course, it might have been temper) and judged, regretfully, that it was time to intervene. He forgot as he stepped forward about his injured shoulder, but of long habit it was his left hand that came up to cover Brent's wrist, and to twist it suddenly, painfully. Brent gave a gasp that was part surprise, but mostly because he had been hurt: Audrey jumped back a pace, and stood rubbing her arm; and Antony, feeling rather foolish now, kept his grip and reflected with rueful amusement on the fate of those who catch the tiger's tail. Apart from other considerations (and his own helplessness came back to him forcibly now) Brent was at least two stone the heavier; and it was scarcely feasible that they should stand thus all night.

They had all three forgotten John Barclay, who came forward now, saying sharply, "I should really prefer it if you would conduct your brawls in some more convenient place. I am quite capable of controlling my own household, Maitland; and as for you, Brent—"

Antony relaxed his grip, not unthankfully. His adversary eyed him malevolently, so that Barclay said again, "Brent!" in an admonitory tone.

"You needn't worry," said Brent Cassell, who was breathing rather quickly. "I don't waste my time on cripples."

Antony achieved a smile. He was quite unaware that he had gone white with anger. "T-thank you. That quite sets my m-mind at r-rest," he said. He turned to John Barclay, and did not see that the artist himself was equally furious. "My ap-pologies, sir. And to you, too, Miss Barton." He went out without another look at Brent.

He thought he had himself well enough in control by the time he reached the car. Timmy took one look at him, and asked in a scared tone, "What happened?"

Antony told him briefly. Timmy appeared cheered, on the whole, by the narrative; and said, "Damn his eyes!" in quite a pleased tone when the encounter with Brent was reached. Antony, finding himself at the point upon which he had no wish to elaborate, finished quickly, "So I came away." The younger man looked at him curiously; but then, remembering, asked with some anxiety:

"What do you suppose he meant?"

"I haven't the faintest idea. But I expect we'll hear only too soon."

"Well, meanwhile, ought I to go in and see Brent?"

"Good heavens, *no!*"

"Well, I thought . . . I can't have him bullying the girls."

"He can't very well while Barclay's there," said Antony, reasonably.

"Then I'll ring up Grandfather, and tell him where I'm staying." Timmy sounded determined; the decision had evidently cost him something. "Would that do, do you think?"

"Admirably, I should say."

"Then I'd better do it at once." Timmy fumbled for the ignition key, and said with his attention on starting the car, "I don't want to, you know. But he can't make me go home, after all."

"You can use our phone," said Antony. "Jenny's expecting us for supper . . . do you remember?"

"That's all right," said Timmy, as the car slid forward gently. Then he chuckled, with an abrupt change of mood that reminded Antony that he was, after all, very young. "I do wish I'd seen Brent's face," he said.

Sir Nicholas, having taken one horrified look at the cold collation with which it was his housekeeper's habit to regale him on Tuesday evenings, had fled upstairs to Jenny's more hospitable board. Antony, hearing of this from Gibbs (a disagreeable old man who had served Sir Nicholas's father, and now declined to be pensioned off; without prejudice, of course, to his right to regard his continued activities as a grievance), sent Timmy into the study to telephone in privacy. The old manservant departed, muttering, for his own quarters (probably he was having a cold supper too), and Antony sat down on the stairs to await his companion's return.

It was about five minutes before Timmy came back; his

lips were set in a thin line, and he was silent as they went upstairs; but he roused himself to say, as they neared the top landing, "He wants me to go home."

"Are you going?"

"Not on your life. It wasn't a—a peace offering, you know."

They found Jenny and Sir Nicholas relaxing over their sherry. Antony went to change, and returned to find that Jenny had gone to the kitchen, and the other two were deep in conversation. Timmy stopped talking as he went in, and looked guilty. Sir Nicholas gave him a black look, and said coldly, "I have been hearing of your—er—encounter with Brent Cassell. I was enthralled!"

"Well—" said Antony, who had his own reasons for not wishing to pursue the subject. Timmy, looking from one to other of them, remarked:

"I wonder what Brent was talking about." His air of innocence was exaggerated a little, so that Sir Nicholas eyed him suspiciously before allowing his attention to be diverted.

"Probably nothing at all." Antony had been making a round with the decanter, and now brought his glass and put it down on the end of the mantelpiece. "It's just the sort of thing people *do* say," he added.

"We'll take your word for it." Sir Nicholas turned again to Timmy. "What did you think of your brother's solicitor, Mr. Herron?"

"He seems a good chap," said Timmy. "I thought he seemed very capable." He sounded diffident, as though doubtful of the value of his opinion, and Sir Nicholas gave him an approving smile.

"He will do very well, very well indeed," he agreed.

"My uncle means," translated Antony, "that Horton will allow *him* to do just as he pleases."

"Well, perhaps. But only because what I do is so eminently sensible," said Sir Nicholas. "Are you going out again to-night, Antony?"

"Heaven forbid. We might have a session later; I've a good deal to report."

"Very well. I shall be in court all day to-morrow; and you'll have your hands full with that Hemingway business, because Mallory tells me it will probably come on Thursday.''

"And Horton wants a conference in the evening. Tomorrow evening, I mean. I told him to come here; was that right, sir?"

"Certainly." He seemed about to say more, but glanced at their guest, and then back at his nephew. Antony, accustomed to his ways, thought him perturbed; a state of affairs so unusual that he was, himself, conscious of a stirring of anxiety. Timmy went out just then, in response to a call from Jenny that there was a tray to carry. Antony said:

"Uncle Nick—?" and the telephone rang. He damned it fervently, and went across the room.

"Maitland?" inquired the telephone. The voice was familiar, and he identified the caller in the same moment as he gave his name. "Robert Wayne here."

"Good evening, Mr. Wayne."

"Good evening. I hope you don't mind—"

"I was going to get in touch with you to-morrow, anyway."

"I suppose that doesn't mean *you've* anything to tell *me?*"

"I'm afraid not."

"Then it means more questions." The deep voice was expressive, sad but resigned. "Well, I've got one for you now. Do you know where young Timmy is?"

"At the moment," said Antony, "he's in the kitchen here, helping my wife to dish up supper."

"Good lord! Look here, I want to see him."

"I'll tell him."

"Well, tell him I've had old Mr. Cassell chasing me; thought he might be with me; well, if he *had* to leave home he could have come, you know. But I don't think it's very sensible—"

"He phoned his grandfather about half an hour ago, to give him his address." Antony's tone was deceptively mild. "If that's what's worrying you—"

"Well, I'd still like to see him. After all, he's my cousin, I'd like to help if I can."

"Just a minute." He turned from the phone, to explain to Sir Nicholas and to Timmy, who had come back with the laden tray, what was being said.

"Oh, well, I don't mind seeing Bob," Timmy remarked, though he did not sound enthusiastic. And Sir Nicholas, taking charge of the arrangements, demanded:

"Ask him if he's free this evening. If he can come here you can have your talk with him in the study; and then he can see his cousin."

Wayne was free, and the arrangement was made. He was to come at nine o'clock. "And while you all talk," said Jenny, accusingly, "supper's getting cold."

Wayne was punctual, and Antony took him into the study where his uncle was already established. He showed none of the uneasiness that Barclay had displayed that afternoon, but acknowledged the introduction with every evidence of pleasure, and settled himself comfortably in the chair at the right of the fire-place, saying as he did so: "I wasn't sorry to be seeing you again, you know. I've been concerned for the twins, as you can imagine; and I must admit, too, to my fair share of curiosity."

"I hope you're not counting on having it satisfied," said Sir Nicholas with a smile.

"Well, hardly. But you'll tell me this much: are you still representing Paul?"

"Oh, yes. He decided he would prefer a solicitor of his own choosing," explained Sir Nicholas easily. "The briefs, however, are still to come to us."

"I see. But if you've abandoned the idea of Paul being mad I don't see how I can help you."

Antony embarked once again on the explanation he had given Barclay that afternoon. Wayne seemed to find it specious enough, but shook his head sadly as it came to an end, and said, half to himself, "So it's still in the melting pot. And I must resign myself to the possibility of giving evidence, as you explained when first we met. I think, perhaps, Maitland," he added, "I did not seem very helpful on that occasion."

"Very few people like answering questions," said Antony. "It's nothing new, I assure you."

"Well, I was reluctant to start going over all that again. But I do see your point about covering everything."

"I've been asking Timmy about any other possible sources of information."

"I honestly think I'm as good as you'll get. We were in a way a compact group, though we each of us had, of course, friends and acquaintances outside that small, intimate circle."

"You are referring to the Herrons—"

"Yes, Matthew and Mark. And Ruth, of course. Then there was poor Marian; and John Barclay; and myself." He stopped, and his thoughts seemed to be sad ones. After a while he went on, "They were an extraordinarily nice couple, you know: Matt and Ruth. It all seemed to fit so well, and Mark always seemed part of the family, never an outsider. He and Matt were identical twins, you know; it always seemed to me that they were closer than ordinary twins—than, say, Paul and Timmy are. But I was saying, their friendship meant a great deal to me, because that was a time of my life that wasn't easy: the year after *this* happened." He gestured as he spoke, so that it was obvious he was referring to his facial injuries. "I spent a great deal of time with them; I suppose I was unduly sensitive, but it was the one place I felt really welcome. John Barclay was another frequent visitor during the last months, but he had not known my cousins as long as I had. They were older than I, but I was with them a great deal, even when we were children."

"Do you remember Mrs. Barclay?" Antony threw in the question, as he seemed to have fallen into a brown study.

"Indeed I do. Ann Foster she was, a quiet little thing, her daughter is very like her."

"And was she known to the Herron family?"

"Oh, yes, we'd all known each other for ages. I remember at one time my mother thought that Mark was fond of her; and she always thought John Barclay and Marian would marry."

Sir Nicholas said with a smile, "In a moment, my nephew will be asking if he can interview your mother. He is a great believer in thoroughness."

"Well, can I?" said Antony.

"She died, I'm sorry to say . . . even before John and Ann were married. But I was telling you about Matt. I'm not surprised John noticed nothing; or that he thinks now I imagined there was a strangeness. But he did change, so little, so imperceptibly that I never thought about it till later; but still, there was something different . . . a look . . . an occasional sharpness of tone . . . nothing to pin down.'' He was silent for a while, and then looked up with the smile that twisted his face so oddly. ''It's a long time ago,'' he said quietly.

''Eighteen years,'' agreed Sir Nicholas.

''And eighteen years since William Cassell had been home,'' said Antony. He spoke idly, but it seemed to him, after he had spoken, that the words were full of meaning. Neither of his companions seemed aware of this.

''I wish I could help you.'' Wayne was regretful. ''But you won't want hearsay evidence.''

''I had a talk with Barclay. He knew Uncle William well, but wasn't able to help me. His recent knowledge is hearsay, too.''

''So I suppose. It may seem odd I never met him, but my connection with the Cassells has been closer since my cousins died than it was before.''

''Yes, of course.''

''You never thought,'' Sir Nicholas asked, ''that there could have been any foundation for Matthew Herron's suspicions?''

''That Ruth and Mark—oh, no, that's quite ridiculous.'' He spoke shortly, but controlled himself after an instant. ''What I think is that Matt *knew* it wasn't true, but couldn't stop himself from thinking it *might* be,'' he said. ''I know that isn't precisely sense, but—''

''I see what you mean.''

''Well, I went round to the flat the evening before they died. John says Mark had been there, but left just before I arrived. We just sat and talked, you know how it is when you know each other well . . . there's always plenty to talk about.''

''Barclay says—'' Antony began, but was interrupted by Robert Wayne, who said irritably:

''I know John thinks I imagined it, but Matt *was* odd that evening. And Ruth had a headache; well, I know that's nothing very unusual, but one thing might have led to the other, don't you think?''

"She was an attractive person, so I understand," said Antony, and Wayne shot him a look.

"John again?" he asked. "It's true enough, anyway. She was extremely attractive: a little thing, very pretty and lively—"

"And wearing a new red dress," said Antony meditatively. (For some reason the mention of Barclay seemed to aggravate the visitor, and it amused him to prod gently the source of the irritation.) "Mr. Barclay has a good visual memory," he added. "Comes of being an artist, no doubt."

"Well, that's not very difficult," said Wayne, with a note of derision in his voice. "Dark red, burgundy I think Marian called it; and her ring showed up well against it, an opal ring, and it was glowing so that I thought it must be true they look best on people who were born in October." He paused, and gave his interrogator a challenging look. "Helpful, isn't it?"

"No," said Antony. "However, you never know till you try. I'm grateful, Mr. Wayne."

"Well, I would if I could, you know. Now, what about young Timmy? Is he still here?"

"Yes, he's upstairs. Before I fetch him—"

"I wanted to ask you what the police are up to?"

"Biding their time, so far as I know. *I've* wanted to ask *you*—"

"Well?"

"You do realise, Mr. Wayne, that somebody arranged for Miss Cassell to take an overdose of her sleeping tablets? And if we assume that Timmy didn't do it—"

"I find the thought distasteful, but it has to be faced, though I've done my best to believe it might have been an accident. If Timmy didn't do it, someone else did."

"And that being so, can you add anything to what you said on Sunday? Any impression, even—"

"There's nothing." Wayne's tone was one of controlled violence. "I don't think Timmy would . . . but I can't believe it of any of the others either."

"All right. But if you do think of anything—"

"I'll tell you. Of course." He added, angrily, "It's a damnable business, Maitland."

"And there I agree with you." Antony got up. "If you'll wait here a moment I'll fetch Timmy. You can talk here."

"Don't worry, I'll take him off your hands now. It's getting late, I may as well run him home, and we can talk as we go," said Wayne.

Timmy was fetched. He had been playing beggar-my-neighbour with Jenny, and came downstairs complaining bitterly at being dragged away in the middle of a game that he was winning. His manner changed as his cousin came out of the study. He greeted him in a friendly enough way, but his tone had its reservations.

They went away together. Antony, standing in the doorway, heard Timmy's voice as he crossed the pavement. "Well, so long as you don't start talking to me for my own good—" The words were cut off by the slamming of the car door. There was a pause, during which Antony imagined the argument was continuing. Then the car drove away, and the square was silent again.

CHAPTER 15

THE NEXT DAY was a busy one. Sir Nicholas disappeared at a comparatively early hour in the direction of the Law Courts, accompanied by old Mr. Mallory and the most junior of the clerks. Antony, by shutting himself into his own room and snarling at anybody who approached him, succeeded by lunch time in producing the opinion for which Watterson and Company had been waiting hopefully since the previous week. "And much good will it do them," he remarked to the second most junior of the clerks, who was gathering up the closely-written sheets which were strewn over the desk. "Not what they wanted to hear," he added, with gloomy malice.

The afternoon he spent with the affairs of one, Arthur Hemingway; they seemed pretty hopeless, but he persevered with them until past six o'clock. Geoffrey Horton was due in Kempenfeldt Square for a conference that evening; Sir Nicholas was already at his desk when Antony took the solicitor into the study, surrounded by a regular barricade of books and documents, his glasses on the end of his nose, and a procession of stout ducks marching across the blotting-pad. He threw down his pencil and remarked bitterly by way of greeting:

"If either of you have given any thought to this matter you will have some idea of what I am being asked to do; it is impossible, quite impossible!"

"Surely not, sir." Antony waved a hand to indicate that Horton should seat himself, and pulled up another chair at the far side of the desk. Sir Nicholas looked at him in an overwrought way, and shuffled his papers until a sheet appeared on which there were words as well as ducks.

"First, we have our client's own story. You will not, I take it," he added, looking accusingly at Horton, "expect me to put it to the court without such support as may be obtained."

"Of course not, sir. I have—"

"Yes, no doubt. You are going to tell me that you have witnesses to the fact that this sleep-walking was not at all unusual."

"That, of course," said Geoffrey. He looked at Antony, and then back at the older man, and added defensively, "It seemed to me—"

"And quite correctly," interrupted Sir Nicholas with sudden cordiality. "But does that make my task any easier?" ("Yes," said Antony.)

"But we must—" said Horton. Sir Nicholas replied with a great appearance of reasonableness, "That's what I'm complaining of. We must." He turned a hostile eye in the direction of his nephew, and added, "How am I to produce this evidence in corroboration of Paul Herron's story without at the same time creating in the mind of the jury a strong doubt as to his sanity?"

"You can't, of course," said Antony, promptly. "And once that doubt exists it creates in its turn a strong presupposition of his guilt."

"I'm glad," said his uncle coldly, "that you have so much grasp of the situation in which you have entangled me." Horton began to look anxious, but Antony remained unmoved.

"You'd better tell us what you've been doing," he said, encouragingly to the solicitor.

"Well . . . corroboration of the sleep-walking: there's the cook, not the present one, she's only been there three years; and a chap called Canning, who was the twins' housemaster. He remembers very well, and is inclined to think it was genuine, but—"

"And when we have done our worst with this substantive detail . . . what next?"

"The housemaid, Rose, saw Paul come home. About ten past nine, she thinks. Timmy says he looked into his room and saw him asleep 'about ten o'clock'. The others are vague about times, but there's no real disagreement."

Antony looked down at his handful of notes. "There's the rifle," he said, "and why it was in Wimbledon, and who knew it was in the cupboard? Then there's the fingerprints; there seems no doubt that under Paul's prints, the older ones are badly smudged. That *could* be because someone handled it who was wearing gloves."

"Inspector Blank," said Sir Nicholas, looking at the ceiling, and giving a fair enough imitation of a policeman's court-room delivery, "said there was nothing to show, either way; and he couldn't say different, not for anybody."

"Very likely. Then I think, Uncle Nick, whatever your opinion really is, we'd better try to demonstrate the sheer unlikelihood that William was killed instead of his brother."

"As against that, the Crown will certainly point out that at ten-thirty in the evening Ambrose was habitually in his study."

The slips of paper went back into Antony's pocket. "Paul hadn't seen Uncle William; Paul had quarrelled with his grandfather; Paul had, certainly, the best of opportunities," he said; and he sounded angry.

"And you don't think he did it?" asked Horton. His tone was flat, unsceptical; but Antony's answer came with something of a snap.

"No!" he said. He got up restlessly, and wandered round the desk to take up his favourite position in front of the fireplace. "And I'm increasingly of the opinion that I know who did."

"Who, then?" Geoffrey's tone was eager. Sir Nicholas shook his head at him.

"Not of interest, unless he can prove it." He looked at his nephew. "Can you?" he demanded.

"Not even to my own satisfaction, sir."

"Then we had better defer our theorising until Cobbold's report is to hand, and return to your . . . cook did you say, Horton?"

"Yes, sir."

"What sort of a witness will she make?" inquired Sir Nicholas, picking up his pencil again, and pushing his spectacles up to their correct position.

"I've no idea," said Horton frankly. "Woolly . . . I should think."

"May heaven forgive you," remarked Sir Nicholas; and added a shawl and sunbonnet to one of his ducks which he felt (wrongly) had rather a feminine air.

They adjourned at ten-thirty. Antony saw Horton to the door, hesitated a moment at the foot of the stairs, and then went slowly back to the study. Sir Nicholas had left his desk, and was looking along the book-shelves; he turned as his nephew came through the door, and laughed gently at his expression.

"What devotion to duty! Go to bed, Antony. To-morrow is also a good day."

"Which reminds me," said Antony, disguising his relief that his uncle was not proposing to start another session, "Horton says Manuel Calleya is coming to London. He's due on Friday."

Sir Nicholas took down a book, turned off the desk light, and came purposefully towards the door. "I hope he can help us."

"So do I." He did not sound hopeful. "Oh, well, who lives may learn. Good night, Uncle Nick."

He went upstairs slowly; he had reached the degree of weariness where even this slight effort was a formidable one; his mind was empty, he felt he would never be capable of constructive thought again. And as he opened his outer door there came from the living-room the sound of voices. He went across the hall and pushed open the door.

Jenny was sitting in her favourite corner of the sofa. She turned to smile at him as he went in. There was a girl beside her, whom at first he did not recognise. Then she, too, turned her head, and he saw it was Ann Barclay. She looked at him questioningly, unsmiling, and then got up.

She was wearing a dark frock, obviously her office dress, in which she looked slighter and even more fragile than in the less formal clothes he had seen her wearing at the week-end. Timmy pulled himself up from the wing-chair at the far side of the hearth, and stood behind Ann, also looking across at the newcomer. Antony pushed the door shut, and contemplated his visitors. Ann's eyes were steady, but he thought her composure was hard-held. She said as he came across the room, "Mr. Maitland, I'm sorry. But we had to talk to you."

Antony smiled, and then looked past her at her companion. "More trouble?" he inquired.

Ann seemed to find this matter-of-fact attitude reassuring. She said, "Do you mind? I told Timmy—"

"She *would* come," said Timmy, apologetically.

"Well, suppose you tell me what's the matter," said Antony. "If you sit down again we can be comfortable." As the visitors obeyed him he looked at Jenny, who seemed to have lost some of her customary serenity. She said:

"It isn't really so bad, but I told them to wait."

"Yes, of course." He looked inquiringly from one to the other of the two young people. "Well?" he encouraged.

"It's what Brent was hinting at," said Timmy. He looked down at the hearth-rug, with every appearance of intense concentration. "It's about the 'Drowse' tablets," he added.

Antony transferred his attention to the girl. "Suppose you tell me," he said.

"Somebody ordered a box, on Saturday morning. Not from the usual chemist Aunt Marian goes to, but another one quite near. It wasn't Timmy, of course . . . but he said he was."

"And the tablets were delivered, about twelve o'clock. Rose remembers the package, and she put it on the table in the hall." Timmy looked up as he spoke. "The police have been asking questions, of course; but no one seems to know what happened to it."

"And that's how Brent knew," Ann put in. "He told Audrey, and Audrey told me."

"Well, now," said Antony. "You say the person who placed the order gave Timmy's name?"

"He said, 'I'm speaking for Miss Marian Cassell—' and gave the address, and asked for the tablets to be sent round. So the chemist asked who was speaking, and the man said, 'I'm her nephew, Timothy Herron. You'll be sure to send them, won't you? She needs them to-night.' And that was all."

And quite enough, Antony considered. He said, thoughtfully, "I don't suppose that will make the police look on you with any less suspicion; but you mustn't exaggerate the evidential value.''

''That's what I said,'' agreed Jenny. Her husband smiled at her, but in rather an absent-minded way.

''But it *will* make them suspicious!'' There was more than a hint of desperation in Ann's tone now. ''And they want to see Timmy again to-morrow morning.''

''Of course they do. That's nothing to worry about.'' Timmy looked up from his study of the hearth-rug, and said quietly:

''Well, perhaps not. But will you—''

''I'll be in court all day. But this is what you have a solicitor for . . . remember? You'll find Horton very helpful, it's his line of country, after all.''

''You don't think—?'' said Ann. She stopped, and looked at him imploringly.

''I don't think they'll arrest Timmy, at least until after Paul's trial,'' said Antony, responding to the appeal. ''But I'm not infallible, you know.''

Ann got up. ''We're grateful,'' she said. And added, with an air of inconsequence, as Timmy scrambled up to stand beside her, ''Audrey isn't going to marry Brent.''

''Is she not? When did they—?''

''At lunch time to-day. He told her about the new inquiries the police are making; and I don't know what made her cross, but something did. So she broke it off.''

''And a good thing too,'' said Timmy. Antony saw that he had undergone one of his sudden changes, and that his spirits were mounting rapidly. ''I never could see what she saw in him.''

''Well—'' said Ann, a little doubtfully. Her eyes filled with tears, and she bent down to pick up her gloves which were tucked down the end of the sofa where she had been sitting. ''Anyone can make a mistake,'' she said. ''But I do wish, Mr. Maitland, there was something I could do.''

''I'm afraid—'' Antony began formally; but interrupted himself to say, with sudden decision, ''You could look for the letter.''

''Eighteen years ago,'' said Ann, when the letter had been explained to her. She sounded doubtful, but not undecided. "There are some bundles of old correspondence down in the strong-room. I'll look, of course."

Timmy put out a hand, and took her arm; it was the first time, since the first evening at Wimbledon, that Antony had seen him touch her. "We ought to go," he said.

Antony came upstairs for the second time to find Jenny stacking cups and plates on the draining board. She came into the hall, and shut the kitchen door firmly. "You look as if you'd had quite enough of to-day, darling."

"Too much," he agreed. "Those are nice children, don't you think?"

"Very nice. But I'm glad they've gone," said Jenny. "Poor Paul," she added after a moment. "But you know, I don't think Ann is at all cut out for a farmer's wife."

"Well, that at least is not our worry," said Antony, thankfully. "Do you realise," he added, making for the bedroom, "that I've to go into court to-morrow to try to obscure with a rose-coloured mist the behaviour of one of the biggest scoundrels—"

"Surely there's something to be said for him." Jenny might have been being charitable, or merely encouraging.

"Oh, yes, to be sure there is," said her husband, with an inflection of sarcasm in his voice. "I hope he gets ten years!" he added spitefully.

CHAPTER 16

ARTHUR HEMINGWAY didn't get ten years; in fact, the jury gave him the benefit of the doubt. But that, said Sir Nicholas (who had arrived in court half-way through the afternoon) was no thanks to the way his case had been presented. Antony was impenitent, and not really dissatisfied with the result of his labours; and when on their return to chambers he found a fat envelope awaiting him from Geoffrey Horton, he followed his uncle without ceremony into his room and announced his intention of returning home with his trophy.

"Will you be free later on this evening, Uncle Nick?"

"I'm having dinner with you; didn't Jenny tell you?"

"Oh, does she know?"

"As it happens, yes. So I shall have plenty of opportunity of hearing the results of your research."

"I shall count the moments," said Antony, in no very dutiful tone. Sir Nicholas grinned to himself as the younger man left him; but was interrupted to take up an argument with Mr. Mallory (who grew ever more tyrannical with age) on the disagreeable, continually recurring subject of fees.

By the time dinner was on the table, Antony had already digested the detectives' report. "Any help there?" inquired Sir Nicholas, watching with an approving eye as his nephew filled his glass.

"There's plenty of it," said Antony, grudgingly. "But where it will lead us, I really can't imagine." He took his place at the table and watched with an absent eye while Jenny ladled vegetables. "To begin with, there were differences of opinion between Ambrose and William—policy differences. It seems Uncle William chose to absent himself, to allow himself to be overruled. But suppose he decided to assert his views? We know nothing of his reasons for coming to England just now. A family visit? But why now?''

''You're still baulking at the idea that William Cassell was killed in mistake for his brother. I agree the point must be made, as forcibly as possible. But in view of what the Crown can prove, do you think they'll have any difficulty in persuading the jury to draw the few remaining (though unprovable) conclusions?''

''No, I don't. Who's got it, by the way?''

''Halloran.''

''Well, I'd back you against him, any day. But the odds are too heavy, and what have we got? A little gossip, unconfirmed conjectures—''

''Is that the best Horton's detectives can do for us?''

''Just about.'' Antony regarded his plate gloomily, and seemed surprised to find it empty. ''They've been digging round the firm's employees, and the picture that emerges is by no means one of a family completely in harmony. But that's a far cry from murdering each other.''

Sir Nicholas smiled. ''Indeed it is. Is this leading anywhere, I wonder? Or are we merely making conversation?''

''You said,'' put in Jenny, ''that you were coming to supper because you wanted to know what was in the report.''

''That was remarkably rude of me.''

''Well, frank anyway.'' Jenny smiled at him.

''So I mustn't blame your precious husband if the facts I crave are missing? Well, fair enough. What next?''

'' 'Lovely rice pudding','' replied Jenny, maddeningly literal. ''And you'd better eat it quickly, because Mr. Horton's coming.'' She vanished in the direction of the kitchen, and Sir Nicholas gave his nephew a companionable grin.

''Evidently it is not done to allow the instructing solicitor to see counsel eating rice pudding,'' he said. And added, as the younger man's expression did not lighten, ''Don't take this too much to heart, Antony. That's no way to win cases.''

''No, sir.''

''You were telling me what Cobbolds' report had to say.''

''Yes, well . . . not much, really,'' replied Antony, diverted. "Ambrose is not popular; though, funnily enough, more popular with the staff than Gregory is. Gregory is believed to live beyond his means. The gossip from Midhurst also confirms that when they first went to live there they were pretty hard up. And it wouldn't surprise me to hear that Grandfather keeps a tight hand on the cash-box; Aunt Agnes has a passion for new clothes."

"You didn't tell me that," said Jenny, returning with the pudding.

"You'd never know it to look at her," said Antony. "But it seems she's inclined to run up bills."

"What fun! Mind that plate, Uncle Nick, it's hot!"

"As for Brent," said Antony, "the girls are inclined to think him wonderful. The men say he's an able business man; opinion's divided as to his personality."

"What about the twins?"

"Not considered very important by the men. Timmy is the favourite with the girls. A good deal of uninformed gossip . . . not helpful. They tried the domestic staff, too: Rose and Cook, and the char who's a little odd, it seems, and pretty deaf into the bargain. We know what Rose has to say; Cook disapproves of everybody on principle. Well, I could have told them."

"And the others? Barclay and his household. And Wayne?"

"Well, there's a certain amount of interest there, but if you ask me whether it's helpful—"

"I didn't."

"No, that's right. I'll start with Wayne, though the stories tie up, as you'll see. His father was a diamond merchant, Hatton Garden, prosperous enough, but not one of the famous names. Our Wayne was brought up to the trade, and was only about twenty when his father died and he took over the business."

"I thought you said he's a stockbroker."

"So he is. However, he continued in his father's business for four years, about. Then he suffered a rather spectacular burglary, in the course of which a night-watchman was killed, and he himself received the facial injuries which I, at first, put down to the war."

"What really happened?"

"The premises went up in flames one night. Nobody thought anything but that it was an ordinary fire. They got it under control pretty quickly, but inside was badly burnt, of course. The police were trying to get in touch with Wayne at his home, when the firemen discovered both him and the night-watchman in one of the workrooms on the first floor. Both were badly burned; the old man was already dead, and it wasn't until some time later that they found he'd been shot. That encouraged them in their inquiries, as you can imagine; they found the safe had been robbed, and a valuable collection of stones was missing . . . along with other, smaller, items."

"Hum!" said Sir Nicholas. "What about insurance?"

"What a nasty suspicious mind you have! He was insured, of course, but only to the amount of the stock he usually carried: the diamonds I mentioned were a special order, and by an oversight—"

Sir Nicholas looked at him, as though puzzled by his tone. "A bad business, then," he said. "And how did Wayne come to be on the premises?"

"It was some time before he could talk, of course. He went in to get some rubies he had a possible customer for; said he was knocked over the head as he went into the room, and that was the last he knew till he came to in hospital. He suspected the night-watchman; which might be fair enough, even in the circumstances."

"What about the man who was interested in rubies?"

"Well, he'd disappeared by the time they heard of him from Wayne and started making inquiries. But that could have been quite natural, too, in view of the length of time that had elapsed."

"How did the fire start? And what did the police think had happened?"

"As for the latter, who am I to say? To judge from what was said at the inquest they thought the night-watchman had conspired with one or more accomplices to rob his employer. That was borne out by the fact that he shouldn't really have been in Wayne's office at that particular time; he did the rounds of two other houses, as well; was due to punch a clock in one of them at about the time the fire must have started. Granted that, it all seems simple enough;

Wayne arrives unexpectedly; they dispose of him; they take the doings, probably using his keys, and then there is a falling out of thieves and the watchman is shot. To try to hide that part of the evening's proceedings, they fire the premises.''

"All very fine," agreed his uncle. "But there's a snag . . . isn't there?"

"The snag is the fire department chap swore there was nothing that suggested arson. He could have been wrong, of course; the ground floor was pretty well burnt out, and—"

"Well, that's all very fine; it seems Wayne had plenty of cause to be sorry for himself." He broke off to frown at Jenny, who was removing empty plates with an obvious attempt to be unobtrusive. "No washing-up to-night, my child. Can't Mrs. . . . Mrs. Thing do it in the morning?"

Jenny laughed. "All right, I'll leave it. But you'll let me fetch the coffee?"

The men moved over to the hearth. Antony shivered, and bent down to put a match to the fire that was already laid. "The first time this year," he remarked. "But I think it's cold enough, don't you?"

Sir Nicholas disregarded the query. He said reflectively, "You've told that story at some length. Is there a sequel?"

Antony watched the flames leap upward among the logs. "In a way there is," he said.

"You told me Wayne gave up the diamond business. I suppose he was discouraged."

"Very likely. He went into an office first, and set up on his own a little later. That wasn't what I meant, though."

"Well?" His tone was sharp. Antony looked up at him, and grinned.

"John Barclay went bankrupt," he said.

The older man frowned again. "I don't see why that should interest you," he complained.

"Don't you, sir? I'm interested in the reason."

"It must have been about the time his wife died. Maybe he was too worried—" He broke off, and looked at his nephew with dawning comprehension.

"Too worried to attend to business? But what business?" said Antony. He scrambled to his feet again, to take his favourite position with a shoulder propped against the mantel. "The report doesn't specify, but I must say I find the question intriguing."

"And so do I," agreed Sir Nicholas. And turned a blank face to Jenny, who came in at that moment with the coffee. Geoffrey Horton was just behind her carrying a tray, and Antony pulled forward a table to accommodate it, saying apologetically:

"We didn't hear you come."

By the time they were settled, and greetings had been exchanged, Sir Nicholas had thrown off his abstraction. Jenny, pouring coffee and passing the cup to her husband, asked, "What about Timmy? Did you see him, Mr. Horton?"

"I did, indeed," he replied, accepting a cup from his host and shaking his head at the offer of the sugar-bowl.

"He isn't . . . they didn't—?"

"He isn't under arrest, Mrs. Maitland. But to be frank, I think he would be were his brother's case not pending."

"Well, I'm glad of that. But I don't see why—"

"Tactics, love," said her husband, briefly. "What did this new evidence amount to?" he added, turning to the newcomer.

"Damn all!" said Horton. "But it doesn't sound good, you know, on top of everything else."

"And how were our friends, the gendarmes?"

"We only saw Conway. I expect they know well enough how much real value this new development has." He turned to Sir Nicholas. "Have you seen Cobbolds' report, sir?"

"I have heard the gist of it from my nephew."

"It isn't very helpful, I'm afraid," said Horton. He spoke apologetically, as though the deficiency of evidence might somehow be blamed on him.

"It has its points," said Antony.

"But you wanted a motive—"

"Well, I didn't expect one to be supplied to order. They may have something more for us in a few days. I took the liberty of phoning them . . ." He stopped, and sipped his coffee. "There is meanwhile the question of opportunity which we might discuss," he said. And pulled from his pocket the usual untidy sheaf of papers, which he eyed vaguely and in some surprise. "There was a plan," he added. And looked round for enlightenment.

Jenny produced the plan, and spread it out on the hearth-rug with the sugar-bowl and cream jug to stop it from rolling up. The discussion was exhaustive, and unhelpful; and not at times without strain between the two younger men. "There's one thing I should like to know," said Horton at last. "When you talk about motive, are you taking Ambrose or William as the intended victim?"

"I just don't know." Antony bent to retrieve his notes, which were scattered by this time across the face of the plan. "William . . . I think. It sticks in my gullet, somehow, this business of killing the wrong man. Besides—"

"You have some hare-brained notion of linking up William Cassell's death with what happened to his niece and her husband, all those years ago."

Horton looked at the older man curiously. "You don't agree, sir?"

Sir Nicholas removed his spectacles, put them in their case, and snapped it shut. "I have learned," he said, unfairly, "in the interests of a quiet life, to give my nephew his head."

"I see." The solicitor did not sound as though he found this statement enlightening. He looked from one to other of his companions, and added doubtfully, "We don't seem to be getting anywhere. I suppose we may as well call it a day."

"You'd better take the report home and brood on it," said Antony. "There are points in it that I would recommend to your consideration."

"What, in particular?"

"The financial affairs of John Barclay," Antony told him. "And don't say I'm not being helpful, because I am."

"Thank you," said Horton, bitterly. "I'll remember you in my prayers."

Antony grinned at him. He seemed to have regained his spirits now, to a quite remarkable degree. "I'm sorry," he said. "Really I am!" But his tone belied his words.

CHAPTER 17

FRIDAY MORNING was grey and chilly. Antony grumbled, "Nice day for prison visiting!"; took his raincoat under protest; and went out with only the most half-hearted of smiles to acknowledge his bad temper. Jenny, who was driving Sir Nicholas that day, followed him downstairs, and endeavoured to derive some comfort from the reflection that a good deal could still happen before the trial started. This was not, in fact, very consoling; as Sir Nicholas pointed out, the delay before the case came on only meant so much longer for them to endure her husband's moods. He relented, however, when he saw that she was really disturbed; and when they left the house together a little later they did so in perfect amity.

Antony, meanwhile, had made his way to Brixton, and found nothing to cheer him in the bleak room where he awaited his client. Paul, when he joined him at length, was pale but composed in manner. Antony, eyeing him closely, thought he showed now more signs of strain; but he had himself well in hand.

He looked about him inquiringly as he seated himself, and Antony said, "I came on my own. I thought perhaps—"

"You thought I might talk more freely, I suppose? I'm quite in your hands, but I don't see what else I can usefully say."

"Don't you?" said Antony. Paul gave him a look that might almost have been one of apology, but said inconsequently:

"Did you tell Timmy what Sir Nicholas said?"

"Horton did, at some length."

"I'm glad of that. And can you give me news of Aunt Marian?"

"Still good, I'm pleased to say. They're hoping to send her home before too long, but the doctors still won't say when she'll be able to talk."

"Is that important?"

"Well, why did someone try to kill her?"

"I don't know; because she knows something—" He stopped, with an anxious look. "I never thought: they might try again."

"Don't worry about that. Superintendent Forrester has promised—"

"But you said the police think Timmy did it."

"So they do. That won't prevent them from taking due precaution."

"Do they still—?"

"They have a little new evidence." He outlined the chemist's story and added, bluntly, "Not proof of anything, of course. But not a good thing, in the circumstances." Paul took his time considering this, but maintained his air of serenity. Antony said, into the silence, "If you want the rest of the family news: Timmy has left home, and is living in lodgings in Earl's Court."

"I suppose things were pretty difficult at home."

"I imagine so. He assures me his means are adequate for the present, so there's nothing for you to worry about there."

"Very well." Paul was still unnaturally calm. He added, with something near amusement, "While you're in such an informative mood, how is Ann? And Audrey?"

There were limits, Antony felt, beyond which frankness should not be expected. "Both well," he replied cautiously. "Audrey has broken her engagement."

For the first time that morning Paul Herron seemed moved by this announcement. He looked at his visitor in a considering way, and then said abruptly, "So . . . if I were free—" He looked away again, at the dusty window, and the grey walls beyond. "I suppose you think," he added wearily, "that this is neither the time nor the place to be thinking about girls."

"It all depends—"

"Well, would you . . . if you were me?"

"I shouldn't," said Antony, with sudden exasperation, "have got engaged to the wrong girl in the first place." The other seemed a little taken aback by this bluntness, but said mildly, after a moment's pause:

"It seemed a good thing to do at the time; and Audrey was going to marry Brent."

"Well, if you think I'm going to involve myself," said Antony tartly, "you'd better think again. You'll have plenty of time to sort your own muddles out later on."

Paul smiled at him. "I suppose it will have to be done. If the occasion offers . . . and do you think it will?"

"That brings us back to where we left off last time," said Antony. Paul's eyes shifted; he said evasively:

"You haven't told me—"

There had been, Antony considered, quite enough delay in reaching the point of his visit. The subject was, besides, one he particularly disliked; all the more reason for introducing it without delay. He said firmly, "I want to know what you remember about the night your parents died."

"I told you . . . nothing!" Paul's tone remained calm, but still he did not look at his companion.

"Have you thought about it at all since we were here on Tuesday?"

"I wish you'd tell me; why do you want to know?"

"May the Lord give me patience! What difference does that make?"

"A good deal, I should have thought."

"Then listen to me for a moment! I want to know because I think the information might be of help to my uncle in planning your defence; you've been charged with murder—remember?—and if we can't put up a more effective defence than your unsupported story of what you were doing on the scene of the crime the jury will think you mad . . . and guilty *because* you're mad." He paused. Paul was looking at him now, and his breath was coming more quickly, but he made no comment, and his look was questioning. "I understand, only too well, that there are things it's easier to forget. I don't enjoy badgering you—"

"I'm sorry," said Paul.

"Then, try to think—"

"I was only six years old, you know."

"Yes, I know. I can believe, very easily, that you remember nothing to the point. But you must have *some* recollection, and until I know—"

"But what is the point?" He sounded at once stubborn and apologetic.

"I don't think your grandfather was the intended victim." Paul looked up quickly. "So I'm looking for a motive for someone to have killed Uncle William."

"Why should anyone want to? He hadn't been home—"

"He hadn't been home for eighteen years. He hadn't been home since your parents died. You saw him that night, do you remember that?"

"I . . . I think—"

"And if you don't care about yourself, you might spare a thought for your brother."

"Timmy? You think they'll accuse him of trying to kill Aunt Marian?"

"I'm damned sure of it. If you're convicted, they'll arrest him for that. If you're acquitted, on the other hand—"

"Well?"

"They'll charge him with the whole works. Killing Uncle William, and the other." He paused, seeing Paul's stricken look. "I'm sorry," he added, more gently. "But if you think about it you'll see the argument: if he shot your uncle and you were blamed, it would explain why he tried to prove your innocence by such drastic measures. A student of logic wouldn't think much of that train of reasoning. But it wouldn't be difficult to impress a jury with it."

Paul was horrified now, and made no attempt to conceal what he was feeling. "Oh, my God," he said. "I didn't know." And put up a hand to hide his eyes.

It was an hour later when Antony left the prison. Outside the gate the world looked unfamiliar. He found his hands were shaking, and shoved them angrily into the pockets of his raincoat. There should be a taxi if he walked towards the main road. He became aware of a figure at his elbow, and turning saw, without surprise, that Timmy Herron had fallen into step beside him.

"I was waiting," said Timmy. "How is Paul?"

Antony laughed. "As well as can be expected," he said; and became aware of his companion's curious look. "I've been conducting an experiment," he explained. "I find I haven't the stomach for it."

"You'd better come in here and have a drink," said Timmy, practically. He indicated a dingy café, and added hastily, seeing Antony's look of revulsion, "It's warm in there, and you can drink Bovril if you don't care to risk the coffee; and nobody'll look at you."

"Admirable," said Antony. He essayed a smile, and Timmy pushed open the door invitingly. There was a rush of warm air; a smell in the dark little room that was indescribable, but not unpleasant. They took a table by the window, and presently a fat man in a greasy apron (who seemed to recognise Timmy) brought thick mugs full of hot Bovril which he placed before them with an air of respectful sympathy.

Antony laughed again, and put out his hands to warm them round the mug. Timmy, hearing this time a note of genuine amusement, relaxed his watchful look and leaned back in his chair. He said, after a moment: "You didn't answer my question. At least, not properly."

"How is your brother? Honestly, Timmy, I don't know how to answer that."

"What's the matter?" He was anxious, suddenly; more than that, perhaps . . . afraid. "He hasn't . . . ? He isn't. . . ?"

"He told me this morning what he remembers of the night your parents died; and it is a good deal more than you were able to tell me."

"But I didn't know—"

"I made him think about it, for the first time. God knows if I was justified."

Timmy hesitated, and finally said, as though he were half afraid of the question, "Didn't it help?"

"I don't know. He confirmed what I suspected, that's helpful, I suppose. But as for proof—"

"I see." Timmy was very pale now. "I expect you mean they were murdered," he said, and he spoke as if every word were an effort. "It's funny, really; that doesn't seem to matter now."

"At least," said Antony, with more energy, "it has laid this insanity nonsense once and for all."

"Yes, of course. But proving it, I mean. If Sir Nicholas can get Paul out of this mess, I wouldn't care about that."

Antony looked at him in silence, but his thoughts approached panic. He was aware that he had identified himself foolishly, uselessly, with Paul's struggles to remain (however uncomfortably) oblivious of the past; now he must face the realisation that if Paul were to go free it would be at Timmy's expense. Short of proof to the contrary he could see no way out of that. "There's got to be proof," he said at last, aloud.

"That doesn't seem so easy." Timmy seemed puzzled by his vehemence.

Antony drank some of the Bovril, and said with a fair attempt at a normal tone, "Horton tells me you came through your interview yesterday pretty well."

"Did he think so? I didn't enjoy it much," said Timmy. "Come to think of it, it isn't the sort of thing that really happens . . . all this."

"And it won't now!" Antony set down his mug with a thump on the damp-circled table top and spoke with sudden decision. "You haven't been home, have you?" he inquired.

"No. I couldn't!"

"Couldn't you, Timmy?"

"I . . . well, if I had to."

"It may not be necessary. Have you any news this morning of Aunt Marian?"

"They want to send her home at the week-end. The police have talked to her, I think; but they won't let anyone else." He was drawing with his spoon on the stained table, but looked up anxiously as he spoke. "Do you suppose she's still in danger?"

"Well, if they send her home."

"Then I'll have to go back, of course."

"I admit, I'd like you to. On the other hand, if anything happened to her it might be better for you to be out of the way."

Timmy shrugged. "And live with myself afterwards. No, thank you."

"Very well, then. But keep in touch, whatever you do." He got up as he spoke, and pulled out a handful of change; regarding it blankly, and then selecting a florin with an air of great preoccupation. "I'm meeting Bellerby for lunch," he added. "And afterwards I've an appointment to meet your cousin Manuel Calleya. If we can find a taxi, I'll give you a lift back to town."

"A penny saved is a penny earned," said Timmy. "I say, do you think Manuel will be received into the family circle? After all, Grandfather *is* his uncle!"

"So he is. How distressing for both of them. But I think it very unlikely—"

"I do wish Grandfather were human," said Timmy, crossly. "He seems to have no natural curiosity at all!"

Senhor Manuel da Costa Calleya spread his hands and eyed Antony apologetically. He was a dapper little man, and Antony was amused to observe in him something of the look of old Ambrose Cassell underlying the mannerisms of his native land. "What can I say, *senhor?* How can I help you?"

"If you can suggest, *senhor,* some motive for his death?"

"Nada nao! Who should wish to kill him? And who in England, where he has not been for so long?"

Antony shrugged, in unconscious parody of the other's gesture. "You see, *senhor,* I do not know; and so I come to you."

"There is nobody. Once perhaps, but now—"

"Once?"

"Ah, *senhor!"* His eyes were wide and mournful. "You ask me for my family secrets, my bones in the closet. But perhaps already this so-helpful *Senhor* Bellerby has told you that William Cassell was my father."

"I understand you were the principle beneficiary under his will," said Antony, with caution.

"Then all explains itself." Manuel evidently took this for agreement, and appeared to be gratified, rather than otherwise. He peered anxiously at his companion. *"Combinado?"* he queried.

"Well," said Antony. "As a matter of fact, no."

"No?" said the other, sadly. He reflected. "There is no scandal, you understand. My mother died when I was born;

her husband is my father while he lives, but perhaps, once, he has not been happy because of this.''

''Perhaps not.'' Antony could not keep a touch of dryness from his tone. Manuel smiled at him, with amused self-deprecation.

''This is not helpful, I know. She is dead since many years; and though there are relations, also . . . as I have said, there is no scandal. Why should they care?''

''Why, indeed. But I have thought, *senhor,* that perhaps William Cassell, spoke to you of his family here in England.''

''But, of course. They are, after all, my kinsfolk. Then, too, he was pleased to tell his brother of my existence: I think this 'Uncle Ambrose' has his shirt stuffed, as you say; he is, too, a hypocrite . . . of that I am sure.''

''And the others, *senhor?''*

''My cousin, Gregory—he is dull, I think. But Marian, who is now so ill, her I should like to know. My father laughs at her, always; but he loves her too.'' He stopped, and again favoured his companion with the full melancholy of his expressive brown eyes. Antony said quickly:

''She is recovering, I believe.''

''So I am told.'' He seemed cheered by the thought, and went on briskly, ''And that is all of the family, *senhor.* The children, after all, he does not know.''

''But he knew his niece, Ruth, and her husband. Surely he spoke of them?''

''Oh yes, indeed. It was a sad memory of his last visit here, he spoke of it often.''

''Can you remember, *senhor,* when first he heard what had happened?'' Antony did not trouble to hide his anxiety, and Manuel looked at him curiously.

''Twenty years ago . . . was it not? But yes, I remember.''

''Then—''

''You wish that I tell you? He returned from his trip (that was not long after I first made my home with him), and there were tales to tell; you can imagine, *senhor.* I do not know whether I remember the things he told me then, or what he has said to me later when we spoke of his family here. He was fond of both his nieces; and there were the three children, the twins and the older boy.'' He stopped, and again gave Antony the odd, apologetic look which was so much at variance with his rather ebullient manner. ''I think he delighted in them, and buying toys for them, because in *my* childhood, *senhor,* he could have no part.''

''And when the news came—?''

''It was . . . stunning. How could it be else?''

''Did he tell you of the last time he saw Matthew and Ruth Herron?''

''The evening before he left he was with them. And the brother, too, was there. He left them all together, and never thought that all was not well with them.''

''It was never suggested that he should come back to give evidence?''

''But what could he tell? He knew nothing!''

Antony got up suddenly, and the restless movement brought his companion's eyes sympathetically on him. ''There is something you wish me to tell you? But I do not know—''

''It's so long ago! It doesn't seem worth while—''

''If it will help you, let us explore further.'' Antony looked at him with wonder.

''You are the first person, *senhor,* who has not asked me . . . why . . . why . . . why. . .?''

''But you have told me you wish to help the young man, my cousin Paul Herron.'' He stumbled on the name, but went on without regarding its difficulty. ''And if I should know more, surely you will tell me.''

Antony grinned at him, and came to sit down again. *''Muito obrigado, senhor!* Let us by all means explore together!''

''But it wasn't much use, really,'' he said that evening, in Sir Nicholas's study. ''He was the soul of patience, and was able to tell me a great deal about Uncle William's visit to England when asked the right questions.''

Sir Nicholas looked up at his nephew, who had taken his favourite position on the hearth-rug. ''Nothing to the point, however?'' he asked.

''I heard again about the ring he gave Ruth, and the teddy-bears for the twins. Aunt Marian had a dressing-case, and Brent had Meccano: I won't weary you with the rest of the list.''

"Good," approved Sir Nicholas.

"I learned too of old Ambrose's reaction to William's revelation that his son was living with him." He broke off, and grinned at his uncle. "That was a comic set-up, sir. The relationship was generally known, but there was no scandal because it was never admitted!"

"Very proper."

"Well, Ambrose moralised, I gather; and William retaliated by disagreeing with the firm's policy. Not that he'd a leg to stand on there, after all, he made his home abroad of his own choice. There seems to have been a good deal of heat generated on both sides: but nothing, you know, to lead to murder, eighteen years later."

"It certainly seems unlikely—"

"There was just one thing, not worth mentioning really. Matt and Ruth lived on the third floor of a block of flats at Putney; Manuel says that as he left that evening Uncle William saw a man coming up the stairs on to the landing. He remembered because there was a lift, so it seemed a bit odd. But the man might have been going farther up; or to one of the other flats on the same floor."

"And, of course, it wasn't anyone he knew?"

"Well, no. I think he might have considered that worth mentioning, don't you? For the rest, I heard a good deal about Uncle William, and what he meant to do *this* trip, poor old boy. Manuel's a nice chap, and pretty upset about the whole thing. I'm glad to think he now owns William's share in the firm; not a very large one, as it happens, but at least old Ambrose won't be able to wash his hands of the whole connection."

Sir Nicholas sat up. "Talking of 'the firm', there's a nice little Madeira I'd like you to try." He twisted in his chair to look across at a side table. "I told Gibbs . . . yes, it is there. Do you mind—"

"It's a pleasure." Antony's tone was absent. He returned a moment later with two glasses, and stood looking at his uncle in a troubled way, holding the wine just beyond his reach. "You were carrying on the other evening about the prospect of making a satisfactory defence, sir. I like the prospects even less, now.'' He looked down, and seemed surprised to see the glasses he was holding. He handed one to his uncle, and placed his own on the mantelpiece.

Sir Nicholas sipped his wine, and put the glass down carefully on the table at his elbow. "What, especially, is troubling you?" he inquired.

Antony gestured with his left hand; an indecisive movement, very expressive of his state of mind. "I have what we need, but I don't see my way," he said.

"You have intimated before that you know who killed William Cassell," said Sir Nicholas, unmoved.

"I have thought I did for some time; what Paul had to say confirmed it. But how can we use that? The memories of a child of six . . . the evidence of a man on trial for his life!"

"As you say, these things are of no use to us."

"Well, I must tell you, sir, I don't expect now to get any further confirmation of what really happened. We can bring evidence to show that Paul's sleep-walking story *could* be true; we can prove that other people knew where the rifle was; we can probably make the court believe that the blurring of the fingerprints on the rifle *could* have been caused by someone handling it with gloved hands. And where will all that get us?"

"There is still the possibility of a further report from the inquiry agents."

"But proof, Uncle Nick! It isn't even enough, now, if we manage to get Paul off. I don't need to tell you that."

"No, I had appreciated Timmy's position. I think it possible we should approach the police in this, you know, even at the risk of revealing the slenderness of our case."

"Yes, I've thought of that. But I don't know—"

"It offends every instinct," agreed his uncle. "And I'm inclined to think they'd laugh at us. But short of definite proof, all this would be dynamite as part of a defence."

"I know it never goes down well, to try to shift the blame," said Antony gloomily. He paused, listening. "I wonder if that's Jenny. She said she wouldn't be late."

"If it is Jenny," said Sir Nicholas, picking up his glass again, "she seems to have someone with her."

Antony started across the room, but the door opened before he reached it. Jenny came in, and behind her was Ann Barclay.

"We met on the doorstep," Jenny explained. "I thought most likely you'd still be talking."

"How well you know us." Sir Nicholas came to his feet, and smiled encouragingly at Ann. "Come over to the fire, my dear. You look cold."

Ann came forward slowly. She was nervous, but trying hard to hide it. "It's nice to see a fire," she said. "I don't know, perhaps I shouldn't have come." Her hands were shaking, and she clasped them on her lap as she seated herself. Antony took his glass from the mantelpiece and handed it to her.

"I haven't touched it . . . it'll warm you up," he remarked. "Will you borrow Uncle Nick's, Jenny. Gibbs doesn't seem to have allowed for you."

"And, of course, you daren't ring for him," said Jenny, scornfully.

"My dear, it's ten o'clock!"

Jenny laughed. "Well, I know where they're kept."

When she returned a few minutes later she found the two men were giving the visitor the benefit of their undivided attention. Ann was sitting rather straight in her easy-chair; and, having evidently drunk a little of the wine, was looking somewhat flushed. She was saying, "I made an excuse to work late to-night; so I had a key, and I went back after everyone had gone. I thought perhaps it would be better than Saturday morning, but I didn't really like it much, on my own there. And it was stuffy and dirty downstairs, I didn't stop to wash." Ann held out a pair of undeniably grubby hands, and looked up at Sir Nicholas apologetically.

"But did you—?" said Antony. He stopped as his uncle scowled at him.

"It took ages," said Ann. "And all the time I didn't think it would be there." Antony moved restlessly, and she added, "I'm sorry, Mr. Maitland. Only, I don't—"

"You have no need to be afraid of what you have to tell us, Miss Barclay," said Sir Nicholas, gently.

"I didn't tell Timmy I was going back to-night," said Ann, inconsequently. "I said I was going to wash my hair. And now . . . I don't know how to tell him. Or how to tell you. But I must, because of Paul." She shivered, and drank the rest of the wine, and set down the glass firmly. "I'd better explain," she said.

None of the others spoke. She looked from one to other of them, and then went on with more decision. "The letter was filed at the office because he had written a long one about business before the news came, I took a copy of page three, you'll see some of it is business, then he says he'd just heard the news; it sounds as if he was so shocked he hardly knew what he was doing." She was fumbling in her handbag as she spoke, and now produced a folded sheet of rather stiff paper. She held this out to Antony, who was nearest. "There!" she said. And began to cry.

When Jenny and Sir Nicholas between them had coped with the situation, and Ann had been sent home in a taxi, uncle and nephew were left regarding each other across the rather badly-made photostat.

Antony said, disgustedly, "And no help, really. Confirmation to us . . . not proof for a jury."

Sir Nicholas looked at him with rather a twisted smile. "Proof enough for that poor child," he said. He thought for a moment, and then went on briskly. "The situation is rapidly becoming intolerable. I think . . . I really think you must take drastic action of some kind to-morrow!"

CHAPTER 18

IT WAS IN pursuance of this advice that Antony found himself, at ten o'clock the following morning, greeting Superintendent Forrester in the latter's room at Scotland Yard. The detective received him with his customary placidity; and though he demonstrated his surprise it was in the gentlest way. "No more complaints, I hope, Mr. Maitland. I think your instructing solicitor has a very fair picture—"

"No complaints at all, Superintendent. I'm here off the record, so to speak." He looked round, carefully, and added with a grin, " 'Are we alone, and unobserved?' "

"You alarm me." Forrester did not sound perturbed. "Perhaps I should have asked Inspector Conway to join us."

"I think," said Antony hastily, "we'll do very well as we are. It's about Miss Marian Cassell."

Forrester picked up a pencil, and twisted it between his fingers. His eyes were alert now, and perhaps a little angry. "Is it, indeed?" he asked. "I'm not likely to be taken in a second time on *that* score, Mr. Maitland."

Antony frowned. This wasn't going to be easy. "I can't let that pass, Superintendent. Taken in?"

"You know well enough what I mean, I believe."

"I know what you *think* you mean. Strange as it may seem, the request I made to you was made in good faith; I thought it necessary that Miss Cassell should have protection; and I still think so . . . if you're interested."

"Frankly, I'm not." Forrester was blunt. "What happened must be obvious to any unbiased person. And I'm no fonder than the next man of being made a fool of."

"I see. However, that's beside the point."

"Perhaps if you told me—"

"In view of what you say, it may not be necessary to trouble you. Am I to take it you have removed all surveillance from Miss Cassell?"

Forrester leaned forward, and eyed him closely. "You want to see her . . . is that it?"

"Yes."

"Well, I've no one with her now, Mr. Maitland. But the hospital authorities have refused to allow visitors—"

"That was at your instigation, surely?"

"I admit to having taken certain action in the matter, after we talked on the telephone." His tone implied regret, and still, faintly, annoyance. Antony grinned at him.

"And having put ideas into the heads of the hospital authorities, you cannot now remove them. What fun!" he said.

"I'm afraid I don't share your amusement, Mr. Maitland."

Antony got up. "Now you're cross," he complained. "Well, it seems I must try my powers of persuasion on the doctors—"

The detective looked at his watch, and came to his feet in his turn. "Unless you're very quick . . . in fact, I don't think you can possibly do it. They're sending her home at eleven o'clock." His ill-humour seemed to have vanished. He sounded smug. "So you'll have to exercise your wiles on Mr. Ambrose Cassell, I'm afraid."

"Hell and damnation!" Antony turned back, and his consternation was very evident. "Look here, Superintendent—"

Forrester spread his hands. "What can I do, Mr. Maitland? No doubt Mr. Cassell—"

"You know perfectly well I'm *non persona grata* at The Laurels." He was beyond fencing now.

The detective replied, and did not trouble to hide his amusement. "You will, of course, be entitled to see a copy of any statement she makes to the police: but only if your client is charged with the attempt on her life."

"You won't ask her the right questions." He had thrust his hands into his pockets, and was striding about the room as he spoke.

"We shall do our poor best," said Forrester, with spurious meekness.

"No doubt." Antony came to a halt beside the desk, and glowered at his companion. "You won't ask her, however, about the events of eighteen years ago."

Whatever Forrester had expected, it was not this. He sat down again, suddenly, and looked up at his visitor blankly. "Whatever you mean," he said presently, "you can't mean you're going back to the idea of Paul Herron being insane?"

"No, I am not," snapped Antony; and was momentarily too angry to consider the wisdom (or otherwise) of the course he was taking. "If you'll take that d-damned grin off your f-face, I'll tell you what I *am* doing." (Which was a fine piece of injustice, as Forrester was now perfectly serious.)

"I should be glad to hear."

"Well, then: I want to know why Matthew, Ruth, and Mark Herron were killed, eighteen years ago. And I want to know what Uncle William knew about it . . . at least, I do know, but I'd like to be able to prove it." He stopped short, glaring at the detective, who said invitingly:

"Having gone so far—"

"I may as well go all the way? Well, why not?" He hooked the chair towards him with his foot, and sat down again with his elbows on the desk. "I said I couldn't prove it, but I'm going to," he said. "And you're going to help me!"

"Am I?" queried Forrester faintly.

"Certainly." He paused, and gave the detective a friendly grin. "I say, Superintendent, I *am* glad you didn't have Inspector Conway in! He makes me nervous," he complained.

It was nearly twelve-thirty when he came out again into Whitehall, and almost at once he caught sight of Timmy Herron, who was standing watching the gateway with an expression at once hopeful and apprehensive. He joined him, and inquired, "Are you tailing me, by any chance? And if so, what if I'd come out on to the Embankment?"

"Well, I had to risk that." Timmy's grin was disarming, but he was still doubtful of his reception. "I went round to

Kempenfeldt Square, and Mrs. M. told me where you were. She said to wait, but I thought perhaps . . . and anyway, I felt restless. I hope you don't mind.''

"On the contrary, I want to see you." They fell into step together, and walked up the street.

"Any news?" said Timmy, eagerly. "Or something I can do?"

"The latter, I'm afraid."

"Afraid?" He stopped, and looked at Antony, who took his arm and urged him forward before they caused an obstruction on the crowded pavement. "That means it's something beastly," he added; and his voice was even enough, but did not reflect the attempted lightness of his words.

"Yes," said Antony. "Aunt Marian's going home this morning, and you said—"

They walked on in silence for a moment. "I'm glad, of course," Timmy said at last. "And, of course, I'll go. Only it takes a bit of believing, that someone still wants to hurt her—"

"Then you can take it from me," said Antony bluntly.

"But . . . who? Look here, I've tried not to annoy you by asking questions, but—?"

"Are you aware that you have a very expressive face?"

"No, have I?" Timmy's look was suddenly blank.

"Well, I don't doubt your discretion, my lad, but I wouldn't trust your acting ability any farther than I could throw it."

"I suppose that means, you won't tell me," said Timmy. "Well, what do you want me to do, after I've gone home?"

"Well, mainly, arrange for a gathering of the clans there this evening. Can you do that, do you think?"

Timmy looked doubtful. "Well, I think Uncle Greg and Brent are fixtures for the moment. At least, I can let you know if they'll be in."

"And Barclay, and Wayne?"

"Bob is likely to come in if he knows I'm home again. I could let him know, if you like. As for John, he'll come if he thinks he can see Aunt Marian."

"Then tell him he can."

"I'll phone Ann. But when I rang her this morning she sounded odd."

"I shouldn't worry too much about that."

"But she wasn't at the office, after all."

"No, she found the letter last night. There was nothing we could use, I expect she was disappointed and felt you would be, too."

"Oh, well." Timmy sounded dispirited. "I don't expect it matters, anyway."

"I'll be round this evening, but you don't expect me, of course. And don't let it appear that you're pulling strings—that'd be the end."

"I'll be careful. Let's see: Grandfather, Uncle Greg, Brent, Bob, and John Barclay. Am I supposed to like this?" asked Timmy.

There was no comfortable answer to that. Antony watched him go; and felt, himself, at that moment, uncommonly like a murderer.

At eight o'clock that evening he scrambled out of a taxicab at the gate of The Laurels, and had found change and satisfied the driver by the time Geoffrey Horton joined him in the driveway. The solicitor was inclined to linger as they rounded the corner which brought the house in view, "for it doesn't look," he remarked, "like the sort of place where things happen." But Antony urged him on impatiently.

"Wait till you see the people," he invited.

"I'm all agog." Geoffrey followed obediently, but Antony threw a doubtful look over his shoulder.

"Don't forget I brought you with me to lend an atmosphere of respectability to the proceedings," he warned.

"Trust me." Horton's tone was sober enough, but his companion was aware that he was enjoying the expedition, and was irrationally annoyed by the knowledge.

Rose looked doubtful when Geoffrey asked for Miss Cassell. "I'll have to ask the master, sir," she said.

"Well, tell him I'm Paul Herron's solicitor." Horton produced a card. Rose took it, and stood back to let them enter.

She was gone only a moment. Ambrose Cassell came into the hall at her heels, surveyed the visitors with a marked lack of cordiality, and said at last, "Well?"

Antony achieved a deprecating smile, and waved a hand towards his companion. "We hoped—" he began.

"I'm afraid it is quite impossible for you to see my daughter." The old man turned towards the solicitor, who sustained his hostility calmly enough.

"I should not wish to upset Miss Cassell in any way," he said carefully. "But Dr. Hearn assured me—"

"I'm afraid," said Ambrose Cassell again; and was interrupted this time by Brent, who came out of the drawing-room behind him, and stood lounging in the doorway.

"Perhaps we could help Mr. Horton," he drawled. "After all, he's Paul's solicitor." He glanced briefly in Antony's direction, without obvious unfriendliness. Antony concealed his misgivings, and spoke with enthusiasm.

"That's very kind . . . don't you think so, Horton? I'm sure when we explain to Mr. Cassell—" He was moving across the hall as he spoke. Ambrose gave him an angry look. "Yes, I was sure you'd agree with me," Antony murmured gently and without meaning as he passed. He reached Brent's side, and they stood a moment, their eyes level; and this time the look they exchanged was one of unveiled dislike. Then Brent took a step backward.

"Come right in!" he invited. Antony walked past him into the drawing-room. From the hall he could hear a murmur of voices: Geoffrey 'playing propriety,' he hoped; but his attention was on the three men who looked up as he went in.

John Barclay was there, as he had hoped. He was lounging on the sofa at the far side of the fire-place, and looked as though he had been there for some time; he waved a casual greeting, but his lips tightened ominously and he had a wary look.

Gregory Cassell got up fussily, and murmured what might have been a welcome. He was obviously at a loss what line to take, and relapsed quickly into an unhappy silence, though he continued to hover uncertainly in the middle of the room. Antony's eyes went past him to where Timmy Herron was sitting, a little withdrawn from the others. He had a copy of *Punch* on his knee, obviously for the purpose of camouflage; Antony thought he had rarely

seen an expression at once so controlled and so distressed.
Brent spoke at his shoulder.

"You see our prodigal has returned, Maitland. You find
us celebrating . . . quietly of course, in view of the circumstances. Now I wonder, can you use your influence with my
young cousin here: I believe you are by way of being a
friend of his, and I must admit we are all curious to know
why he has chosen this moment to—er—return to the fold."

"An interesting field for speculation," said Antony
(whose chameleon-like behaviour in the face of other people's mannerisms had often led him into trouble). "Surely,
however, it must be regarded as his own affair?"

"I told you," said Timmy doggedly, his eyes on Brent.
"I ran out of cash."

"Oh, I know what you *said.*" The words were an insult.
Timmy, who could not be accused of any great facility in the
art of prevarication, flushed scarlet; his eyes rested re-
proachfully on Antony's face for a moment, and then he
looked away. Brent shrugged, and turned.

Horton and old Mr. Cassell were talking in low tones, and
Uncle Greg had joined them. Brent moved a little towards
the fire, and said to Barclay, "Maitland came on the same
errand as you did, John. And is equally unfortunate."

Barclay said lightly, "Well, perhaps to-morrow—" and
was interrupted somewhat sharply by his host, who had
broken off his conversation to listen to what they were saying.

"The nurse may agree to a short visit from you to-
morrow, John. But I cannot on any account allow Marian to
be badgered with questions."

Antony said, with sudden earnestness, "One question
only, sir, and I assure you it is of the greatest importance."

"In what way?" The old man was stiff. His son echoed
the query, with a note of querulousness.

"Surely there can be nothing more! And what do you
wish to establish?"

Antony looked round. The room was suddenly silent.
"Well, I know who killed William Cassell," he said, almost apologetically. "I only want proof."

"Very nice," said Robert Wayne, approvingly, from the
doorway. "Dramatic," he added. His eyes sought his

cousin across the room. "I thought I'd better come, Timmy."

Timmy looked sullen. Old Mr. Cassell said testily, "You, I trust, haven't been encouraging this foolishness?"

"On the contrary, I'm very glad to see him home again."

"Rubbish," said Barclay suddenly. "The boy would be better on his own."

"How can you say so?" Brent returned to the conversation, and his tone was sweetness itself. "Away from his loving family?"

Barclay uncoiled himself from the sofa. "Away from his family," he amended. He looked round, from Ambrose Cassell to his son, and then back to Brent again.

Timmy said into the silence, "Aunt Marian—" and Brent swung round on him fiercely.

"I suppose you're going to tell us that's why you came home. As though we'd let you go near her!" Timmy looked at him blankly.

"No, that'd be too much to expect," he said after a moment. And looked at Antony without putting words to the anxious inquiry that was obviously in his mind.

"We might get back to this statement of yours, Maitland." Barclay remained standing, and looked across at him challengingly.

"This has gone far enough." Ambrose Cassell spoke decisively. "I have no interest in this theory, and no intention of allowing you to see my daughter . . . now or any time," he added.

Antony moved to face the old man. "I'm sorry you take that position," he said quietly. "I would have liked to spare your grandson the weeks in prison before the trial can come on; and the additional anguish of the trial itself."

"You are trying to tell me that you can *prove* Paul's innocence?" The old man's tone was incredulous.

"With Miss Cassell's evidence; oh, yes, indeed!"

"I don't believe—"

"Well . . . never mind." He sounded weary. "She'll be called at the trial, you know. And I don't expect we shall find her unwilling to give evidence."

"We shall see!" Old Ambrose was clearly concerned with effect only, blindly indignant that his opinion was being disregarded, and not considering the import of his words.

"May I ask," put in Brent, "whether this defence of yours rests on Aunt Marian's evidence alone?"

"You may, of course." Antony was cordial. He looked at Geoffrey Horton. "But I think enough has been said, don't you?"

"Quite enough." Horton was emphatic.

"I think you're bluffing," said Brent.

"But why should I bother?"

"That's what I'm wondering."

Ambrose Cassell said sharply, "I see no point in this discussion. If Sir Nicholas has finally decided to reject the obvious line of defence, it is difficult to see what other line he can take."

"Maitland says," put in Barclay, from his place near the fire, "that they can prove Paul's innocence."

"Which brings us back to my original query," said Brent. "What other evidence have you, besides what Aunt Marian may (or may not) tell you."

"Enough, at least, to create a 'reasonable doubt'," Antony retorted. He stopped, and looked quickly at Timmy and away again. Horton was tugging at his sleeve.

"Leave it there," said the solicitor urgently.

"Very well." He looked at old Ambrose and added, "But perhaps even you may have second thoughts—"

The old man's hands were shaking. He said, with unusual uncertainty, "But someone tried to kill me—"

"No," said Antony, and turned towards the door.

"Mr. Maitland! I must insist . . . I must ask you to tell me—"

Antony turned slowly. "Somebody was afraid of William Cassell, and that person killed him," he said.

"But he was a stranger here, after so many years—"

"A good many things happened eighteen years ago," said Antony. "For one thing, your daughter was murdered."

Ambrose moved to find a chair and sat down heavily. "But that was all explained," he said.

"Did you never doubt the explanation? Never once, in spite of your surprise at what had happened? Did it never occur to any of you that they might, all three, have been murdered?'' His eyes moved from Ambrose to his son; to Robert Wayne, who was still standing a little apart from the group; to John Barclay who had resumed his comfortable seat on the sofa by the fire.

Barclay muttered, ''No . . . no!'' None of the others spoke. Antony went on:

''Then think about it now. Think of what it would mean to the killer, who had thought himself safe for so long, to know that the one man who could upset that safety was returning to England . . . that he could not avoid a meeting with him . . . and that inevitably he would remember—''

Ambrose looked up, ''You are saying, are you not, that this man is our familiar friend?''

''I am saying,'' said Antony clearly, ''that he is in this room.'' Again his eyes moved from one set face to another. ''Well?'' he said. ''Is that worse than accusing your grandson?''

''I cannot believe—'' The words came stiffly.

''You believed in Paul's guilt. Would it be more unnatural to accuse one of your friends, your son even—?''

''But the boy is mad—'' His tone was almost pleading.

''If I am right about his parents' death, you could have no reason for saying that.''

The old man looked up, and all his assurance had left him. ''What proof have you—?'' he said at last.

Antony said slowly, ''I know a great deal about your affairs . . . eighteen years ago. I know that your firm was in difficulties, that your brother blamed your handling of the business, that you quarrelled.''

Gregory said stiffly, ''This is intolerable—,'' and Antony swung round to face him.

''I know your position at that time, too. You were in need of money, your father could not help you, even if you nerved yourself to appeal to him. Did you do that, I wonder?''

''I—'' said Gregory. He looked at his father who was sitting very still now, only his eyes seeming alive and angry in a face that might have been carved in stone. ''No,'' he added, and shut his mouth with a snap.

"But you weathered the storm," said Antony. "Your associate was not so lucky. Were you, Barclay?"

The artist was feeling among the cushions: a now familiar gesture. He paused to look at Antony . . . angry, merely puzzled? . . . the younger man could not tell. Nor was his voice any clue when he said evenly, "That's a long time ago, Maitland."

"My point precisely," said Antony.

"I was bankrupt . . . my wife died . . . does that help you?" he asked abruptly.

"There was a good deal of ill-luck about just then," said Antony. "You were in trouble too, were you not?" he said to Wayne.

"As you see." Wayne smiled his twisted smile. "I've no doubt you know my story."

"Well!" Antony paused to reflect for a moment. "You can see that I wanted a motive . . . for the killing of three people. When I heard about your burglary it seemed too obvious . . . and then I learned the diamonds which formed the largest part of your stock had not been insured."

"Which left me again without a motive. How distressing for you," said Wayne lightly. Gregory said suddenly, as though he had not been listening to this exchange:

"May I ask if you propose to bring all this out at Paul's trial?"

"Only so much as will serve our purpose. And if I get Miss Cassell's evidence . . . I told you (do you remember?) that it might not be necessary to go to court at all."

"But what could she tell you?" Brent's voice was rough.

"She could confirm what Uncle William said in his letter to you sir." Ambrose Cassell looked up at him, and said doubtfully:

"You asked about that letter—"

"And now I have a copy of it. Besides the matter on which I want Miss Cassell's confirmation, it tells us what Uncle William saw as he left the Herrons' flat on his last night in England."

"But he knew nothing—"

"Didn't he, Mr. Cassell? He saw the murderer . . . that night."

"He would have said—"

"He thought nothing of it at the time . . . he said in his letter he had seen nobody as he left, *except* a man who was coming up the stairs to the third floor."

"But why should he have thought—?"

"He didn't. As you say, why should he?"

Barclay said, frowning, "Are you asking us to believe that he saw the murderer; and that, after all this time, this man thought he might be recognised?"

"I'm telling you," said Antony positively.

"But he knew us all; and someone he didn't know he couldn't possibly have recognised later—" His voice died. He sat up suddenly, and looked around at the others.

"Precisely, Mr. Barclay." Antony spoke very quietly now. "There was one person he didn't know; and that person of sufficiently distinctive appearance to fear recognition, even after so long."

There was a silence; there was disbelief, and doubt, and hostility. There was fear too, but it was well hidden. The man with the disfigured face gave back look for horrified look, and then turned back to Antony.

"Prove it!" said Robert Wayne.

CHAPTER 19

THE SILENCE lengthened. Old Mr. Cassell got up slowly. "Robert—?" he said, questioningly.

Wayne looked at him, and laughed angrily. "No, of course I'm not admitting it," he said. "But I'd like to hear more of this . . . this fabrication—"

Barclay was frowning. "You can't stop there, you know," he pointed out. "You have made an accusation—"

"In point of fact, that isn't true. You made certain objections to my theory, and I pointed out there was one person to whom those objections did not apply. But I'll be pleased to go further if you wish; on the understanding that it is an intellectual exercise only, and that I am not responsible for any conclusions you may draw." He looked around at the company. "Well?" he asked.

"I think we must ask you to continue," said Ambrose Cassell.

Antony took his time looking around him. Horton was anxious, but met his look with one of encouragement. Old Ambrose seemed bewildered; Gregory had the appearance of one who has been affronted; Brent, for once, looked wholly serious, and almost as puzzled as his grandfather. John Barclay was sitting up now, and his eyes were alert; Wayne had a wary look, but was discouragingly calm. Timmy, more shocked than any of them, met his friend's look with one of appeal. Antony shook his head at him, and turned back to his audience.

"To go back to the beginning: I started out, as all of you did, with a strong prejudice in favour of Paul's guilt. Even then I would have been happier about it, if he had killed the right man; but as he was reported insane that didn't worry me too much. But it wasn't going to be easy to prove; all I could get were unsupported allegations of his oddness, nothing to back them up; only the sleep-walking, and that might be taken as confirming his own story. So I wondered—" Timmy made an abrupt movement, and knocked an ash-tray off the table at his elbow. Nobody even looked in his direction.

"Well, I started inquiring into the death of Matthew and Ruth Herron. I can understand that nobody doubted the obvious solution at the time; murder is outside most people's calculations. But here was I, with an undoubted murder in mind; and the old affair just didn't make sense. Looked at coldly, which was more likely: that a normal, happily-married man should up and shoot his wife and brother? Or that the three of them should have been the victims of some other person? Fantastic, perhaps. But so was the alternative.

"So there were the rest of the family to think about; and any friends sufficiently intimate—"

"Anyone could have shot him through the window," said Timmy. "Or do you mean, sufficiently intimate to have a motive?"

"Well, barring a maniac, he wasn't shot by a stranger," agreed Antony. "But really I was thinking of the rifle; somebody had to know about that, and whether Grandfather or Uncle William were the victim, someone had to know the ways of the family."

"Yes, I see," said Timmy. He put up a hand to cover his eyes.

"On the score of opportunity, if I ruled out Paul his cousin Brent was the most likely suspect. But he was another member of the younger generation, and certainly couldn't have had a motive for murdering Uncle William—"

"Thank you," said Brent, with something of a return of his former manner.

"Next, Grandfather could have done it. But if the motive lay in the events of eighteen years ago, it was hard to visualise any knowledge Uncle William might have had about his brother which would suddenly have become dangerous because he was coming home; and the more I thought about it, the more I saw that applied to the other people he had known. But, what could a stranger have against him?

"So I thought about possible motives, and I didn't get very far at first. Uncle William had been at the Herron flat the night they died; but if he knew something it must have been some fact not obviously incriminating. His evidence was not available. There was some talk of a letter, but it seemed to be missing. And the twins remembered little or nothing of what had happened."

Timmy said accusingly, "But you said—" and Antony answered without looking at him:

"Yes, but that was later. Just then I was thinking about motives: suppose Uncle William had seen somebody. And I made the same objections you did, Mr. Barclay. And answered them as I did just now."

Barclay nodded. "As I did, also," he admitted. "But I don't agree with your premises; not yet."

"Nor did I, at the point I am speaking of. I considered possible motives for killing the Herron family, and first I thought I'd found one if the burglary at the Hatton Garden premises was part of an insurance swindle. Only the greater part of the booty wasn't insured."

"I don't see how you got round that one," said Brent. "Even as an 'intellectual exercise'."

"But I think your father does; don't you, sir?" Gregory Cassell made an indeterminate gesture. "Well, I'll tell you what I thought about it: I thought, here were three men, well known to each other, and all in financial straits at the same time. Admittedly, the thirties weren't easy; but you, Mr. Cassell, had a salary which should have taken care of your needs; and you, Mr. Barclay, went bankrupt, which suggested business dealings of some kind. Certainly dealings outside your own career as an artist. So I wondered—"

Gregory found his voice. "That was acute of you," he said. "When Bob told us he had the chance of doing a good deal in diamonds, but hadn't cash for the stones he needed, John and I found the money for him."

"He put up one third himself," said Barclay. "I thought he was hit as badly as we were."

"Well, look at it this way. He bought the stones with your money; they were stolen, and as they were uninsured you lost all you'd put in. The fact that there was no insurance prevented any suspicion of fraud. But if the burglary were a fake, *Wayne still had the diamonds.*

"You see, it wasn't an insurance swindle (I think the Herron brothers might have forgiven that, and connived at their cousin's getaway, if not at his retaining the proceeds); but it was a deliberate betrayal of familiar friends. And then there was the night-watchman."

"Yes, the fire. That doesn't tie in, surely."

"I think it was an accident, and I think the watchman saw it and came haring in to see what was up and found Wayne on the point of leaving. He hadn't the stones on him, of course, they were already stowed away safely; not expecting the fire, he'd been doing whatever was necessary to make the burglary look like an outside job. I don't know what it was caught the watchman's eye, of course, and made him suspicious. It was the act of a desperate man to shoot him, and I think afterwards he was dragged to the room he was found in to suggest the story that eventually gained credence—that he was part of the burglary. But by that time the fire had got too strong a hold, and nearly disposed of Wayne as well."

"But then—" Gregory glanced at Wayne, and said with a return of his former uncertainty, "But I don't want to seem to suggest . . . I was only wondering—"

"As I am," said Wayne, cordially. "First we have 'if' and 'suppose'; and now we've reached the coincidences. However, it's ingenious. You must admit that."

"I'm glad to be amusing you," said Antony. Up to this moment he had been sustained to some degree by excitement, but now he felt chilled and uneasy. "Shall I go on?" he inquired. And there was in his voice no betrayal of his thoughts; nothing but a mild politeness, as he might have asked, perhaps, if he was boring the company.

There was no reply to that, only an uneasy exchange of glances between Gregory and his son. After a moment's hesitation old Mr. Cassell nodded abruptly, and Antony went on with his tale.

"Well . . . there could be a motive in all that, if either Matthew or Mark Herron had got wind of what had happened. An unsatisfactory state of affairs, until to-day.'' He paused, and looked round; Timmy said hoarsely:

''What happened to-day?''

''I read a further report from the firm of private detectives who were employed by Horton in this connection. One of them has talked to the man who investigated the robbery and the fire on behalf of the insurance company. He hadn't much to say about it, only he had his doubts. But because only part of the stock was insured; and because there was no indication whatever of arson, the company preferred to pay up rather than start a full-scale inquiry. However, there was just one interesting point: this man knew Mark Herron well, as a business acquaintance; though there's nothing to show that he knew of the relationship between him and Wayne. If ever he spoke to him of his doubts, it's obvious that Mark, with his more intimate knowledge of his cousin's affairs, would have been well placed to find out what had really happened.

''However, long before all that came up there was the attempt on Miss Cassell's life. That was a bit of a facer, it didn't seem to fit in either with the police theory of the first crime, or with my alternative. The police, however, were able to evolve a theory which dovetailed neatly enough into their solution of William Cassell's death. And I, of course, also thought up for myself an explanation in accord with my own ideas. I had, I think, evoked a certain amount of consternation with my inquiries; whoever the murderer was, it must now be apparent to him that I wasn't going to take Paul's guilt for granted, and I'm very much afraid that my expressed intention of asking Aunt Marian for more information was the cause of her life being in danger. Ironically, at that time my questions could hardly have elicited any useful replies, as I had very little idea to what points they should be directed.''

Gregory Cassell said, in his worried way, ''If Marian had known anything, she would have been only too happy to tell you.''

''The fault was mine, sir; I didn't know the right questions to ask.''

''But now you do?'' said Brent. There was a trace of a

sneer in his tone, but Antony was inclined to put it down to habit rather than to any present intention to annoy.

"I think I do," he admitted. He looked at Wayne, and added deliberately, "I want to ask her exactly when Uncle William gave Ruth his parting present—?" Wayne made a sudden movement, and was still again. Timmy looked at him, and then at Antony, and asked:

"What was it?"

"An opal ring; her birthstone." He looked at old Ambrose, who said in a strained voice:

"It was on her hand . . . I had never seen it before."

"Well, I don't know, of course, what Miss Cassell will have to say about it; but the letter mentions the gift, and the inference is that it was given at their last meeting. And Paul remembers quite well that after Uncle William had given the twins their presents he took a little box out of his pocket; and he remembers his mother's face as she opened it, and how she held out her hand to admire the ring on her finger—"

Timmy said abruptly, "I can't stand this! I—"

"You must. You told me once that Uncle William had brought presents for you the last time—"

"That won't help you," said Barclay, suddenly. "They were only six years old."

"That's why I want Miss Cassell's evidence. And if she confirms what her uncle seems to say in his letter—"

"Well, what then?"

Antony smiled. He was beginning to feel sick, partly with apprehension, partly with a kind of queer regret for the part he was playing; but he smiled and said, reflectively, "Nobody could have known of the ring except from Uncle William, or from seeing it on Ruth's hand. Wayne never knew William Cassell, he told me so on at least two occasions; and he said he did not go to the Herrons' flat on the day they died. But he described the ring quite graphically to me, and to my uncle."

Wayne said, "You're mistaken." It was, perhaps, something to have provoked him to denial; but he still looked calm enough.

Antony shook his head. "I'm right . . . or I'm lying. But Aunt Marian may not remember, you know."

"Oh yes, she will," said Brent. "A thing like that—"

"That's what I hope, of course."

"And is that all of this . . . this fairy-tale?" inquired Wayne.

"Not quite. I didn't mention the other thought I had when Aunt Marian was poisoned; I thought that anyone in the family would have known of the doctor's prescription; so that perhaps the man we were looking for was one with familiar knowledge of her ways, which was, even so, not quite up to date."

"Fanciful!" said Wayne. And laughed.

"Perhaps so. It is fortunate I don't set much store on it," said Antony. Wayne's laughter, disconcertingly, had a ring of genuine amusement. "There is still what Paul remembers."

Old Mr. Cassell got up then, and went out without a word. Gregory turned as if to follow, and Brent put a hand on his arm to detain him. Barclay said, "You spoke of that before. I always thought—"; and Timmy moved a little nearer to the rest of the group. Wayne's eyes were watchful, but his expression did not betray him. Only his hands clenched as he listened; Antony watched them as he spoke . . . and wondered—

"I persuaded Paul to tell me what he knew. That was yesterday. He didn't want to tell me." He sounded matter-of-fact, but in his ears was still the sound of Paul's voice hurrying desperately over his story; as though now, after so long a delay, it could not too soon be told. "He was excited, that night, and couldn't go to sleep. He heard Uncle William go, and watched through a crack in the door. And just a few minutes later the bell rang, and his father went to the door, and he heard a voice he knew. Your voice, Mr. Wayne."

"He was dreaming," said Wayne, casually.

"It was a vivid dream in that case. He went back to bed then, and he began to get frightened because he heard men's voices, quarrelling." He paused, and frowned, and went on slowly, almost reluctantly, "In a way, that was for him the beginning of fear, that has stayed with him ever since. But then he fell asleep, as children will, and he doesn't know how long it was before something roused him again, or how long after he woke up he heard the front door close. He lay for a long time, too scared to move; and then he got up and went into the sitting-room; and then he went back to bed again.'' Antony found Wayne's eyes fixed on him now intently, and met his look and held it for a long moment before he spoke again. "He says it seemed a long time till morning," he added. And the room was very silent, so that his words seemed to echo there, as though with a life of their own. And then Wayne laughed.

"And what is the next move, Mr. Maitland. Your 'intellectual exercise' hasn't taken us very far, has it? And how will it sound in court?"

Antony was aware of Horton at his elbow; of Gregory Cassell's air of shocked surprise; of Brent's frowning look, and John Barclay's uncharacteristic alertness. And of Timmy Herron, whose face had a greenish pallor, and who sat down suddenly on the arm of the chair beside him, as though his legs would no longer support him. He said evenly, "We've gone far enough, I think. And far enough for the court to take some notice—" He realised as he spoke that Wayne knew he was lying; that even when they had Aunt Marian's evidence, it was feeble enough for all that. Unexpectedly, his present audience were with him; but a jury, in the cold light of reason, would be more likely to think Wayne victimised than guilty. "And you haven't explained—"

"Listen!" said Brent. There were voices in the hall, and the door opened suddenly to show Rose looking scared, and in the hall behind her, as though he had just come down the stairs, Ambrose Cassell.

Rose said, breathlessly, "Mr. Maitland, there's a foreign gentleman—" and the hubbub of voices rose to a crescendo behind her as she spoke.

Antony looked at Horton, "Wait, do you mind?" and then glanced at Brent, who nodded his comprehension of the unspoken appeal and lounged across the room to cover the way to the door. Antony went out, and shut the door firmly behind him.

The scene in the hall ought by rights to have amused him, but he was too worked up to see the funny side just then. Grandfather Cassell was standing at the foot of the stairs, and his expression of concern was overlaid with a look of outrage; inside the front door, Manuel da Costa Calleya waved expressive hands and spoke volubly to Superintendent Forrester, who in his turn looked as near harassed as was possible for one of his somewhat phlegmatic disposition.

"Well, now, Mr. Maitland, it seems to be you this gentleman wants—"

"*Senhor!*" Manuel spun round, and beamed a welcome. "I am come to help you, perhaps you are pleased to see me?" And he darted an indignant look at the old man who was standing, stiffly indignant, at the foot of the stairs.

"*Boas tardes, senhor.*" Antony could not quite conceal his bewilderment, but Ambrose Cassell, in no mood to consider the fine shades of meaning, pounced as soon as he spoke.

"Are you responsible for bringing this person to my house?" he demanded.

Antony turned. "Not precisely, sir. We are acquainted, but I did not hope to have the pleasure of introducing your nephew to you." He turned to Manuel. "Your Uncle Ambrose, *senhor*. And the other is Superintendent Forrester, of the police."

Manuel bowed, suddenly on his dignity. "If I intrude, then I am sorry," he said. "But I have been to your home, *Senhor* Maitland, and when I told him my business with you *Senhor* Harding has sent me to find you. On no account take no for an answer." He spread his hands. "Behold me," he said.

Antony felt a stir of excitement. He looked at the detective, who shrugged and said good-humouredly: "I'm no wiser than you are, Mr. Maitland. I'm here as I promised you, and I found *Senhor* Calleya on the doorstep before me. He seems to have something on his mind."

Old Mr. Cassell exclaimed impatiently, and Antony turned back to him, saying earnestly, "I owe you an explanation, sir. I asked the superintendent to come here because I was afraid . . . because I thought—"

"Mr. Maitland told me he thought there would be another attempt on Miss Cassell's life," Forrester interrupted. "He said her best chance of safety was in certain facts being put before her family. I'd no power to stop him doing what he wanted, though I'm a long way from admitting his justification. But there was just a chance there'd be trouble, so I agreed to come along.''

"I also hoped, to be honest, to get a new light on events. One or two points did emerge, but nothing like legal proof.'' Antony sounded despondent, and Ambrose eyed him curiously.

"Nevertheless, I have spoken to my daughter—''

"Yes, sir?''

"She confirms that Ruth received the opal ring on the day she died. William had shown it to her (to Marian, that is), and told her when he came back from the flat that night of her sister's pleasure in the gift.''

Antony looked at the detective. "Well, Superintendent?''

"Added to what you told me, I find that . . . interesting, Mr. Maitland.''

"No more than that?''

"I grant the ingenuity of the case you have put together; though I suggest that if you, yourself, were concerned to disprove it you could bring a host of arguments to bear on the other side—'' (Antony grinned reluctantly) "—and there is still the undoubted fact that the case against your client is the stronger—''

Manuel had been hovering urgently on the brink of this exchange, eyeing first one and then another of his companions with a bright, inquiring stare. Now he could bear his exclusion no longer, but interrupted explosively, "I do not know why you will not listen to me. *Senhor* Harding has said 'that is proof . . . proof positive'. Do you not wish to see?''

"*Senhor*—?''

"You have been kind enough to tell me, *Senhor* Maitland, what you wished to do for my young cousin, who is now arrested. But you wished proof, you said. Am I not correct?''

"Only too correct,'' said Antony.

"Well then, I help you. I speak on the telephone to my assistant in *Lisboa;* there is this letter you spoke of—if indeed there was business mentioned will there not be a copy?''

Antony frowned, and spoke without thinking. "But my uncle knew—''

"Ah, yes, he told me you had seen the original. But wait, *senhor!* When my assistant had found this copy he spoke to me again, and when I heard what he had to say I told him to come here . . . immediately . . . on an aeroplane." He paused, deliberately dramatic, and his listeners drew a little nearer. Even old Mr. Cassell had forgotten his grievance as his interest grew in what this unlikely nephew of his had to say. "He arrived two hours ago, and brought me . . . this!"

The paper was a little dog-eared, but the carbon impression was clear enough still. Antony took the folded sheets, and opened them slowly. Something there must be, since Manuel knew he had seen the original . . . he seemed to have lost the ability to think; and then he saw, at the bottom of the last page, faint but unmistakable . . . a pencil sketch. He looked up, and the blaze of excitement in his face silenced Manuel, and brought Forrester to his side with a sudden look of eagerness. He held out the paper to the detective.

"There you are, Superintendent. William Cassell tells in that letter of his last visit to his niece and her husband; and he mentions the man he saw as he waited for the lift. And on his copy he drew a sketch, it wasn't a face he was likely to forget, and I was told he had a gift for taking a likeness."

Ambrose Cassell said, "May I see, Superintendent?" and turned away with a look of distress as the detective held up the tattered sheet. William Cassell had had a decisive way with a pencil, there was no mistaking the subject of his sketch.

"I'd better be having a talk with Mr. Robert Wayne," said Forrester heavily. And crossed to open the drawing-room door. Antony hesitated only a moment, and then followed him. This was what he had worked for, after all; and now it must be gone through.

CHAPTER 20

IT WAS THREE days later, about eight-thirty on Tuesday evening, when the twins arrived to pay a visit in form in Kempenfeldt Square. Antony recognised it as such from Timmy's unnatural decorum, both of dress and demeanour; and they had been talking for some minutes before he was certain that the solemnity of his young friend's manner was a good deal more than surface deep. By comparison, Paul had an air of serenity that might have been considered surprising; perhaps, after all, he had found his passive role in the recent events less harrowing than his brother's more active, if not more intimate, participation?

It was Paul who said, as the stream of conventional remarks which will carry any group of people over the first moments of meeting seemed to be in danger of running dry, "You heard he's dead?" He gave Jenny a look that might have been an apology, turned back to Antony and added abruptly, "I can't say I'm sorry."

The sentiment did not seem to Antony to call for any apology. He looked inquiringly at Timmy, whose attention seemed to be concentrated on the hearth-rug, but who remarked as though in reply:

"They say he had the stuff on him. Do you suppose he'd been afraid, all these years?"

"I suppose he hoped to find a chance of finishing off Aunt Marian," said Antony bluntly. "Why the devil do you suppose I put on that performance, and with Uncle Nick's connivance! It wasn't for fun!"

Timmy looked startled. Paul said slowly, "I didn't think of that. What would have happened if Manuel hadn't turned up?"

"I thought perhaps you hoped he'd lose his nerve." Timmy sounded curious.

"Well, if I did, I wan't fool enough to expect it," said Antony. "He might have sued me for slander, but I don't think he'd have had the nerve."

"I wouldn't have put it past him." Timmy seemed oddly cheered by this pronouncement. "But I'd have thought you could have said all that at Paul's trial; it sounded awfully convincing."

"There wasn't anything approaching legal proof, you know."

"But he knew about the ring," said Paul. There was in his voice, even now, a chill of recollection.

"And Uncle William *did* describe him in his letter," added Jenny.

"Well, as to the ring, pretty well anything that depends on human recollection is open to question," said Antony. "As for the letter—"

"Ann told me," said Timmy. "He said he'd seen a man as he left the flat. And when she read the description she realised—"

"She was upset when she was here on Friday evening," Jenny put in, sympathetically. "I've been wondering how she is now." She looked at Paul as she spoke, but a little uncertainly. And it was Timmy who answered.

"She has known Bob Wayne all her life," he said. "Of course it was a shock."

"Of course," Jenny echoed.

"But people don't turn into monsters, suddenly, when you've known them for ever." Timmy was addressing himself to Jenny, and he spoke earnestly, as though it were immensely important that she should be made to understand. "I mean, I *know* what Bob did: five murders, and trying to kill Aunt Marian, and trying to get Paul hanged, too. But what I *feel* is that he used to be kind to us; and I'm glad he's dead because the trial would have been so beastly. It's no good trying to hate people to order; it just can't be done."

"Well, I'm glad too," said Paul. "But I don't understand how it happened. They searched me pretty thoroughly—"

"That's the theory of it," said Antony. "In practice,

of course, things can get overlooked. It isn't the first time.''

"And they did find one lot of poison," said Paul. "I suppose it was what he meant to use on Aunt Marian. What was it this time?''

"Strychnine. And he'd kept a still larger dose for himself." Antony exchanged glances with Jenny, who knew well enough what he was thinking. Robert Wayne had found the means of poisoning himself during the night before the Magistrate's Court hearing which should have freed his cousin and seen his formal committal for trial. He had died in the prison hospital only that morning. And just as well, if you wanted to be callous, it saved everyone a lot of bother; but there was Timmy's viewpoint, too, and it was one with which both the Maitlands found themselves uncomfortably in sympathy.

Jenny said into the silence, "You didn't tell me if Miss Barclay—''

The twins, in their turn, exchanged glances. "Well, you see, Mrs. Maitland," said Paul, "she's had a good deal to think about—''

"Of course," said Jenny, soulfully. "She must be *so* relieved to have you back!" Antony, seeing Paul's look of alarm, could cheerfully have slapped her for this piece of mawkishness, deliberate though he knew it to be; but Timmy, who was better acquainted than his brother with their hostess's ways, cheered up suddenly, and said with a grin:

"Well, she was! She wanted to break their engagement.''

"And did she?''

"Oh, yes." Paul's tone was carefully casual. "She's going to marry Timmy." He caught Antony's eye, and laughed at his deliberately uncomprehending expression. "You'd like to say 'I told you so', I expect. I didn't think it'd be this easy." He looked at Jenny. "I'm going to marry Audrey," he explained.

"And what next?" Antony asked. "Business as usual, or—''

"Not that." Paul was definite, but his tone was a little uneasy. "I've got what I wanted, I suppose I shouldn't complain—"

"Grandfather threw us out," said Timmy. "I don't exactly know why, but I don't care, of course."

Antony, thinking of the shaken old man he had seen on the evening of Robert Wayne's arrest, thought he could have explained very well. Once over the shock of what happened, the presence of his grandsons would have been a continual irritant to Ambrose Cassell, a continual reminder of how wrong he could be. That was something not to be borne, galling beyond endurance. He smiled at Jenny, who was indignantly incoherent, and said peaceably, "It doesn't matter, after all. You didn't want—"

"No. I can join Harry straight away; and start getting the cottage in order. We thought we wouldn't get married until Aunt Marian is well enough to come, she'd hate to miss it, you know. But Audrey can stay with Harry's mother meanwhile."

"It sounds a very good arrangement. What about you, Timmy?"

"I need a job." He tightened his lips, as though at a suddenly disagreeable thought. "I did get an offer, from one of the newspapers, but there were . . . strings."

"I can imagine."

"Yes, well—" Perhaps it was the understanding in Jenny's eyes, or just the feeling of being in sympathetic company, that made Timmy relax and say, quite naturally, "I talked to Cowan—he's my publisher. He said I couldn't expect anything else for six months, anyway, but after that he could give me some introductions that ought to lead somewhere. So I thought—it'll be a couple of weeks before Aunt Marian is well enough, but as soon as she is Ann and I will get married."

"And then—"

"Well, I rather thought of a protracted honeymoon. As a matter of fact, we're going to Alcantara; Manuel seemed keen, and after all he is my cousin."

"I expect he's lonely," said Jenny. "But what about the meantime, until Aunt Marian is really better?"

"We're down at Haslemere at the moment," said Timmy. "I always thought Uncle Greg was a bit dim, but he's been pretty decent about all this.'' He hesitated. "It was comforting to have somewhere to go, in the family, I mean. I don't know why. And even Brent is trying to be friendly.''

"In spite of his broken engagement?" Antony looked inquiringly from one to other of the brothers.

"He took it very well," said Paul. "He even offered to be my best man.''

"A little hackneyed," said Timmy, apologetically. "But we're encouraging him, because he means well." He paused and looked at Paul, and then went on with an air of resolution, "I said Grandfather threw us out. He's winding up the trust so that we get what there is to come from our parents' estate right away."

"I'm glad to hear it."

"So you see . . . we told Horton to send in his bill," said Timmy. He met Antony's eye, and wilted a little under its blank look. "Well, you were pretty helpful," he said defensively.

Antony said solemnly, "The briefs were marked . . . nothing on earth can alter them now." ("Except Mr. Mallory," said Jenny, under her breath.) He grinned at Timmy's downcast look, and appealed to Paul, "Honestly, I couldn't face Uncle Nick with such a suggestion."

"No, I see that. But there's our point of view as well. Sir Nicholas was more than helpful, he was very kind to us. And so were you."

"Well, so I should hope!" Jenny sounded matter-of-fact. "But you can't go back on the agreement now."

"We only wanted—"

"Well, if you're going to Alcantara, Timmy, you could send Uncle Nick some port when you get there. He'd like that.''

The twins looked at each other; they seemed to be taking counsel. "All right," said Paul at last. "But I hope you know we're grateful—"

"Let's take it as read." Antony got up and made for the cupboard. "We'll have a drink on the bargain. And if you're not careful,'' he added warningly, ''I'll offer you a Colonial sherry.''

Timmy began to laugh; and after a moment Paul joined in. Jenny said, ''We haven't really got any.'' But neither of them was listening to her.